Don't Think Twice

Book One of the

Call Me Rab Crime Series

by

Ron McMillan

Prologue

The girl awoke to a scream that bounced around the dark room. She was bathed in sweat, and the scream was her own. The dream often reduced her to a sodden wreck, stumbling around the house, terrified to close her eyes in case nightmare thoughts lurked in the shadows.

The setting never repeated itself and the heart-wrenching conclusion never changed. This time she ran as if through invisible treacle in pursuit of a woman who strode the busy platform of a forbiddingly large, dimly lit railway station where no heed was paid to the girl's distress. When darkness embraced the woman, the girl voiced her despair in one long, throat-rasping scream. She stretched out in a final hopeless gesture, her other wrist locked behind in a searing grip. The girl was going nowhere and, as ever, her mother left without looking back.

The lingering grief was normal. The horrible pain in the arm trapped in the dream was not. She lay on it with her wrist above and behind her, somehow locked in place. It took excruciating minutes of struggle to turn over and free the aching limb from the weight of her torso. She was battered and bruised, but the real pain came as circulation returned to the arm, still locked behind her.

In the throes of the dream, could the arm have become snagged between the bed and the wall? She could see nothing to support the theory, but worse, she already knew it was wrong. Her bedroom was at the front of the house, where the powerful streetlights of Alexandra Parade seeped through the merest gap in the thick curtains. She was never in total darkness, but now the room was coal-cellar black. And her bed was too hard. She felt with her free hand. Where there should have been the comfort of linen on an expensive mattress, was hard wood.

Only when she brought the hand to her face was she finally struck dumb with terror. Her head was encased in thick fabric fastened tightly around her neck. This was not her bedroom, and she most certainly was not in her own bed. She tried to think back to the night before, and vaguely recalled turning out the bedside reading light and her head hitting the pillow. From that point, until the nightmare, nothing.

Urgent now, she ran her fingers around her head, but detected no way to free the sack. She got a fright when a fingernail pierced the mask and scratched at the corner of her mouth. An opening reinforced with heavy stitching. What little air she could detect coming through the hole gave scant clue to where she might be. Stale, with dust and a hint of old fish.

She swept the free hand over the wooden floor, earning a painful splinter in the web between thumb and forefinger. She raised the hand to the hole in the sack and got her teeth around the skelf with enough purchase to tear it out. Warm blood crossed her palm as the hand touched on something new. There. Solid but movable. Plastic, cylindrical, some kind of bottle. Restricted to the use of one hand, fingers sticky with blood, she looked for a way to open what felt like a sports bottle of the type cyclists hang from the downtubes of bike frames. For the first time since awakening, she felt thirsty beyond belief. Night sweats did that.

When she swallowed hard at the cool water she felt pain. *Down there*, as one of her older schoolteachers referred to it during a special class on sexual abuse. Three of her friends managed to skip the lesson due to complaints from church-going parents adamant it would encourage daughters to become sex-hungry deviants. The joke was on the parents, who had no idea two of the three were already screwing boyfriends with much-discussed regularity, and the third was in a long-running lesbian relationship.

Oh no. One of the warnings drummed into them during the lesson was about date-rape drugs. Roofies, the more street-aware kids called them. They rendered victims unconscious, unaware of anything being done to them – and later, unable to recall what went on.

Odourless and flavourless, the teacher said, impossible to detect. It gets slipped into your drink, and you don't remember a thing.

Too late, the girl dropped the bottle and spat out the last mouthful, which caught on the inside of the sack and ran down her chin onto her neck. She cried herself into unconsciousness.

Chapter One

Glasgow City Centre, 1993

The two neds in Le Coq Sportif tracksuits took turns tugging manfully at a shared cigarette as they watched Rab wrestle the old Datsun into place. The rare good fortune of finding an empty meter on Pitt Street still left him with the challenge of parking. Three attempts later, he had one foot on the road before he remembered to tuck the flattened Bisto Gravy box under his arm.

One of the scruffs angled his gel-slicked head at the Datsun's nearside tyres, squashed against the high kerb.

'Three tries,' he said, 'and that's the best ye can do?'

'The handbrake's jiggered and I need the car to be here when I get back,' said Rab.

'We could look efter it fur ye,' said ned number two.

Rab pretended to consider an offer common on streets surrounding the city's football grounds on match days, when any motorist wanting his paintwork to remain intact knew to pay off trainee protection racketeers a lot younger than these two.

Ned 1 met apparent indecision with an outstretched palm.

'You're on,' said Rab. Instead of cash, the ned got a painfully strong handshake and a wink across the road at the Glasgow Police Headquarters building. With the forefinger of his other hand, Rab tapped his turban in mock salute. 'Detective Sergeant Singh, CID,' he said. 'I won't be long.'

Rumour had it even the Chief Constable of Scotland had to show his warrant card before he got past PC "Sticky" McCorrisken. In a building full of big men, McCorrisken was a giant whose nickname came from being a stickler for the only rule he ever had to enforce. Today, he opened the door and shook his head when Rab reached for his inside pocket. Word had reached HQ's most notorious gossip.

'Sorry to hear this, Rab,' he said. McCorrisken was also the only uniformed officer in the building who routinely called superiors by their first name.

'Thanks, Sticky.'

The corkboard above the lift buttons had the usual dog-eared announcements from the union and a reminder to carry warrant cards at all times. Some joker had added a yellow Post-It note warning staff not to miss DI Malloy "entering the Lion's Den" on BBC's *Crimewatch* at seven o'clock. Rab didn't need reminding.

His arrival on the CID floor was met with a hush, conversations stalled or reduced to whispers. He picked his way through desks crowded with typewriters and computer terminals. The corner of the Bisto box clipped a paperwork stack, sending a helter-skelter paper spiral to the floor. Rab paid it the same attention he gave the silent stares.

His own desk was so cluttered, he had to take to his knees to assemble the box and reinforce it with tape from a drawer. The regulations said personal items only. A few books, a Partick Thistle scarf from the bottom drawer and some newspaper clippings went into the box, topped by a framed photo of two young boys which Rab first dusted with his

7

sleeve. After closing the box with more tape, he turned around to find PC Jane Ross standing over him.

'Sergeant Singh,' she said.

Rab looked around. Eavesdroppers everywhere.

'Inspector Ferguson wants a word,' said Jane.

'Something wrong with her legs?'

'Excuse me?'

'She couldn't take ten seconds to come over here, had to send you?'

'A private word. In her office.'

As an inspector in the uniform branch, Sheena Ferguson merited a glass-enclosed corner space with windows overlooking the architectural smorgasbord of downtown Glasgow. Scotland's biggest city rewarded pedestrians' upward glances with some of the country's most striking buildings, many commissioned by 18th century tobacco barons made obscenely rich by the slave trade. When Rab entered without knocking, the dark-haired beauty who first made his head spin in secondary school stepped away from the window to sit behind her neatly ordered desk. A framed copy of the same photo Rab had packed into the Bisto box occupied one corner, angled to make clear to all visitors the inspector's priorities.

'Was that your idea of revenge?' he said, 'sending Jane Ross to deliver the come hither message?'

'Do you think making her squirm qualifies as revenge for screwing my husband and broadcasting it to the whole of HQ?'

She had a point. 'What's so important you want to talk with me in private?'

'Have you forgotten about the boys?'

'Of course I haven't.'

'They're upset you're going.'

'Did you tell them?'

8

'Could you blame me if I did? You're about to leave town without talking to them. Anyway, not guilty.'

'Aw no,' said Rab as he put the box on the floor and dropped into the visitor's chair. He didn't like the word estranged, but here he was, sitting across the desk from his estranged wife of 12 years, who outranked him.

Sheena teased an errant strand of hair back over one ear.

'Correct,' she said. 'Darling Ruby made sure I didn't get to choose how they found out. She dropped round "to help take her grandsons to school" because she "never did like the idea of how we made them go all that way on their own". She launched straight into one of her one-woman melodramas and made it sound like Dunoon was the far side of Karachi. At least she saved golden boy the trouble of telling his sons about his drastic career move.'

'It's not like I had a choice,' said Rab. 'It was either go down the coast or leave the force.'

'Did you punch Ken Malloy?'

'Not really.'

'That's not an answer.'

'I took a swing at him, but missed. No witnesses, his word against mine.'

She shook her head in what others might have interpreted as disbelief. Rab knew better. It was more like disappointment.

'OK, why Dunoon? It might not be the other side of Karachi, but it's still the back of beyond.'

'It gets me out of the way for a while, stops Malloy pushing for my dismissal. It's close enough so I can still get back to see the boys, take them to games at Firhill.'

'You have to talk to them. You're a screw-up, but you're still their dad.'

'Tell them their screw-up dad will phone tonight.'

'Malloy was here a few minutes ago. He wants to see you.'

Rab, sad-eyed, lifted the box and elbowed his way out of

Sheena's office.

As he picked his way through CID, most of the room avoided eye contact and only Wullie Boyd left his desk to intercept him.

'Sorry to see you go, Rab, but this is temporary, right? You'll be back,' he said.

'Thanks, Wullie. Don't know about coming back.'

Wullie's eyes flicked over Rab's shoulder. 'Here comes your favourite short-arse,' he said out of the side of his mouth, like a ventriloquist. With an affectionate pat on his friend's shoulder, he left.

Rab took one step towards the door before the inevitable happened. From behind came the voice of Inspector Ken Malloy.

'I told Inspector Ferguson I wanted to see you before you ran out.'

Rab turned to look down at Malloy, who, when he joined the force must have teetered on his tiptoes to scrape past the rigid height requirement. A bog-brush Nigel Mansell moustache failed miserably in its attempt to divert attention from the station's worst comb-over.

'Must have slipped her mind,' said Rab, his tone intentionally dismissive, conscious of the rest of the room inching closer, hoping to catch a snippet worth sharing. Aware of them, Malloy, too, moved in closer, which made the need for him to crook his neck all the more obvious.

'If I'd had my way, Singh, you'd be out of a job,' he said in a low growl surely calculated to intimidate. Rab met it with a smirk and inched forwards until their chests touched. He spoke at a volume nobody else in CID would miss, spraying his superior's face with a fine mist of spit.

'But you didn't, and I'm not. Is that why you wanted to talk to me? Did you want a chance to savour your sour grapes? Leading by example as usual, Kenny?'

'Sir to you. You think the transfer doon the watter is temporary? You're finished. I'll make sure of it.'

'Like you made sure we found Ashna? Four years today since she vanished. Four years – and what have we achieved for her family? Not a thing. If the BBC doesn't hang you by the balls tonight, *Inspector,* maybe I will. Now shift your arse. Sir.'

Malloy stepped backwards involuntarily and his voice rose to a near-shout to match the rage in his face.

'Did you just threaten me, Sergeant?' He spread his arms, open palms a plea for witnesses or sympathy. Eyes averted, colleagues' sentiments were clearly with Rab, who headed for the lift, exchanging nods as he left behind a city and a job and a woman and two boys he loved.

Chapter Two

The neds in track suits were still sharing a smoke even though the pavement at their feet was littered with cigarette ends. Rab unlocked the driver's door and dropped the box on the back seat.

'Ho,' said one of the neds. 'What happened to your stereo?' He pointed at the centre of the dashboard, where wires dangled from a jagged hole.

'I gave up after the third one was stolen,' said Rab.

'That's outta order, so it is.'

Rab fired up the engine and reached casually behind a flap attached by Velcro to the underside of his seat. A touch of one button made the neds jump when Elvis Costello wailed about Watching the Detectives through custom speakers secreted at four points in the Datsun's cramped interior. It was true. He had lost three stereos to thieves, but since he left the yawning gap in the broken dashboard and hid a new system under the driving seat, he often didn't even bother locking up.

The Isley Brothers accompanied a frantic mid-afternoon dash along a Clydeside Expressway designed for times when two-car families were the exception, and at last the Datsun escaped through a sweeping cement canyon to the Clyde

Tunnel. Damp year-round with rainwater running into the smog-yellowed gloom, the tunnel was a 90-second down-and-up where Rab's dad, at the wheel of his ex-Post Office Morris van, challenged teenage Rab to try and hold his breath until they got out the other side. A generation later, Stuart and Ronnie relished Rab's challenge to do the same. He was forever amused by how the boys never twigged that, like his own dad before him, Rab did it so he could enjoy 90 seconds of peace and quiet.

On the south side of the tunnel in the flat grey of Glasgow in March, the Victorian Southern General hospital glowered at traffic fighting for position on the approach to clover-leaf flyovers to and from the city centre. Rab circled towards the M8 motorway heading west and within a minute or two skirted Paisley, the neighbouring town he only ever seemed to visit when Partick Thistle played away to St Mirren.

The motorway soared over the White Cart Water, treating him to views first absorbed from the window seat of a Lufthansa 737 cutting a smooth vector in the opposite direction from the coast and along the Firth of Clyde before touching down at Glasgow Airport. It was 1971, and 11-year-old Rabinder Singh fizzed with excitement at the twin prospects of being reunited with his father and experiencing his new home. He remembered dancing nervously in the crowded aisle while ground crew took forever to roll a stairway to the jet, and recalled how frightened he was when its platform wobbled as he and his mother finally stepped out the door. Ruby stopped to wave frantically at the rooftop viewing deck. There, hand raised over the glass barrier, was Baldeep, 8mm film camera held to his eye, capturing a shaky moment while passengers behind them were forced to a standstill by Ruby's complete absence of awareness of anyone else around her.

'Take your time, dear. We've got all day,' said a man in a smart business suit who waited at the head of a tight line of impatient passengers.

'Fuckin' Pakis,' said another voice. Welcome to Scotland.

A stewardess swept a gloved hand towards the bus on the apron below.

'Please,' she said. Ruby scowled, grabbed Rab by the wrist, and down they went.

At last, they stepped through automatic doors in the main building, and there was his dad, movie camera still running. Rab's instinct was to run and leap into his father's arms, but Ruby's unrelenting grip locked him behind a trolley with a dodgy front wheel determined to go in any direction but straight ahead. Baldeep moved to the end of the barrier that channelled arrivals towards family members, waiting drivers and tour guides. To the faint whir of the movie camera, he pecked his wife on one cheek before turning to formally shake Rab's hand. If any onlooker knew the trio hadn't set eyes on one another for more than four years, they would have thought them a strange lot. For Rab, it was the beginning of a new life in a strange land.

The ferry pier at Gourock had a smattering of cars and vans waiting for the next departure for Dunoon. Rab added his car to the line and headed for a phone box perched on the edge of the Clyde, weather-scored windows looking across the water towards Ben Lomond. He dialled a number from memory and waited for the sound of his mother's voice before battling to get a coin into the slot.

'Hello Ruby.'

'Rabinder. How many times did I tell you? What's wrong with "Mummy"? Where are you? What's this nonsense about you leaving Glasgow without telling your own mother? That woman was gloating today, rubbing my poor nose in it.'

'That woman is the mother of your grandsons. I'm sure Sheena didn't mean to gloat.'

'There you go, letting her tread all over you. She has done nothing but play Mrs High-and-mighty ever since she forced you from the family home. If I had a pound for every time she—'

'Enough, Mother. I'm in a phone box, and don't have much time. Sheena told you I have been transferred to Dunoon. It's just a few months to cover for an officer who is injured.'

'Injured? What happened to him? What are you letting yourself in for? When are you going to spare a thought for your mother?'

'Are you taking your medication, Ruby? The officer broke his pelvis on a mountain rescue exercise. They need a replacement for a few months.'

'And you have to be the replacement? Do you think I came up the Clyde on a banana boat? I know you punched a senior officer. See what being a policeman has done to your good character? Your father and I never wanted you to join the police. What was wrong with medicine or law? How many times did we—'

'Too many times,' said Rab. He rubbed his face wearily. This was how every conversation with his mother went. 'The people at the temple must have to hide their sniggers every time they see you.'

'Exactly. I'm the laughing stock of the entire Indian community. Your dear father will be turning in his grave. And what about this television thing tonight? How can you help Ashna's parents if you are marooned in the back of beyond? Where is Dunoon anyway? Don't tell me, it doesn't matter, since you might as well be on the moon for all you care about Ashna's family. Or your own mother.'

At last, the telephone made the urgent beeping sound.

'Run out of money, Ruby. I will call you.'

The connection was cut. He looked at the line of coins in his palm and put them in his pocket.

Chapter Three

Simran Gupta was nothing if not insistent. When he declared driving to be a waste of time because parking at the BBC would be a nightmare, he and his parents Dilip and Lala set out on foot to cover the ten minutes from their home in Dowanhill. They crossed Great Western Road where the Victorian Botanic Gardens sat back from a busy intersection shadowed by a deconsecrated but unoccupied parish church and the toney Grosvenor Hotel, constructed anew behind the original sandstone façade after a suspicious fire tore through it in the 1970s. Simran led them over the crowded pedestrian crossing with the confident authority of youth. His parents trudged behind with markedly less enthusiasm.

Queen Margaret Drive had long been synonymous with the BBC's sprawling complex of studios and offices perched on a giant swathe of some of the most valuable real estate in the city. Entry from the street meant dealing with uniformed security men, but their names on a priority entry list meant they were soon escorted to a reception area and asked to wait on comfortable seats arranged around coffee tables littered with tattered copies of the Radio Times.

'I am not happy about this,' said Dilip. Beside him, his wife was mute.

'Dad, we already discussed this and I explained what we are doing and why we are doing it,' said Simran. 'This is all about taking the initiative.'

'So because your university professor shared with you her "crisis communications strategy" we have to take our story back onto national television? Hasn't that already been done to death? And to what benefit? Our Ashna is still—'

'Four years,' said Simran. Out of the corner of his eye he watched his mother pluck a handkerchief from her sleeve and dab delicately at meticulously applied eye make-up under imminent threat of tears. 'We all know today is the fourth anniversary of Ashna's disappearance. It's why we are here, it's why the TV people are prepared to cover the story yet again. Four years of assurances from the police they are doing everything possible, and what do we have? Nothing. It's time to force the police to raise their game.'

His father looked suspicious. 'What do you mean, "force"?'

Simran was saved by the arrival of a young woman carrying a heap of file folders threatening to tumble from her arms, a possibility which had clearly not occurred to her, going by the way she extended one hand out from under them in welcome.

'Mr and Mrs Gupta? Simran? Thank you so much for coming. I'm Sally, production assistant on the Glasgow feed for tonight's programme.'

If she expected a response, it failed to arrive. She pressed on.

'My first job is to do some quick checks to ensure nobody gets your names wrong and to sort out what London puts on screen when you are being interviewed on camera. After, I'll show you the studio, give you an idea what to expect – and take you into make-up. No need to be nervous. This way please.'

Simran and his mother got to their feet, but Dilip remained

seated, elbows on knees, eyes towards the floor.

'I think we are making a mistake,' he said.

Sally made a show of being not in the least put out.

'Don't worry, Mr Gupta,' she said, 'you would be surprised how many people get butterflies at the prospect of facing—'

'Nothing to do with nerves, my dear,' said Dilip without looking up. 'My wife and I – and my son – have stared resolutely into the cameras a hundred times since our Ashna disappeared. And did that help? No.'

'Oh, but *Crimewatch* has helped thousands of people over the years. Even after a long time like this, the retelling of the circumstances of a crime, sorry, of the circumstances of an *event*, especially such a distressing one as yours, will attract many calls from members of the public, fresh leads for the investigation.' She stopped talking when she saw Dilip's body language speak of determination, a mind made up. Panic creased her face as she contemplated telling producers in Glasgow and London she had lost a key player in tonight's episode, 90 minutes before they were due to go live on one of the week's most-watched shows.

Lala moved to Dilip and bent over. She put fingertips beneath his chin and softly raised it until their eyes met and she kissed him lovingly on the tip of his nose.

'Let's go, darling,' she said.

Dilip didn't react immediately, and Sally's half-step forwards was stopped by Simran bringing one palm to rest on the files.

'We're OK,' he said, quietly.

As Dilip stood, Lala spoke, her lips close to her husband's ear:

'We need answers, my love. Let's go create a fuss for Ashna.'

The short procession to a door marked "No Entry Unless Accompanied by a BBC Staff Member" passed a lone figure at

18

another table. Detective Inspector Ken Malloy looked up expectantly. They blew past as if the chair was empty.

Chapter Four

Rab nosed his car out of the Dunoon Ferry Terminal onto the Esplanade and under the stern, moonlit gaze of Highland Mary. The bronze statue of Mary Campbell, one of the poet Robert Burns's many lovers and the subject of songs and poems by the Bard, was installed to mark the centenary of his death in 1896, according to a tourist brochure Rab had read four times on the ferry.

The road curved around a stubby headland before it left the shore to pick through ever-narrowing streets. Rab found what he needed on a hill lined with businesses that looked like they struggled to make the rent. Without having to think, he went through the routine of parking with two wheels hard against the kerb. Maybe life in the wee town could be quiet enough for him to get the handbrake fixed.

The Lobster Creel bar's dimly lit interior was blue with tobacco smoke. Far from being devoted to a display of coastal fishing kitsch, the pub was as bare as a factory canteen. Walls and ceiling had been given a rough coat of flat grey emulsion slapped over nails and hooks from forgotten wall hangings; bare fluorescent tubes cast a sickly glow on plain metal and plywood tables and chairs in a fetching shade of black. A threadbare carpet sucked at the soles of Rab's shoes. The odour was classic smelly Scottish pub, a nauseating mix of stale beer, third-hand smoke, and unwashed bodies. About a dozen customers dotted the room, all male except for one old dear wearing a hat like a tea-cosy. She sat alone with both hands clasped protectively around a whisky glass, her feet swinging clear of the carpet. Three drinkers occupied a table cluttered with empty pint tumblers and an overflowing ashtray. One of them reacted to Rab's entry with a double-take straight out of a silent movie.

'Ho!' he called out, 'Ah don't remember sendin' out for a curry!'

Rab glanced over in time to catch the wannabe comedian, arms spread wide, trawling the room for appreciation. Rab could list a dozen variations of the racist joke, but it still earned the comic a few smiles and a gratifying spray of foam from a drinking partner who appeared to have choked on his beer.

'Never mind that eedjit,' said the lone barman. Early 40s, shoulder-length red hair, barely-controlled 1970s sideburns and Ian Dury & the Blockheads t-shirt. 'What can I get you?'

'Apart from the number for your decorator?'

'Christ, another funny man. The owner took over an empty shell and got everything he needed at an auction after the American base closed shop. With this sort of clientele, he's in no hurry to fix it up.'

At least that explained the battleship grey paint.

'Half-pint of lager shandy, please.' Rab pointed at the television suspended on a frame above one end of the bar, the reason he was in this dive waiting for a drink he didn't want. The screen showed a darts match in progress with the sound muted.

'Can you switch the channel? There's something I want to catch on the other side.'

While excess foam sluiced down the sides of a lager glass tilted to offset too much gas in the mix, the barman fished a clunky remote from beneath the bar and slid it along the counter top.

'Be my guest. Fresh off the boat?'

Rab nodded as he fiddled with the remote.

'I hope you ate on the ferry,' the barman said. 'Fussy folk have been known to starve to death in here. Soggy hot pies, four different flavours of crisps, that's yer lot. We're even out of brown sauce for the pies.'

'I'm alright.' He managed to change the channel to BBC1 and found the button to increase the volume in time for the opening credits for *Crimewatch*.

Right on cue, the loudmouth bellowed.

'Haw, Ben! We were watchin' the darts. 'C'mon tae fu—'

'Baxter,' said Ben, 'you and I both know this is the last pub in Dunoon you're not barred from. If you want to go for the full house, keep talking.'

As Rab took a tentative sip at the shandy, a cloud of stale fumes arrived from behind.

Baxter was in his late 30s, short-cropped hair greying at the temples, eyes blurred, the corned beef complexion of a man who took too much drink too regularly. He put a calloused hand on the bar and extended one accusing finger towards Ben the barman.

'Y'mean some Paki turns up, never been here in his life before, and he takes over the place? Who does he think—'

'I know exactly who I am,' said Rab. 'And I remember you.'

He pushed his warrant card under the other man's swollen red nose. Baxter's eyes crossed as he tried to focus on it, ire dissolving to be replaced by fear and frustration. Busted.

'The legendary Jim Baxter,' said Rab. He turned to Ben. 'The other one. This fine specimen is from Glasgow's east end

– Celtic territory – where he was stuck with the same name as the best footballer ever to pull on a Rangers jersey. I never forget an arrest.'

'Awright, awright,' said Baxter. Too late. This genie wasn't going back in the bottle.

'Second offence, wasn't it? What did you get? Three months in the Riddrie Hilton?' He pointed with his full glass at Baxter's friends across the room. 'I bet your mates don't know anything about it. Will we tell them?'

Palms front in surrender, Baxter reversed unsteadily towards his drinking buddies. Rab turned his attention to the television, where the attractive BBC *Crimewatch* presenter spoke earnestly to camera:

'Welcome to *Crimewatch*. Tonight, as well as highlighting crimes around the country the authorities seek your assistance to solve, we will return to the mysterious disappearance of a young woman from Glasgow, exactly four years ago. But first, we go to Birmingham, where a disturbing series of break-ins has targeted the homes of elderly residents in a tight-knit housing estate close to the centre of the city.'

Ben the barman couldn't resist:

'What did Baxter do to get the jail?'

Rab kept his eyes on the TV. 'You're asking me to be unprofessional,' he said.

'He called you a Paki.'

'I was thinking today how I got called the same thing even before I stepped off the plane at Glasgow airport. How long has Baxter been in Dunoon?'

'Three or four years. Did you see the hands on him? Bricklayers can easy find work around here. He sometimes disappears back to Glasgow for a while, but keeps turning up like the proverbial bad smell. Three months in Barlinnie, eh?'

Rab raised his glass towards the television screen, where a second presenter sat with one bum cheek on a desk, foot

23

dangling, papers in hand.

'Sorry. Got to see this,' said Rab.

The presenter put on a serious face.

'Now to Glasgow where, four years ago tonight, Ashna Gupta, aged fourteen, disappeared without trace. Today police renew their call for help from the public.

'Ashna Gupta was a popular student at her secondary school in Glasgow's west end. She excelled in her studies and was particularly drawn to drama and dance, passions which police suspect might have brought her into the company of someone responsible for her disappearance. Live from our Glasgow studios, we welcome Ashna's parents Mr Dilip Gupta and Mrs Lala Gupta, and her brother, Simran. Also in Glasgow we have Detective Inspector Ken Malloy, who has headed the investigation from day one.'

The screen shifted to Ken Malloy, sweat glistening his brow, the look of a man who knew he was in for a hard time.

'Inspector Malloy,' said the presenter, 'four years into the case, is it fair to say your investigation has drawn a blank?'

Malloy unwittingly gave the game away with a sideways eye flicker. Malloy was about to lie. No surprise there.

'Police forces throughout Scotland have devoted countless hours to what is very much an ongoing case,' said Malloy, irritation already obvious in his voice. 'While it's true we are hungry for new evidence, we remain confident of solving Ashna's disappearance.'

The presenter nodded as if Malloy wasn't 400 miles away and hadn't sidestepped the question. Time to give the inspector some more rope.

'For the benefit of viewers at home who may be unfamiliar with the intricacies of a case you know so well, Inspector, please summarise what you know about the night of Ashna's disappearance.'

Malloy leaned forward, hands clasped. This much he had

prepared for.

'On Friday, March 17th, 1989, an engagement party saw people from Glasgow's Indian community gather at a reception in the Hilton hotel on Great Western Road. Ashna's family attended, and she was expected to join them. Instead of going with her parents, she agreed to come later, after first meeting with someone. Despite exhaustive investigations, no trace of any meeting involving Ashna has been found. We don't know who she met, or where any meeting took place. Unfortunately, we still don't even know the purpose of this alleged meeting. None of her school friends know anything, and nobody from her dance or drama circles recalls seeing her over the course of the evening; nor do they recall any mention by Ashna of such a meeting being planned.'

The screen cut momentarily to the interviewer, whose look said *get to the point, pal.*

Malloy, looking directly at the camera, went on. 'The absence of information surrounding Ashna's disappearance has never been explained. This is why it is vital for us to ask members of the public who were anywhere in Glasgow on the night of Friday, March 17th, 1989, to cast their memories back. Did anyone cross paths with Ashna on March 17th, or at any other time in the run-up to March 17th, or even thereafter? It is important to remain open to the possibility there might not have been foul play involved, and indeed Ashna may have run away of her own volition. Bearing this in mind, we ask members of the public to look closely at the photographs – taken when she was fourteen years old – and let us know if they think they might have encountered Ashna at any time in the last four years.'

If Malloy hoped for more time to shine, he was disappointed. After a few seconds showing a selection of photographs of the teenage Ashna in school uniform, in casual clothes and with her family, the interview turned to Dilip and

Lala Gupta, and rapidly became painful to watch. Rab lowered the volume. Ben the barman hovered nearby.

'You'd be the replacement for Willie Duffy,' he said.

Rab considered and rejected the idea of another sip of shandy.

'Is he the Sergeant Duffy who fell off a mountain?'

'None other. Wouldn't listen to anyone who said he was too out of shape for mountain rescue work,' said Ben while he ran a grubby towel over the already dry bar. 'A mate of mine is on the rescue team – says the rest of them were lucky he didn't drag them off the cliff with him.'

'What made you think I was here to replace him?'

'Dunoon's a wee town. Everyone knows you're coming, and you gave me clues. The Glasgow accent, the warrant card you stuffed in Baxter's face—'

'And the fact I'm a turban-wearing Paki?'

'I never said that.' Defensive.

'Don't worry about it,' said Rab. 'For the record, my family's Indian.'

Ben looked relieved to be off the hook.

'You'll be staying at Mags Henderson's B&B,' he said.

'I will?'

'New arrivals usually do.' He looked over to where the old dear in the tea-cosy hat soundlessly raised an empty glass clouded with handprints. 'Right with you, Marilyn,' he said. Ice crackling in the oily rush from the Famous Grouse optic, he went on:

'Mags used to be married to one of the uniformed sergeants, Neil Henderson. Everybody calls him Hen. Know him?'

Rab was keeping an eye on the TV.

'I expect he knows me, since it looks like the whole town's been briefed on who to expect.'

Ben delivered Marilyn's fresh drink and, on his return, set

about washing her old glass in sink water coated with soap scum. Dirty water flew off his thumb as he jerked it in the direction of the television.

'Tell the truth, I recognised you from when the Glasgow case first made the news,' he said.

'Wasn't my case,' said Rab.

'Because you were a family friend.'

'I was a go-between for the Guptas. Because we were friends, I wasn't allowed to get any closer to the investigative side of things.'

'Any way you look at it,' said Ben, 'it's a bloody tragedy.'

Rab silenced him politely with a raised hand. On the television, the original presenter was sitting in London, interviewing Simran Gupta and Ken Malloy in Glasgow. The presenter straightened her skirt before she addressed Simran.

'Your parents have chosen to leave us, Simran. Can you explain why?'

Simran squared his shoulders and took a deep breath.

'My parents were born in Glasgow, but our community's culture remains deeply traditional, and what I am about to show you pains them. However, they are desperate to learn what has happened to Ashna; not a moment passes when she is not foremost in their minds. That will remain the case no matter what comes to light.'

The gaze of the presenter sharpened. Something unexpected was going on here, but she was quick:

'Do you have new evidence to share?'

'I do,' said Simran. He glanced sideways at Ken Malloy, who looked increasingly uncomfortable as Simran continued: 'Something we discovered a couple of days ago, a clue the police missed.'

Malloy now had all the confidence of a burst balloon.

'This must be painful for you,' said the presenter. 'Please go on.'

27

Simran flourished a brown A4 envelope and extracted a partial 8×10-inch black-and-white photograph encased in a clear plastic bag. About one third of the photograph was missing, leaving a ragged lower edge. He held it to the camera.

In the photograph a heavily made-up young woman pouts with exaggerated sexuality. She is wearing a 1930s burlesque outfit; a tight-waisted one-piece with a push-up bra doing its best to accentuate small breasts. Her shoulders are bare, her hair in tumbling ringlets held in place by a feathered band. A lacy garter belt shows a lot of thigh before attaching itself to black net stockings.

The rip in the photo cuts through slender stockinged legs. One ornately gloved hand clutches a long black cigarette holder, the cigarette freshly lit, its curling smoke artfully illuminated from behind.

Simran glanced around the studio to make sure he was facing the "live" camera.

'This is Ashna,' he said, his voice cracking. 'We recently discovered this photograph in her room.' He shot an accusing look at Malloy. 'It might have been taken shortly before she disappeared. Ashna made no secret of wanting to be in the entertainment world, or perhaps a model. This may have been for some kind of portfolio we, the family, were unaware of. The photographer is unknown, and we have no idea where to look. We beg the photographer to come forward and identify him or herself. Likewise, if anyone in or near Glasgow is aware of anyone doing portrait work like this – or perhaps recognises the costume or the props used here – we beg you to inform the police.'

He looked expectantly around him. 'Viewers can see the number?'

In London, the presenter nodded vigorously. 'The hotline number is now on screen. If anyone has any knowledge which might assist in solving this perplexing mystery, no matter how trivial their information may seem, we ask you to call the number on screen. Everything shared will be treated with the utmost confidence. Simran?'

At the edge of the screen, Malloy continued to squirm. The surprise photograph reflected badly on his investigation, and it looked like there was more to come.

Simran took a deep breath. Rab guessed he was either milking the moment, or cleverly upping the tension, adding fresh drama for the millions of viewers at home around Britain.

'The Indian community throughout Britain has come together to offer a reward for information leading to Ashna being found. After all this time, we are aware of the possibilities. Our beloved Ashna may be dead, but even if so, we want to know – we deserve to know. Any caller providing information leading to Ashna being found will be able to claim a reward of ten thousand pounds. The cash is ready and waiting. Please call the number on screen.'

Ken Malloy looked like he wished for a hole to crawl into. Rab changed the channel to find one fat darts player with bad tattoos celebrating victory over another fat darts player with bad tattoos. Cue muffled curses from Baxter's table. Rab turned to Ben.

'How about directions to Mrs Henderson's B&B?'

'I'll trade you for a clue about what got Baxter locked up.'

Chapter Five

Sitting down to breakfast in a B&B dining room always made Rab feel like an intruder, and the contrast with the minimalist Lobster Creel bar could not have been more complete. Except for the table, every possible surface in the Crest dining room was crowded with intricate glass ornaments arranged with obvious care and no little degree of precision. How they remained intact and sparkling and free of dust was a mystery that would have sent Sherlock Holmes back to Baker Street with his tail between his legs. Rab sat at the one place set at the table, thankful to have the room to himself and not to have to make small talk with sales reps or holidaymakers.

Mags Henderson backed through the door with her arms full. She was tall, what Scots called "heavy set", and radiated warmth and motherliness. Which made her about as different from Rab's mother Ruby as it was possible to be.

'Good morning, Sergeant Singh,' she said.

'Please call me Rab, Mrs Henderson,' said Rab.

'I will,' she said, 'if you call me Mags. I didn't ask you last night. Ben at the Creel said you arrived in time to see *Crimewatch*. What did you think?'

'I think DI Malloy will have some explaining to do to his

superiors this morning. Rather him than me.'

'Maybe you're best away from Glasgow for a while. You'll find things here a bit quieter.' She carefully lowered a metal tray painted to look like a fluttering Scottish saltire. At its centre was a plate loaded with so many arterial threats it should have come with a health warning. She raised precisely-plucked eyebrows at Rab's turban.

'My full Scottish breakfast is quite famous around here; I'm glad your faith doesn't prevent you from enjoying it.'

'Not half as glad as I am,' said Rab. He was famished.

A brisk old-fashioned telephone bell cried out from the hallway. 'You tuck in, Rab,' said Mags as she backed out the door.

He was still contemplating which delicacy to attack first when Mags reappeared.

'That was Hen. My ex. His real name's Neil, but everyone calls him Hen. He says they need you at the station right away. I said surely they can wait until you finish your breakfast, but apparently not.'

Heavy silver cutlery, still locked in a roll of starched linen, went back on the table.

Having to see two boys off to school every morning meant Inspector Sheena Ferguson's work day seldom started much before nine o'clock. She was used to finding the floor her office shared with CID buzzing while the fresh overnight workload was absorbed into existing duties, but the level of activity this morning was on an entirely new scale.

Nobody viewed *Crimewatch* with more interest than police officers whose cases were being put through the media grinder, and although Sheena's uniform branch was only peripherally involved, there was the family connection of Rab's and Ashna's parents being close.

She had bought an hour free of distractions by granting the

boys unexpected video game time. Glass of wine in hand, she settled back to find out what the Guptas had to say on national TV. The timing of the show, four years to the day since Ashna's disappearance, could do nothing but hurt the force's image, but her colleagues would shrug off any amount of finger-pointing if it prompted new witnesses to come forward. What nobody wanted to admit was that, without fresh leads, the case was as good as dead.

Before leaving the office the day before, she had helped organise a hotline station in anticipation of calls following the broadcast. For a cold case, the four lines they installed would normally be enough, but they hadn't anticipated the reward Simran was going to spring on them. Few things sparked fresh memories – real, imagined or spuriously exploitative – better than the possibility of large quantities of hard cash. Now, while four telephones were occupied non-stop, technicians busied themselves installing more lines, as a parade of lower ranks and civilian staff arrived toting collapsible tables and stacked chairs.

At the edge of all of this, Detective Inspector Ken Malloy, bedraggled and exhausted, clutched a coffee mug. Even in a room filled with people who had no time for the man, the sympathy aimed his way was palpable.

Sheena stopped next to him.

'Ashna's brother dropped you right in it,' she said.

Malloy looked into the coffee mug to find it cold and empty. He swivelled and placed it on a desk behind him.

'Up to our necks in it,' he said. 'Twice. Both with the photograph we failed to find in the course of multiple searches of the girl's bedroom, and with the reward he announced without so much as a heads-up. We've had more than two hundred callers certain their "information" entitles them to the ten thousand pounds. Vague, unsubstantiated nonsense we have to scrupulously explore in order to eliminate it as useless.

The gaffers will crap their knickers when they see the overtime this racks up.'

'Nothing of any use at all? Usually there's something worth learning.'

'Bugger all about what happened around the time she disappeared, but loads of rubbish about how she's living everywhere from the Shetland Islands to the Costa Del Sol, doing everything from driving a taxi to singing in a hotel lounge bar. We might have to send someone to Lancashire to check on a report she's an exotic dancer in the Burnley area.'

They both knew he was being unfairly dismissive of information which could prove vital.

'Do you think there's a possibility she's still alive?'

'If you'd asked me yesterday, not a chance. Now, I'm not so sure. It's an investigative nightmare, but how much of this new information would we have if it wasn't for the reward? Maybe something good will come of it.'

'What about the studio photograph?'

'Forensics are on it. More partial fingerprints than the front door of Woolworth's. So far, nothing usable. It's the way it didn't appear until last night that's got the gaffers in a lather.' Malloy's tired eyes met Sheena's. 'You're showing a lot of interest in a case of no concern to you, Inspector. Things quiet in the world of school crossings?'

'You know why. Rab's family and Ashna's were close. They were at the party in the Hilton when Ashna didn't show and the whole panic started.'

Malloy didn't look convinced. 'I like you, Sheena, but your ex-husband has caused me nothing but bloody grief ever since this case landed on my desk. I'm under enough pressure with his mother acting as an unofficial spokesperson. Any journalist stops her in the street, she's spouting soundbites about how badly we are letting down the entire Indian community.'

'Rab's not my ex. We're separated. I'm worried for

everybody involved. Ruby is an interfering old cow, but none of us can ignore the pain people are suffering, especially the Guptas and their close friends. What did Simran have to say about the photograph?'

'Says his mother found it between the pages of a hardback fashion book in Ashna's room.' He gestured towards a nearby desktop where a large book sat in a clear evidence bag.

'We probably flicked through it at least half a dozen times, but if the edge of the photo was jammed into the spine in a book full of black-and-white fashion photographs, I suppose we could have missed it.'

'Good luck trying to explain that away,' she said.

Malloy shook his head. 'Explaining it to the gaffers will be bad enough, but the press scum banging on the door hoping the reward sells newspapers will be worse.'

She left him as he headed off in search of more coffee. Cutting through the room towards her office, she almost felt sorry for him.

Chapter Six

The trip to Dunoon police station took Rab less time to drive than Mags had taken to twice go over detailed directions on how to get there.

The road outside the Crest headed north, following a gentle rise crossed by a handful of intersections in a residential area where prosperity had reigned for a long time. Sturdy semi-detached, two-storey stone properties with impressive bay windows, real slate roofs and low stone walls fronting fastidiously tended gardens, all dating from times when not even the well-heeled required driveways or garages.

Roads tumbling downhill to the east offered glimpses of the narrow Firth of Clyde and beyond, the Scottish mainland. At one intersection, a generous corner plot was home to a looming gothic church, its graveyard crowded with tombstones from centuries past. Rab enjoyed thinking how elder son Ronnie would relish picking through the monuments, doggedly interpreting even the most faded inscriptions. Shit. He had forgotten to call the boys last night. They would be on the way to school by now, disappointed by their dad yet again.

The one turning he had to be sure to remember took him onto Argyll Street, which brought to mind Glasgow's Argyle

Street and the "Heilanman's umbrella", a cavernous dark space beneath the broad swathe of Glasgow Central station's rail tracks. Glaswegians were rightly proud of the welcome they afforded visitors to the city, but the dark space's nickname was built on scorn for fellow Scots from the Highlands, written off as too cheap or too stupid to have their own umbrella. Rab had a lot of sympathy for outsiders written off as lesser beings solely because of where they came from.

Dunoon's Argyll Street was urban, clean, gleaming under blue skies and sadly without the chip shop aroma Rab associated with the Heilanman's umbrella. But it did offer the first sighting of his new workplace.

The police station looked like a small, 1970s primary school. Two floors, flat roof, cement everywhere. Before he left Glasgow, Rab tracked down a colleague who had spent time in Dunoon and who shared some information about the station. A total staff roster of about 25 was divided over four shifts, and he would be the only Detective Sergeant in the whole station.

He wondered about the call Mags had taken this morning. What could be urgent enough to require the presence of the new face who didn't know one end of town from the other? Something more important than a missing bicycle or a broken window, was the obvious answer. He left his car on the street and hurried towards what appeared to be the station's main entrance.

A sergeant who would have made Pitt Street's Sticky McCorrisken feel insignificant lifted his eyes from the newspaper he held against the edge of the reception desk. The paper disappeared and a big hand reached across the counter.

'Detective Sergeant Singh,' he said. 'Welcome to Dunoon. I'm Neil Henderson, duty shift sergeant.'

'Better known in these parts as "Hen",' said Rab. 'Your ex-wife makes a rare breakfast, not that I had the chance to sample it. What's going on?'

'Not for me to say,' said Henderson. 'But the chief wants to see you. This way please.' He buzzed them into the station, where a middle-aged woman thrashing the life out of an IBM Selectric typewriter raised her eyes long enough to be certain the new arrival did not concern her. Sitting at different desks, two uniformed constables, one male and one female, failed to hide their curiosity. Henderson waved at them.

'You two got nothing to do? Want me to find you something?'

Like school kids evading eye contact with a crotchety teacher, the constables dropped their heads. The sergeant's attention shifted back to Rab.

'Have we met before?'

'Don't think so,' said Rab. 'Did you ever work in Glasgow?'

'Couldn't pay me enough to live in that festering den of sin.' He paused at a closed door with a sign announcing the room belonged to Chief Inspector Alexander Woods. 'But I know you from somewhere. It'll come back to me.'

With a hand the size of a heavyweight's boxing glove, he rapped on the door surprisingly softly. A muffled 'Come!' reached them and Henderson stepped aside to usher Rab ahead of him. Two men, one in uniform, the other wearing a business suit over an open-necked shirt, sat facing each other over the only desk in the room. It was a big desk befitting a senior officer.

'Chief Inspector Sandy Woods,' said Hen, 'This is Detective Sergeant Rabinder Singh, newly arrived from Glasgow.'

Without another word he backed out of the open door. The sergeant had known he would not be staying.

Chief Inspector Woods rose from his swivel chair and stretched over one side of the desk to shake Rab's hand. The

37

other man stayed seated and made no attempt to acknowledge the new arrival.

'Welcome to Dunoon, Sergeant,' said Woods, gesturing towards the man across from him. 'This is my friend Archie McCusker. He needs our help. His daughter Zoe is missing.'

Rab patted his jacket pocket and dug out a notepad and pen.

'Sorry to hear this, Mr McCusker,' he said.

'She's a bloody tearaway. Drives me to distraction, has done ever since her mother buggered off and left us. Zoe is the same. Never listens to anything I say, takes every opportunity to defy me. Now she's stayed out all night without a word.'

Woods signalled Rab to pull over a chair from against a wall full of photographs of the Chief Inspector at work in the community, rubbing shoulders with an equal mix of locals and minor Scottish showbiz celebrities.

When Rab was seated, he addressed Archie McCusker directly.

'Z-O-E, correct, sir? How old is Zoe?'

McCusker's scowl deepened. 'What the fuck does it matter how old she is? I just want her back,' he said.

'Archie,' said Woods.

'Sorry, Sandy,' said McCusker. 'OK, you need the basics. She's recently turned fifteen, going on twenty-seven. You name it, and in the last six months she's done it. Smoking, drinking, probably taking drugs – and if she's anything like her mother, laying down for any boy with a hard-on. The joke going around town is she keeps a mattress tied to her back in case she meets anybody she knows.'

No wonder she ran away, thought Rab. 'If your daughter is fifteen and sexually active,' he said, 'any partner she ever had is a criminal in the eyes of the law.'

McCusker actually made a *Pshaw!* sound.

'You're not likely to hear Zoe complaining – never mind any of her so-called "partners",' he said. 'But it's not who she's screwing that bothers me. It's the fact she's missing. I woke up this morning and instead of getting ready for school, she was nowhere to be seen, and her bed's not been slept in. Now are you going to put the bloody notebook away and get out there and look for her, Mr Glasgow CID man?'

Rab wasn't finished, so the notebook stayed out.

'With your permission, I will need to see her bedroom,' he said. 'Is there anyone at your home to let me in?'

'No, there's nobody there to let you in, but this isn't Glasgow. We don't lock doors around here. Sandy will tell you where the house is. I'll be at my office if there's any news.' He got to his feet.

Sandy Woods gave the slightest of nods for Rab's benefit. *We are finished here.*

A knock from the door preceded Hen Henderson's head coming round to address his gaffer in a stage whisper. 'Chief Inspector,' he said, 'there's someone here to see you.'

'Can't you see we're busy, Hen?'

'Sorry, sir, but I think you will want to—'

'Och show them in, Sergeant,' said Woods. The battle was already lost.

The door flew open violently enough to batter against a stopper set into the skirting board, making the photographs and diplomas on the wall shake like tambourine jingles. A teenage girl in school uniform launched herself at Archie McCusker, but stopped short. Elbows out, hands on hips, the classic angry teen.

'What the FUCK, Dad,' she said. 'Three different people on the street have stopped me to tell me you're here reporting me missing!'

The way McCusker bristled, it made Rab wonder if the man alternated between two emotional states. Angry and furious.

'Enough of your lip. Where in God's name have you been? No, I tell you what. Bugger it. Make your apologies to these men for wasting their valuable time, and get yourself to school. I'll deal with you later, madam.' With the slightest of apologetic shakes of his head for the benefit of Chief Inspector Woods and nothing whatsoever for Rab, he stomped from the room.

Rab led Zoe to the staff canteen, where he got a can of Coke from a vending machine and filched a tea bag from an unknown colleague's worn Tetley tin. An inordinate quantity of tea was consumed in police stations, and an urn slightly smaller than a dustbin provided the hot water he needed. Black, no sugar it was. He passed the can to Zoe and sat opposite her at a table with all four edges striped by cigarette burns.

Zoe McCusker had neatly styled, natural blonde hair with platinum highlights, icy blue eyes that made Rab think of Scandinavia, and even white teeth with a hint of an overbite taking nothing away from her attractiveness. If she was Rab's daughter, he'd be keeping watch for would-be suitors. Such were the concerns of any parent who worried about a child's wellbeing, but when Archie McCusker believed his daughter was missing, he had shown anger – and contempt – in the certainty she was sleeping around.

'It's my mother who drives me daft,' said Rab as he squashed the tea bag against the inside of his mug.

Zoe looked around the empty room. 'This must make you Good Cop. You might want to have a word with Bad Cop about his timekeeping.' She snapped open the can and drank greedily.

'You've got me wrong,' said Rab. 'It's true about my mother. She drives me nuts. Even if she means well and she loves me more than anything or anybody – apart from herself, of course.' He watched Zoe carefully. This was the moment when he would discover if he had handled this with any

40

sensitivity whatsoever.

'You're lucky,' said Zoe.

'I am?'

'Archie hates me. Treats me like shit when he's sober, and even worse when he's drunk, which is roughly all the time.'

'I saw how he talks to you,' said Rab.

'He's never going to win Parent of the Month, is he? You don't know the half of it.'

Rab pushed the mug of tea aside. 'Is your father violent towards you?'

Zoe drained the can and crushed it between the heels of her hands. There goes nine heaped teaspoons of sugar into her young system, thought Rab. No wonder Scottish dentists drove flashy cars.

The empty drink can wobbled on the table, no longer of any interest.

'I don't want to talk about him. He's a miserable sod, always accusing me of stuff I don't do ever since my mum went away. He tells anyone who'll listen she cleaned out one of his bank accounts – he's got plenty of accounts, he's loaded, not that I see much of his money. Do you have a cigarette?'

'I don't smoke,' said Rab. 'Our house was full of my dad's cigarette smoke, so I can't stand it.'

'I do it to piss Archie off. Take one out of his pack, light it in front of him.'

'He lets you?'

'Is there a law against it?'

'Do you keep in touch with your mum?' Basic interrogation tactics. Don't let the subject know where the next question is coming from. Zoe ignored it.

'If he's sober enough to catch me, he slaps me around the room. For smoking his cigarettes.'

'You're serious.'

'Serious as a heart attack.'

'That alone constitutes grounds for his arrest,' said Rab. Looking at a partly-unravelled kid whose father talked about her like she was the village whore and who probably beat her, nothing would give him more pleasure. Even if arresting the commanding officer's friend may not make for the ideal first day in a new job.

Zoe might have been reading his mind:

'Arrest Archie McCusker?' She laughed out loud. 'Not while his old pal Sandy Woods still wears a uniform, you won't. Anyway you'd need my help – and if you put Archie away I'd end up in a foster home. I'd kill myself first. I know a kid who bounces from foster home to foster home. The stories he tells—'

'What?'

'They'd bring tears to a glass eye. I need to get to school.'

'Where were you last night?' said Rab.

'At my friend's house. Sarah, Sarah McCrae. She's in my year at school. Mr and Mrs McCrae know Archie is a pain, and let me sleep there any time I need to, so long as I tell him where I'm going. When Archie was getting hammered last night I told him I was going to Sarah's house, and he said he didn't give a fuck where I went. He must have kept drinking and forgotten, and woken thinking I'd done a runner. I can't wait to get away from here. From him.'

'Where would you go?' said Rab. 'To your mum?'

'Maybe,' said Zoe. 'Find out if I really am a chip off the old block.'

In the reception area, Rab saw the way Sergeant Henderson glowered at Zoe.

'Do me a favour please, Sergeant,' said Rab. 'Write down the station's switchboard number and the direct line to my desk. Better write them down twice, give me a copy too.'

He handed one copy to Zoe.

'If you want to talk – about anything – I promise I'll listen. No judgement, no accusations, and no cigarettes.' He tried to read her reaction, but got nothing back.

He watched her leave. Hand on the heavy door, she turned:

'The answer to your question is no. I hardly ever hear from my mum. She hated life with Archie so much, she probably can't face his bitch kid. I don't blame her.'

Chapter Seven

Detective Chief Superintendent George "Quiet Man" Quigley was normally so soft-spoken, rooms routinely fell silent to increase the odds of being able to hear what he said. Today was different, and colleagues throughout CID heard him tear into Detective Inspector Ken Malloy and his offsider, Detective Sergeant Brigida Kosofsky. All work ground to a halt to tune into the raging from the other side of a door that barely had a chance to close before the gaffer let loose.

Office rumour said Quigley got his hair cut every four days. A uniform shade of grey, it was as neat as a Japanese flower arrangement. In his early 50s, he was well over six feet tall and slim enough to slip straight back into slacks he last wore in secondary school. A church elder who had never once been heard to utter profanity, and a stern teetotaller in a building full of heavy drinkers, the closest thing the Quiet Man had to a vice was long-distance running. His office wall had the medals from five consecutive finishes in the London Marathon and the whisper going around was he planned to participate in both Paris and New York in the coming months. As a superior officer, Quigley was scrupulously fair and intensely loyal to his subordinates. Unless they made him look like a fool.

At the side of his desk was Detective Superintendent Bill Donaldson, ten years Quigley's junior, but fading fast. Distended belly, drooping jowls and nicotine stains on hands held behind his back – like an army drill sergeant relishing the undoing of recruits caught climbing back over the wall after an unauthorised night on the beer.

Malloy and Kosofsky, each with a two-handed grip on a clear polythene evidence bag, stood directly in front of the desk staring impassively in Quigley's direction while carefully avoiding eye contact.

'Have you any idea how much, how much *crap* you have dropped on us, Malloy?'

'I understand sir,' said Malloy, 'I can only apologise—'

'Have you never heard of a rhetorical question?'

'Yes sir. Sorry, sir.'

Quigley looked at his hands, spread flat on the crisp, blemish-free desk blotter.

'I have spent the last two hours on the phone having my ears assaulted by the Chief Constable and his ACC in charge of media relations and not one, but three MPs calling from Westminster. Pompous nobodies with salaried flunkies to make their calls for them, keep me waiting for their esteemed Member to come to the blasted phone. Like I'm nothing. Do you think I'm nothing, Malloy?'

Malloy hesitated before responding.

'Another rhetorical question, sir?'

'You can bet your sorry backside it is, Detective Inspector.'

'Sorry sir.'

'I don't need to be convinced of how sorry you are. Here is a question you might be able to answer: How in the name of the Good Lord did your team manage to miss a key piece of evidence for four entire years?'

'Sorry sir, I mean—'

'It's an explanation we want,' said Quigley, in his normal voice.

Malloy had done enough damage already. Kosofsky leaned forward to deter him from making things worse.

'If I could answer sir,' she said. Quigley nodded. *Go on.*

'The photograph was much smaller than the pages of the black-and-white fashion book and it was jammed tight in the spine at a page where it looked like it was part of the book's content. If you look at the page, there is a clear outline of where the photograph was. It obviously didn't move a millimetre in four years, until Ashna's mother found it this week.'

The Chief Superintendent was not convinced.

'Maybe I missed something, Sergeant. Perhaps a decent rationale for you not finding it on day one of the investigation?'

'There is something, sir,' said Malloy, who looked like he was well aware what he said next was not going to help much.

'Go on, man,' said Quigley.

Malloy took a breath.

'We have no evidence the book was in Ashna's bedroom when we searched it.'

'What are you saying, Inspector? Surely you photographed the room before you touched anything?'

'Not immediately, sir,' said Malloy. 'The duty photographer was at a fatal, multiple-vehicle RTA on a Kingston Bridge slip road. Because we didn't know when he would be able to get to the Gupta house, I made the decision to search right away. Ashna had already been missing for more than twelve hours. I felt it was time critical.'

Quigley gave Bill Donaldson a look of disbelief. Donaldson shook his head. He understood. Quigley returned his gaze to Malloy.

'I'll tell you what's critical,' he said. 'The press are all over us like a blithering rash with "blundering plod" stories. City Chambers say we are an embarrassment to the city of Glasgow and want an explanation yesterday. And the Chief Constable and the whole of Westminster are meanwhile gleefully chipping away at what's left of our reputation. Your involvement in the TV programme last night was meant to show how hard we had worked on the investigation, but instead it made us look like idiots who need hard evidence to be handed to us in a BBC studio. What about the reward the brother announced live on national TV? When did you hear word of a reward?'

'Same time as you did, sir, when Simran Gupta announced it during the broadcast. We have talked with the family for months about a reward being posted; Ashna's parents were in favour of it, but there was always something to stop them going ahead. Simran sprung it on us last night without warning, sir.'

'Why on earth would he do that?' said Bill Donaldson.

Malloy hesitated and Kosofsky took over.

'I honestly think it was to make us look bad, sir,' she said. 'In recent months he has been increasingly critical of the lack of progress in the investigation.' She ignored the glance from Malloy saying "Thanks for bringing that up".

'Could anyone blame the boy?' said Quigley. Nobody replied.

'What the dickens happens now?' he said.

Malloy looked pleased. A chance to regroup.

'Sir, one of the forensic team is a keen photographer. He says the photographic paper used and the quality of the printing smacks of a professional printer, or at least a serious hobby photographer with his own darkroom. We are trying to contact every professional in the Yellow Pages. We are already talking to amateur photographic societies and camera clubs to see if anyone recognises the photograph as the sort of work done by someone they know. We will re-interview every one of Ashna's schoolmates to find if anybody knew about when the portrait was taken. Maybe they can tell us something which could lead us to the photographer, because remember, sir, we didn't know about the photograph when we interviewed them four years ago. It was never discussed in any interviews conducted after Ashna disappeared.'

Bill Donaldson chipped in:

'That's a good start, sir.'

Quigley gave it some consideration before speaking.

'Talk to everyone who set foot in the bedroom from the day we were first called in. Find out when anyone took notice of the book for the first time, where they found it, and who remembers flicking through it. Build a timeline of the book's place in the investigation, and try to work out how the heck the photograph managed to evade us until last night.'

'Yes sir,' said Malloy and Kosofsky, in unison.

Quigley looked to Donaldson. 'Where did Singh get sent to? Rothesay?'

'Dunoon, sir.'

'One more blunder from you, Malloy, and you will be walking a beat that makes Dunoon look like Sauchiehall Street on New Year's Eve.'

'Sir.'

'You two get to work.'

When the door closed behind them, Bill Donaldson collapsed into a seat in front of his gaffer's desk.

'They are good detectives, George,' he said.

'I know they are. What kind of name is Kosofsky?'

'I looked at her file. Her dad's a Pole who came to Scotland after fighting for the Allies in World War Two. Used to work for Rolls Royce. A genius with jet engines, apparently.'

'This place is turning into the League of Nations. *Kosofsky.* My wee gran used to say, "A name like that, ye'd be better aff wi' a nummer."'

From his perch on a low wall next to the station car park, Sergeant Henderson watched Rab Singh wander over to sit next to him. He placed his partially eaten sandwich on its greaseproof paper wrapping and unscrewed the cup at the top of a battered thermos.

'You might be able to help me, Sergeant,' said Rab.

'Call me "Hen". Everyone else does.'

'What can you tell me about Archie McCusker?'

Henderson plucked a clean teaspoon wrapped in tissue from deep inside his uniform jacket and used it to stir a packet of sugar into his tea.

'Known him all my life. What do you want to know?'

'Anything,' said Rab. 'The basics, who he is, what he does.'

Henderson took a noisy slurp of tea and dabbed at his lips with the tissue.

'We're the same age, which makes him forty-five. I went through school with him, from primary one until I left when I was sixteen. He went to Glasgow Tech for a couple of years, did some kind of business diploma, came back here and went straight into his dad's firm. His old man died about ten years ago, and Archie has built up the business until now he'd be one of the wealthiest folk in the town. A farm, a haulage company and shares in a couple of lobster boats. The majority share in a private hire cab firm, quite a bit of rental property and who knows what else.'

'He likes a drink?'

'Who doesn't?' He took a bite of his sandwich and washed it down with more tea. 'Archie pours it away, lost his driving licence for a year a while back. It was me who breathalysed

49

him – didn't talk to me for ages after. Now when he's on the bevvy he uses one of his taxis.'

'Zoe as good as told me he beats her,' said Rab.

'Don't Glasgow parents raise a hand to their kids anymore?'

'A lot less than when I was a kid.'

'The world's going soft, but I wouldn't take the daft girl's word for anything. She's a natural-born liar, forever spinning tales to use them to her advantage.'

He screwed the top back on his thermos and carefully folded the greaseproof paper from his sandwich, which he stowed in his pocket. A meticulous man, big Hen.

'Back to the coalface,' he said. 'Those telephones don't answer themselves, you know. Did you get the message I left on your desk? Are you sure we haven't met?'

'I got the message, thanks. And no, I don't recall meeting you.'

Rab watched the big man stroll back towards the station, polished boots splayed wide like a cartoon copper. Remember him? How could he forget?

Chapter Eight

Rab approached the front desk. Hen Henderson pointed a well-chewed pencil at the young officer standing near the door.

'Constable Young?'

'Yes sir. Eric Young. Superintendent Woods asked me to show you around.'

'Lead the way, Constable,' said Rab.

Young took the wheel of the Ford Escort and, with scrupulous attention to traffic laws and the Highway Code, soon took Rab straight past the Crest B&B and the Lobster Creel bar – the two places in Dunoon he remembered knowing. A minute later they parked on a slope next to the Castle House Museum and after Young made sure Rab wouldn't mind, they strolled along a pathway until they stood a stone's throw from yet another place Rab was familiar with, the Highland Mary statue.

The outlook opened up views of the town clustered like a bee's nest on the coast stretching to the north, and the Firth of Clyde reaching towards the mainland. The sky was sparkling blue with puffy clouds from a landscape artist's dream crisscrossed by jet trails pointing at Glasgow, less than 20 miles away. Not quite the other side of Karachi, even if to Rab it felt painfully distant. Constable Young was talking.

'Sorry, I was away with the birds,' said Rab. 'What were you saying?'

'The statue,' said Young, 'it's of—'

'Mary Campbell, otherwise known as Highland Mary,' said Rab. 'Robert Burns's local love, died of typhus when she was twenty-six.'

'You've done your homework, sir.'

'I was stuck on the ferry with nothing to read but a tourist board pamphlet.' He waved one arm at the neat little town. 'Tell me about Dunoon. Anything. I'm embarrassed at how little I know.'

'Not a lot to say, sir. The population is a wee bit north of four thousand, with maybe another fifteen hundred in nearby villages. There were another couple of thousand fell under our jurisdiction until the American submarine base closed last year. The whole area suffered. A lot of jobs disappeared overnight, and we had a spike in crime, mostly drunk and disorderlies, minor outbreaks of rough-house fisticuffs. Sergeant Duffy moaned about having his hands full with a rise in housebreaking and petty theft.'

Rab wandered to the top of steps leading past the statue. He put one foot on the lower rung of a stout railing.

'How long have you been in the job?'

'Nearly five years, sir.'

'What do you call people from Dunoon?'

'No idea what you're on about, sir.'

'Is there an equivalent to Glaswegian?'

'I'm from a village about four miles along the coast. Dunoonites. If I came from the town I'd be a Dunoonite.'

'Must hear a lot of dynamite jokes.'

'First time I've ever heard mention of it, sir.'

Rab's eyes opened wide until he detected suppressed mirth in the constable's expression.

'Got me there, eh?'

'Reeled you in like a haddock, sir. While we're on the subject, do you happen to know the difference between a stick of dynamite and a Dunoonite?'

'I've a feeling you're going to tell me.'

'If handled carelessly, one of them can cause havoc. The other one's an explosive.'

'Not bad,' said Rab.

'You're slotting it away for later use,' said Young.

'I have two sons entirely dependent on me for bad jokes. You went to school with the Dunoonites?'

'Life in the goldfish bowl, though it was a bit different with American military kids in every class. Even at six feet one, I could forget about making the basketball team.'

'What can you tell me about Archie McCusker's wife?'

Young didn't miss a beat.

'The lovely Debbie? She was a looker, and she knew it. Must be about two years ago she upped and went to England. Before she left, we were regulars at their house. Disturbances loud enough to worry the neighbours. Broken ornaments and drinks tumblers thrown around the living room. I remember one night Debbie had a fresh keeker, the eye closed shut, but claimed to have tripped and fallen when she had a drink in her. It was Zoe I felt sorry for, stuck in the middle of it. The lassie never had her troubles to seek.'

'I get the sense her mother leaving might have sent Zoe off the rails.'

'You'd be right, sir,' said Young. 'I don't remember having to deal with anything specifically to do with Zoe until after Debbie left town.'

'I asked Sergeant Henderson if he suspected Zoe's dad might beat her. He seems to think she needs an occasional slapping.'

'Between you and me, sir, Hen's stuck in a time warp,' said Young, 'but I wouldn't put it past Archie. Raising his hand to Zoe, I mean.'

Rab looked at his watch. 'Where do kids like Zoe hang out after school?'

'The ones with too much pocket money huddle at the Cowal. It's run by a grumpy Italian couple, but the coffee and the pastries are top notch.' He pointed north along the shoreline. 'Two minutes away.'

Rab moved to the top step. 'Do they do Empire biscuits?'

They ambled along Argyll Street until an open area with a miniature bandstand separated them from the Firth of Clyde. The Cowal Café occupied a prime spot with a view of the bandstand. Glasgow was full of Italian-run cafés, and throughout his teens and into his student years, Rab had the luxury of the legendary University Café within minutes of the family home. The University was old school – dark wood, intricately-turned wooden posts, all the seating in tight, intimate red vinyl booths.

The Cowal tried to be more modern, with 1970s Formica and metallic chairs, but it did have the requisite espresso machine like a polished steam engine crowding the counter space. Tables and chairs were bolted to the floor, the walls peppered with fading posters and paintings of Tuscany.

Always Tuscany, thought Rab. He had read how most of Scotland's ice cream parlours and chip shops belonged to third- or fourth-generation descendants of immigrants from Barga in Tuscany, who arrived in Scotland at the tail end of the 19th century. Barga was the impoverished hill town where the young Duke of Argyll fell gravely ill while undertaking the

54

customary upper class coming-of-age European Tour. One of Europe's richest men was nursed back to health by kindly locals who didn't have two pennies to rub together.

After he returned home, the Duke pulled strings to bring young unemployed Barga men to work in Scotland, and many of them eventually opened ice cream parlours and chip shops in towns all over the country. Present-day Barga was full of young people with broad Scots accents, bicultural free spirits as much at home in Scotland as they were embraced by the homeland of their ancestors. When Rab first heard the tale, it made him sick with envy. His was a story of a different class of immigrant to Scotland, one whose brown skin and turban marked him as a permanent outsider. On the two occasions he had returned to India, he was met with a mixture of derision for his less-than-perfect Punjabi, and bitter envy over his life in faraway Scotland.

The café was empty of customers except for one old man in a heavy tweed suit with leather elbow patches making breaks for freedom. He had no teeth, and was enthusiastically sucking coffee from a giant mug, lips flapping with a noise that reminded Rab of when kids used to attach ice lolly sticks to the frames of their bicycles to brap against the spokes. The old guy sounded like his bike was missing a few spokes. He paused in mid slurp to give Eric Young a thumb's up.

'Hi John,' said Eric at a volume that suggested John might be hard of hearing. Rab wondered if it was from listening to himself drink coffee.

Rab left Eric at a two-person window table with an unbroken view of the bandstand.

At the counter, a man who looked like an Italian Winston Churchill took Rab's order without a word. After several minutes in awe of the roaring and hissing of steam and frothing of milk, Rab returned to the table toting a round tray with two large cappuccinos and Empire biscuits on a tea plate.

'Four Empire biscuits?' said Eric.

'My all-time favourites. You're allowed one, maybe even two,' said Rab. He sat down just as the door from the street blew open and five school kids piled in, making enough noise to drown John's attempts to suck the glaze from his coffee mug. One of them was Zoe, who winked at Rab as she and her friends sprinted to the counter to place orders, all elbows and adolescent squeals. Even as Rab wondered how you said "dour" in Italian, the proprietor surprised him, not only by putting on a smile, but by changing the music for the benefit of the newcomers. From an Italian opera tenor warbling emotionally in the background to *Take That* belting out a saccharin ballad Rab's boys hated.

While Eric eyed the kids at the counter, Rab took an exploratory nibble at an Empire biscuit. Not bad. 'You're not much older than them,' he said. 'Did you hang out here when you were still at school?'

Young helped himself to a biscuit. 'What I said before about the ones with too much pocket money? I wasn't so lucky. Once in a while I'd be here on a Saturday with a couple of pals, making an iced drink last forever and hoping the girls we fancied would drop by.'

'And did they?'

'Sometimes,' said Young. 'Teenage testosterone fever, eh?'

'It got me into trouble at least once,' said Rab.

'What got you into trouble?' said Zoe. She rested her elbows on the table, brought herself to their eye level.

'We were talking about being teenagers,' said Rab.

Zoe jerked a thumb at Eric Young. 'I can see how he might remember, but you? Too distant a memory.'

'You're funny,' said Rab.

'You think so?'

'No.'

Her friends headed for the door carrying take-away orders and making coo-eee noises. She waved them away with a grin.

'What are you doing here?' she said.

'Constable Young said great things about the Empire biscuits,' said Rab.

'Best in Dunoon,' said Eric.

'It speaks!' said Zoe. 'More like he told you this was where I might be. Do you fancy me or something?'

'You're young enough to be my daughter,' said Rab.

Zoe put one finger to her lips. She might have been trying for seductive, but it only made her look younger.

'Doesn't stop some folk I know,' she said, in a near whisper.

'You might want to choose your next few words carefully,' said Rab.

'You'd be happy if I gave you some names?' Mischief lit up her young eyes.

'If what you're hinting at is true,' said Rab, 'I'll be happy to see them in court.'

'You know that's not going to happen, Sergeant.'

As she hurried off to catch her friends, the background music returned to Italian opera.

A few feet away, old John fished a full set of shockingly white false teeth from his jacket pocket and slipped them straight into his mouth. He stared, faded old eyes glinting at Rab and Eric, and made a clacking noise that might have been laughter.

When Rab looked to Eric Young for an explanation, he raised an eyebrow at the tea plate. The two Empire biscuits were gone.

Chapter Nine

Detective Inspector Malloy felt marginally refreshed after nipping home for a shower and a fitful nap. Inside the door of CID he ignored a young woman who eyed him from one of the chairs set out for members of the public. Wannabe reward hunters were low on his list of priorities.

He saw Detective Sergeant Brygida Kosofsky at her desk. The fatigue in her eyes told him she had chosen not to take a break. He suspected she had remained at her desk as part of a points-scoring agenda.

'Anything important come in?' he said.

'Good afternoon, Inspector,' said Kosofsky.

'Well?'

'More of the same.'

'Any of the callers forget to leave their details, meaning we can't send a reward?'

Kosofsky's face said *Aye, right.* 'More like "let's make sure you get my name and address written down correctly before I tell you a thing".'

A voice called out from behind Malloy.

'Hellooo! I've been here for half an hour with something important.' It was the young woman sitting by the door. She had blue hair and multiple piercings decorating both eyebrows, different parts of her ears, her septum and her bottom lip.

'Maybe I should take it to the newspapers,' she said, 'see if they're interested in what you lot can't be bothered looking at.'

Kosofsky was inured to Malloy's reproachful looks. She paid the latest one no heed.

'Why hasn't anyone attended to this young lady?'

'She arrived with a pencil drawing,' said Kosofsky. 'We've been answering phones and fielding visits from the gaffers. I was going to take a look—'

Malloy turned away while she was in mid-sentence and spoke to the woman:

'Come with me, please.'

The interview room smelled strongly of alcohol and disinfectant, sure signs of a recent episode of vomit, and Malloy detected a damp spot in one corner. He and Kosofsky sat across the table from the newcomer, who made a show of placing a flat package wrapped in newspaper on a scarred table, witness to a thousand interrogations and a fair number of tearful confessions.

'We are extremely sorry for keeping you waiting, ma'am,' said Malloy. 'We've been run off our feet here. What have you got for us?'

'Can you tell us your name first, please?' said Kosofsky. Pissing off Malloy was an art form she was getting the hang of, and his failure to establish the name of a witness right away was an error so elementary not even he could complain about having it pointed out.

'Karen Munro,' said the witness, who spelled it out for Brygida. 'I have a drawing I think you should see. I used to—'

'A drawing.' said Malloy. Not a question, more an expression of disbelief.

'They call it photorealism,' said Munro. 'Art taking on the qualities of a photograph. This one is done entirely in pencil.'

She peeled back newspaper to reveal a framed drawing of a café scene.

'You drew this?' said Malloy.

'Fat chance,' said Munro, 'my nephews pee themselves when I try to draw matchstick men. This used to be gathering dust in a storeroom at the Blue Parrot.'

'The coffee bar on Byres Road that went bust?' said Kosofsky. 'They did great muffins.'

Malloy shot her a sideways look. *I've got this.* Kosofsky pretended not to notice.

'How did the drawing get there?' she said.

'I was a barista there for about a year, and when it closed and we got paid off, the manager said we could take any of the decorations we wanted. Anything except the giant ceramic parrot in the window. There was a scramble for the more flashy stuff, but I had seen this in the store-room. It's been on a shelf in my flat ever since.'

Malloy looked at the drawing carefully for the first time and slapped both palms to the table loud enough to make Munro flinch.

'That's Ashna Gupta!'

'Finally,' said Munro. 'Exactly what occurred to me last night in the middle of *Crimewatch*, and the only reason I'm here.'

This time the atmosphere in the Chief Superintendent's office was different. George Quigley, his deputy Detective Superintendent Bill Donaldson, and Malloy and Kosofsky sat around a coffee table that served as an informal meeting station. The pencil drawing and frame, now separated, lay inside clear evidence bags on the table.

Malloy launched into a detailed description of what constituted photorealism that Kosofsky recognized as a word-for-word regurgitation of Karen Munro's explanation. It prompted a rolling hand motion from the Quiet Man. *Get on with it.* The drawing showed a wide-angle view of a scene inside a coffee shop. The point of view was from close behind the shoulder of a customer who had his back to the artist. Nothing of him was visible other than the shoulder and one sleeve of a crisp white shirt.

On the other side of the table and in front of the man sat a young woman, somewhere between anguish and a full-blown panic attack. It was a sadder version of the same face in the burlesque-styled studio photograph. Undoubtedly Ashna Gupta. The rest of the drawing was of nearby tables stretching towards a window looking out over Byres Road.

'OK,' said George Quigley. 'The key question is: how does this help the investigation?'

Malloy spoke with obvious satisfaction.

'Two things in the drawing are extremely significant, sir. First, the girl close to tears is clearly Ashna Gupta. The second is also important.' He put a finger on the plastic bag covering the drawing. 'On this table next to where they are sitting is a copy of the Evening News. Sergeant Kosofsky made some calls to an editor friend, who promised to keep the enquiry on the QT so long as his paper gets the first call if it leads to something. Thanks to the level of detail in the drawing, we can even read the headline.' He had their attention, and all eyes dropped to where the newspaper front page said:

BULLY BOY POLICE SCANDAL

'My editor contact looked it up,' said Kosofsky. 'The story wasn't about us, by the way — that was Coatbridge's problem. It's the front page from Friday, March 17th, 1989.' She sat back and bathed in her superiors' glow and in the rage emanating from Malloy for having his thunder stolen.

Chief Superintendent Quigley was the first to ask.

'March 17th?'

'The day Ashna disappeared,' said Malloy a little too eagerly. 'The next thing we have to consider, sir, is the drawing might well have been created from a real photograph.'

Detective Superintendent Bill Donaldson got it first. 'Because how else would the artist have captured Ashna's desperation and the detail on the newspaper?'

'Meaning the artist and the photographer might be one and the same?' said Quigley. 'Hang on – you don't think it was the same photographer who took the studio shot Simran surprised us with?'

'We can't be sure,' said Kosofsky, 'but at the moment we think two different photographers are involved. For a start, the photos are of different photographic genres, one a carefully posed and lit studio portrait, the other a candid shot probably taken without the subjects' knowledge.'

'Unfortunately, sir,' said Malloy, 'the girl who brought us the drawing, Karen Munro, was hired at the coffee shop a full year after Ashna disappeared. We're trying to locate the former owners, but it's not proving easy.'

'Is that it?' said Quigley. 'One potentially vital clue and we hit another road block?'

'Not quite, sir,' said Kosofsky. She turned over the evidence bag with the frame. On its back was a printed label.

'The drawing was framed at a shop in Maryhill, sir,' said Malloy. 'Sergeant Kosofsky checked. It's a one-man outfit, still in business, and we'll get over there as soon as we can. Two possibilities spring to mind: the artist could be local, and sold or gave the café a present of the framed drawing; or they received only the drawing and somebody at the café had it framed at the place in Maryhill. The scrawled signature on the front of the drawing isn't a lot of help. Something Brown, first name beginning with the letter A.'

'There must be hundreds of A Browns in Scotland alone,' said Bill Donaldson.

'We hope the frame shop might help us narrow things down, sir,' said Kosofsky.

Bill Quigley nodded. 'Because if the pencil artist based the drawing on a photograph, he or she witnessed a meeting between Ashna and the man in the white shirt, on the day she disappeared,' he said. 'You two get over to Maryhill right away. Seize anything of any help to the investigation, and keep us posted about anything – and I do mean anything – you find out.'

Brygida Kosofsky knew this part of Maryhill well. For years her engineer father had tried to pass on to his only child a passion for the design heritage of his adopted homeland. Long before it became fashionable to be a Charles Rennie Mackintosh devotee he took Brygida on repeated pilgrimages to the architect's more famous landmarks like the Glasgow School of Art and the art nouveau Hill House in Helensburgh. But his clear favourite and the subject of multiple visits was the Queen's Church designed and built on Maryhill Road by Mackintosh in the late 1890s. Despite his client being the notoriously conservative Free Church, Mackintosh managed to infuse design influences from Japan, from Gothic art and from pre-reformation England. Or so Dad kept telling Brygida.

Three doors along from the church, Fraser the Framer occupied a shop at the foot of a tenement block, a miniature trading post that, going by the faded overlapping colours and fonts on the signboard above the window, had changed occupants a few times over the decades.

The man whose name was now above the window was no more than five foot two, and lean as a whippet – not an ounce of fat on a physique unchanged since days as a jockey illustrated in photographs and newspaper cuttings artfully framed on the wall behind the counter. He listened carefully to what they needed before examining the label on the frame in the evidence bag for a moment.

'Easy,' he said. He pointed a varnish-stained fingernail at the label. 'The code beside my logo tells me the year, month and job number. This was the nineteenth job in August 1989, which made it a better than average month. Let's check my work log.'

From under the counter he hauled a bulky, well-thumbed ledger with 1989 written on the spine in blue marker. It took seconds to find the entry he wanted.

'There it is. Margaret Rogers – she was the manager at the Blue Parrot – she lives a wee bit along the road, and gave me a fair bit of work. She brought this one on the 14th of August, a Monday. She collected it three days later, paid thirty-four pounds fifty pence in cash. Shame the Blue Parrot's no more. My wee business loves regular customers like Margaret.'

'I don't suppose you remember what kind of packaging it arrived in?' said Brygida.

'Oddly enough, I do,' said Fraser. 'It was in a big padded envelope from Australia with about twelve stamps on it, and I kept it for my nephew, who used to be crazy about stamps. Next thing we know, he's a collector of pocket knives. No way Uncle Fraser is going to help a Maryhill boy collect blades.'

'Any possibility you still have the envelope?' said Malloy.

'You might be out of luck. We did a big clear-out a few weeks ago. But give me a minute. I know exactly where it used to be.'

He disappeared into a back room, to re-emerge seconds later, carrying a large envelope.

'See what I mean about the stamps?' he said. 'Might be why I couldn't bring myself to throw it away.'

Kosofsky rolled her eyes in disbelief when she saw Malloy pull on latex gloves.

'Please place the envelope on the counter and take a step back,' he said. Fraser the Framer gave Brygida a classic *what the fuck* look that she met with a raised eyebrow.

Using his gloved fingertips, Malloy plucked the envelope from the countertop by the edges and looked inside.

'Nothing,' he said. 'No covering letter.' He put fingertips to opposite corners and let the envelope rotate as he examined its exterior. 'No return address,' he said.

'If there was one,' said Kosofsky, 'it probably was in a letter that went in the bin at the Blue Parrot. What does the postmark say?'

As if by magic, Fraser produced a magnifying glass slightly smaller than a dinner plate and handed it to Kosofsky. She didn't need it to read the pin-sharp postmarks.

'Ulverstone TAS 7315,' she said. 'Tasmania.'

'Not exactly what we were hoping for,' said Malloy.

'It's what folk in our line of work call a clue,' said Kosofsky. Malloy didn't see the wink she exchanged with the smiling Fraser.

Chapter Ten

Rab was at the dining table when Mags Henderson arrived toting a plate filled with enough food to satisfy a family of three.

'You look exhausted,' she said. 'After you rushed out with no breakfast, I bet you had nothing decent for lunch.'

Rab thought about his day. 'You're right. Total nutritional intake was a packet of crisps and an Empire biscuit.'

'I'll leave you in peace. The guest lounge is through there. You've got the place to yourself again tonight, nobody to fight with over the remote control.'

'Do you mind if I use your telephone to call Glasgow? I'll happily pay.'

'I thought you would have one of those mobile things.'

'Mine went with the Glasgow job, and the CID sergeant here doesn't get one.'

'They've been all the rage here since they came out. My friends seem to spend half the day waving their expensive gizmos in the air, trying to get a signal. Are you missing your family?'

'I have to talk to my sons. They're seven and ten.'

'What about their mum?'

Rab's mouth watered as he eyed the shepherd's pie with a side salad and a plate of chips and two buttered rolls. Classic Scottish carbohydrate overload. 'She's a bit older,' he said.

Mags's smile was at least indulgent. 'If it was a comedian you wanted to be, maybe you did the right thing joining the police.'

'We're separated,' said Rab. 'It happened a few weeks ago and I'm still trying to get used to it.'

'What happened?' said Mags. 'Sorry! None of my business.'

'I'm not sure it can be fixed,' he said.

'At least you have your boys. I'll leave you to your food.' She turned to leave but paused when Rab spoke:

'You and Hen didn't have any kids?'

'It was never going to happen. Hen wasn't interested,' she said.

'Some people are like that,' said Rab.

'Like what?'

'They don't want kids.'

'Hen wasn't interested in the bit about making the kids,' said Mags. 'Now he's married to his church. All fire and brimstone and sinners going to hell for the slightest misdeed, real or imagined. Not exactly the place you'd expect a closet homosexual to gravitate, but it's a funny old world. Just between you and me, Mr Singh.'

'Of course. Please call me Rab.'

'The telephone's in the hallway. If you could drop some coins in the jar next to it, that would be good.'

Detective Inspector Ken Malloy replaced the telephone handset and looked at the notes he had scribbled on an A4 pad. To Detective Sergeant Brygida Kosofsky, they might as well be hieroglyphs.

'I'm surprised they were so cooperative,' she said.

'Maybe I got the only helpful diplomat at the Aussie embassy, a bloke called Kevin. Even he admitted they wouldn't normally play research assistant to cops four hundred miles away, but Kevin saw *Crimewatch* and wanted to assist if he could. He also said it helped I wasn't a "fackin' Pom".'

'And?'

'And they have the latest copies of every telephone book for Australia. He found three A Browns in or near Ulverstone, Tasmania. One plain A, one Alex and an Alan.'

Brygida looked at the clock on the wall and did the arithmetic. 'They're eleven hours ahead. Is five a.m. too early?'

'Might mean we catch them before they go out hunting kangaroos, or whatever it is they do in Tasmania.'

'Probably go to work in offices and shops and police stations. Let's take them in the order you wrote them,' said Kosofsky.

Malloy selected the speakerphone and dialled the long number with care. Kosofsky stood closer to him than he would normally tolerate, and they were rewarded with the sound of ringing. The ringing ended, and the gruff voice of a heavy smoker crossed the time zones:

'Whoever you are, this better be good.'

'Sorry to bother you, madam—'

'I'll give you "madam", ya—'

'Sorry sir,' said Malloy. 'I'm calling from Glasgow, Scotland. I'm a police officer looking for an A Brown who is an artist specialising in photorealism and who visited Glasgow in 1989.'

'No fackin' idea what you're on about,'. The line went dead.

'I think we can rule him out,' said Malloy as he dialled the second number on his list. This time the phone rang twice before a more friendly voice, definitely male, came from the other end of the line.

'Who's this?'

'Sorry for the early call, sir—'

'No worries, mate. Early riser, me. What can I do for you? Hope you're not gonna try and sell me something at this ungodly hour.'

'Actually, sir, I'm a police inspector in Glasgow, Scotland. We are trying to trace an A Brown who lives in Ulverstone.'

'Could be me, right enough. Did you say Glasgow?'

'Yes sir. The A Brown we are trying to locate visited Glasgow in 1989, and sent a pencil drawing as a gift to a coffee shop here. Can you help?'

'You're in luck, mate. I'm Andrew Brown, but you're looking for my brother Alan. He took a holiday in Scotland a few years back. What that lad can do with a pencil is amazing. Keep telling him he's wasting his talent working in a factory canning peas.'

When Malloy finally got off the phone, Brygida thought for a weird moment he might give her a high five. Thankfully not.

'About time,' he said. 'I was overdue a break.'

Arsehole.

American office workers shoot the breeze at the water cooler. With Glasgow's tap water tooth-achingly cold year-round, coolers didn't exist, but on Sheena's floor of Police HQ, folk often stopped to talk at the urn, where all-day-long hot water was sought to drag flavour from stale tea bags or make instant coffee drinkable. The urn was close to the photocopier and fax machines, and when Sheena passed through on her way to the lift, Ken Malloy and Brygida Kosofsky appeared transfixed by the silent fax machine.

'Didn't your mothers tell you a watched pot never boils?' she said.

'Don't you have somewhere to be?' said Malloy.

Sheena raised an eyebrow at Brygida. 'What's going on?'

Brygida was happy to engage in idle chat with a colleague her boss wanted to see the back of.

'You heard about the pencil sketch of Ashna looking near to tears while talking to an unidentified male in a Byres Road coffee shop the day she disappeared?'

'No,' said Sheena.

'Someone brought a sketch in. Inspector Malloy and I tracked it to an amateur artist in Ulverstone, Tasmania. We talked to him on the phone, and he's taking the original photo he made the drawing from, and three others he took, to the local police station. They're going to send us faxes of all four. We'll get rough black-and-white copies, but they'll do until the cops over there can get the originals to us by courier.'

'Will you two stop chattering?' said Malloy.

'The fax machine doesn't care how much noise we make, Ken,' said Sheena.

'Enough,' he said. 'Here we go.'

The machine performed its electronic handshake routine with a machine at the other end of the world before it gradually emitted an image burned into thermally sensitive paper. The same process happened four separate times until at last they had four black-and-white high-contrast copies of 5×7-inch photographs spread along a counter top. They formed a line and pored over the images until Sheena broke the silence.

'What else did the artist guy tell you?' she said.

'His name is Alan Brown,' said Kosofsky. 'We caught him for a couple of minutes before he had to go out to work, meaning we have to speak to him again when he gets home. He already gave us three strong leads.'

70

Malloy butted in. 'One, he keeps a diary, and is certain the photographs were taken on March 17th, 1989, the same day Ashna Gupta failed to show for the party at the Hilton. Two, the couple in the photographs left shortly after he photographed them. They were in a rush, and Ashna was distraught, according to Alan. He remembers she kept asking the other guy, over and over, "What am I going to do?" '

Sheena couldn't resist.

'And three?'

Malloy looked smug. 'He was Indian, too, but a lot older than Ashna, and trying to reassure her, to calm her. Alan never saw his face, but he assumed the other man was the girl's father.'

Rab woke with a stiff neck from being folded into an overstuffed armchair in the Crest's lounge. In front of him was a television with the sound muted on a darts match. Maybe it was all they ever showed on national TV. Soap operas, darts matches, snooker tournaments and the occasional episode of *Crimewatch*.

'Rab, wake up.'

He turned to where Mags leaned in from behind the partly opened door.

'You forgot to make your phone call,' she said.

'Oh, sh – shoot,' he said. 'Thank you, it's not too late—'

'There's a call for you now. It's a woman called Sheena, who says she is your wife, and she sounds worried about something. I hope it's not bad news.'

Rab hurried to the phone in the chilly hallway, hoping Sheena was simply angry with him for not calling.

'Hello?'

'Rab?'

'Yes. What's wrong? Are the boys alright? I'm sorry about not calling last night. I was about to call them now. Are they OK?'

'They're alright. You're a bastard for forgetting to ring them, but you know what's the worst thing? They've come to expect you to disappoint them.'

'I'm sorry—'

'That's not why I called. Did you hear about a pencil drawing of Ashna?'

'You mean the photograph Simran surprised Ken Malloy with on the TV last night? Sorry. If you meant photograph you'd have said photograph.'

'Someone who used to work at a coffee shop on Byres Road brought in a pencil drawing a tourist sent them before they went bust. There's only one customer's face visible, but it's Ashna's – and a newspaper on the table next to her puts the date at Friday, March 17th, 1989.'

'You're joking.'

'Listen to yourself. Would I joke about something like this?'

'The day Ashna disappeared. 'What else has Malloy managed to find out? Anything?'

'You know Malloy. If it wasn't for Brygida Kosofsky developing ideas fit for a CID detective, he'd still be stumbling around in the dark.'

'And he isn't now,' said Rab.

'Inside two hours of the drawing arriving at the station, he and Kosofsky were talking to the artist – in Australia – who works from photographs. He took four photos to his local police station in Tasmania, who faxed over copies of the five-by-sevens. He also told Ken and Brygida he remembered Ashna being distressed.'

'Wow.'

'You don't know the half of it, Rab. This is scary.'

72

'What are you talking about?'

'I saw the faxed copies of the four photographs. The artist said the person Ashna was pouring her heart out to was an older Indian man, maybe her father. But because he never saw his face it doesn't appear in any of the photographs.'

'So?'

'It was your dad, Rab, it was Baldeep. The photos show the back of a shoulder and one sleeve of a white shirt. In one of them, the sleeve had exactly the sort of old-fashioned elastic sleeve garter Baldeep always wore.'

'It's your turn to listen to yourself. Maybe older, possibly Indian, and because he wore sleeve garters he must have been my father?'

'There's more,' said Sheena. She sounded reluctant to go on, which terrified Rab. He swallowed the urge to speak and waited for the killer punch.

'There was a bag hanging on the back of the man's chair,' she said. 'You'd recognise it in an instant. The fabric one from the fifties your mother hated and was forever begging Baldeep to throw away or replace with a new one.'

'Oh no,' said Rab.

'Yes, the bag he took everywhere, the one he kept his cameras in. I've only ever seen one bag like it, and the one in the photo is same bag. The man talking to Ashna was Baldeep. The day she disappeared, Ashna was crying her eyes out in front of your dad.'

Chapter Eleven

Experts argue whether there are five or seven stages of grief, and despite the passing years, Rab knew the full effects of his father's death were yet to sink in.

Whenever Baldeep crossed his mind, and it happened a lot, the main emotion Rab suffered was regret. Regret at things beyond his control, like not having a chance to say goodbye because Baldeep was found dead in his attic office, hours after suffering a massive heart attack. Another regret was more painful, the one about not having spent enough time together, and not having paid enough attention to a parent who gave him so much while asking so little. Unlike most parents of his generation, Baldeep not only avoided exerting any pressure on Rab, he ran interference to deflect Ruby's endless meddling. His message to Rab was to do his own thing, follow his own instincts, to explore the roads **he** wanted to travel. It took a long time for Rab to grasp that these were freedoms denied to Baldeep when he was a young man.

One night when Ruby was out playing bridge and after Baldeep had enjoyed a couple or three tots from the Haig Dimple bottle, he ambushed 14-year-old Rab with the *"what do you want to do with your life?"* question.

When Rab admitted to having no idea what lay ahead, his father surprised him by saying there was nothing wrong with that. Baldeep proceeded to vent about the endless competition among parents in the Indian community and how they jostled to present their kids as most likely to become a barrister or a surgeon. Aspiring to be a mere lawyer or doctor no longer impressed the status-obsessed snobs, he grumbled. Unstated was the certainty of his wife being among them.

'And you can forget about it being only us Indians,' he said. 'I went to a parents' night at your school not long after you got here, and do you know what your teacher Mrs Skeggs asked me?' Rab hadn't heard this one, and his father went on, 'She said to me, "Has Rabinder expressed any interest in pursuing a particular profession?".'

'I couldn't believe my ears. "He's ELEVEN YEARS OLD",' I told her. 'If he comes home and says he wants to be an astronaut or a lion tamer, I say "great idea, son!".'

He took a sip of Haig. 'Do you get my point?'

'I'm not sure,' said Rab, who wondered if this was what happened when people got drunk.

'You know how your mother bristles at the mention of Margaret Bourke-White?'

Now Rab was properly lost. 'Who?'

'My hero. The woman in the photo on my office wall. The American photographer perched on a decorative eagle on the 61st floor of the Chrysler Building in Manhattan, in the 1930s. I first saw it in a photography magazine in India when I was about your age. I became determined to be a photographer, and I scoured museums and magazine racks and second-hand bookstores and learned everything I could about the work of photographers like Ansel Adams, Man Ray, Cartier-Bresson and later, Bert Hardy and India's own Raghu Rai. I saved every rupee I could get my little hands on until I bought my first real camera, a Contax II. I still have it. You've used it.'

Rab knew the Contax, was aware how much his father loved it, and always deeply impressed that he was allowed to share it. 'Why didn't you become a photographer?'

'Because my father refused to let it happen. He could have sent me to any university in India, but after I begged him to let me become a photographer, he gave me an ultimatum: study accountancy or law, or get out of the house. And here I am, older than my father was when he died, and I never chased my dream.'

Rab remembered thinking it was the saddest thing he had ever heard. And now photography and photographs were at the centre of the investigation. In one photograph his father was seen with a distressed Ashna hours before she disappeared. And in another, Ashna posed for an elaborate studio portrait Rab now realised must have been taken by his father.

He dreaded what lay ahead, a rabbit hole of peril and uncertainty that could destroy his family and his career.

The first time Sheena watched Rab tie a turban, she broke into uncontrollable laughter. Rab was initially upset because he interpreted her mirth as mockery, but between uncontrollable hiccups brought on by the laughter, she eventually put his mind at rest. Like a lot of people he had met since, she had imagined the turban to be like any other hat, instead of five or six yards of fine cotton cloth requiring skill and patience to create a new turban every time it was worn.

'You're kidding,' said Rab.

'I wish I was,' she said, between more hiccups.

'You've seen me wearing half a dozen colours of turban,' he said. 'Did you think I kept them perched on a row of polystyrene heads on my dresser?'

Laughing out of control, they fell into an embrace and eventually banished the hiccups in a frenzied bout of lovemaking. The turban needed to be ironed and retied when they were finished.

The radio in Rab's room at the Crest played Annie Lennox singing Would I Lie To You while Rab twisted, tied and wrapped a clean orange turban cloth five times round his head in front of an elaborately engraved mirror. The memory must have been from 15 years ago, in Sheena's bedsit when they were students at Glasgow University. He ran his fingers through the short, neatly trimmed beard that, to the informed, marked him as a "*sahajdari*" Sikh, literally a "slow adopter", or unbaptised.

The balance between salt and pepper in the beard hinted at impending middle age and made him wonder, not for the first time, where the years had gone.

Breakfast at the Crest was a quiet affair, Mags Henderson taking great care to deliver food, masses of food, and to make herself scarce to leave Rab with his thoughts.

At least today he was able to eat his fill before going to work, and by the time he carefully folded his napkin and placed it on the table, Rab was fit to burst. At a time in his life when he didn't have much to feel good about, even a full stomach was a welcome boost to his spirits.

Mags insisted on seeing him out, and as she opened the door her attention shifted to a figure standing by the gate at the end of the path. Zoe McCusker, in school uniform. Rab approached the gate, wondering why she was there.

'Walk me to school, officer?'

'I probably have time for that. What's wrong?'

'Something has to be wrong?'

'Yesterday I said I'd hear you out anytime you wanted,' said Rab.

She opened the gate and he joined her on the footpath.

'Which way?' he said.

'Eh?'

'To your school.' He flicked one hand between both ends of the road. 'Which way?'

'You definitely are the new kid in town.' She turned left and Rab fell in step beside her. She moved at a glacial pace, making him wonder if she didn't want to get to school, or if she had something difficult to tell him and needed time to pick her moment. He maintained the pace she set, and she edged closer.

'Did you make it home last night?' he said.

'I did. No panicked visits to the cop shop from Archie this morning, I promise.'

'It's not your dad I'm concerned about.'

'No need to worry about me.'

'But here you are,' said Rab. 'Do you need to tell me something, or can I help somehow?'

'There is one thing,' she said, her eyes dropping to the pavement in front of her feet. She slipped her arm through his and leaned into him. Rab wriggled free, but not before a mother and her school-age daughter stepped out of a doorway and ogled them, the child curious, her mother aghast.

'Go on,' said Rab.

They took a few more paces in silence. Rab sensed Zoe waiting for the mother and daughter to overtake them and move out of earshot. Eventually, with obvious reluctance, they passed and Zoe spoke in a lower voice.

'I told you about my mum, right?'

'You said she has been living in London for about two years, and you want to get away from Archie to go find her.'

'See? That's the reason I'm here, Sergeant.'

'What do you mean?'

'Nobody pays attention to anything I say. You do.'

'It's my job.'

'Does that mean all I am is a crime about to happen?'

'Stop it. I'm listening.'

He waited while she seemed to gather resolve.

'I need you to help me find my mum.' She pulled a photograph from her pocket. It was a close-up of a pretty woman beaming a warm smile. She had blonde wavy hair professionally styled, bright blue eyes and attractive features astonishingly like her daughter's, which made Rab think she must have been young when Zoe was born. Her fingernails bore a clear lacquer and she clasped a gold necklace with Z-O-E in separate letters linked together by a fine chain.

'It's not a lot to go on,' said Rab, instantly regretting his choice of words.

'I wrote everything I know on the back,' said Zoe, already on the defensive.

He cursed himself for not turning it over. The information written in Zoe's young hand was pitifully thin, Name, maiden name, date of birth, town of birth Leeds, Yorkshire. Rab did the arithmetic. She would have been in her teens when Zoe was born.

'The trouble in cases like this—'

'Here come the excuses,' said Zoe, anger in the narrowing of her eyes, the set of her jaw.

'I have to be straight with you,' said Rab. 'I assume your mum hasn't been reported missing. If not, and if she hasn't been involved in a crime, either as the victim or the perpetrator, there will be nothing to find in police records.'

'If you are about to tell me to try the Salvation Army, I'll get myself to school.'

'Are there relatives on your mother's side who might be able to help?'

'So much for you listening!' said Zoe. 'I only know what little she told me. She always said she understood how I felt because she was an only child, too. When I asked about my grandparents, she said they were both dead. She was a mad Leeds United fan, if that's any help. I've got a couple of Christmas cards she sent from London. All they say inside is 'Love Mum'. Still in the envelopes. The postmarks on both are the same. Peckham SE15.'

'No return address?'

'What do you think, Sherlock? Don't you credit me with enough intelligence to tell you if there was a return address? Love Mum. Twice. That's all I've heard in two years.'

While she talked her voice rose and their arrival at the school gate was met with stares from parents, pupils and staff. Zoe looked straight at Rab. Her eyes were moist. 'You'll look for her?'

As Rab nodded, she rose onto her tiptoes, kissed him on the cheek, ran one palm softly across the same cheek as if to second the affectionate gesture, turned and strode confidently across the playground, head high. Every pair of eyes, Rab's included, followed her to the school door. She didn't look back.

Chapter Twelve

As soon as she saw the boys off to school, Sheena Ferguson made a short phone call. One of the benefits of reaching Inspector level was being able to ring a colleague to make it known she would be late for whatever reason she dreamt up. A firm believer in the occasional white lie, today she said she had a doctor's appointment.

Instead of picking through the back streets, she enjoyed wandering Byres Road, past trendy coffee bars, a specialist cheese and pickles shop, two florists, fast-disappearing independent newsagent-tobacconists of a bygone era and at least one public bar whose drunken footprint went back centuries.

Despite being less than two miles from the city centre, this part of Glasgow remained green fields until the middle of the 19th century, when it attracted wealthy merchants eager to escape the grime and overcrowding of the city. Now, after a century and a half of the constant expansion of nearby Glasgow University, the area's prosperity remained gilt-edged, even if many of the proud three- and four-storey terraced homes had long ago been divided into cramped student bedsits.

It was thanks to one such student lodging, the smallest room in a beautiful old three-bedroom flat, that Sheena was making this journey today. She and Rab first dated when they were in secondary school together, and when they both went on to Glasgow University Sheena badly wanted to embrace independent student life by moving into her own place. But since her family home was not far away in posh Bearsden, her father balked at the idea and refused to be swayed until a comfortable room in a secure flat presented itself for a silly price. Sheena moved into a room whose affordable rent was entirely thanks to Baldeep doing his bit to give Rab and his girlfriend a place where they could enjoy some privacy. Ruby never learned the truth thanks to another white lie, the one about how her sainted son, who by then had been dating Sheena for nearly three years, met her for the first time when he helped deliver keys to Baldeep's new tenant.

She had walked this trail hundreds of times. In the past she would happily anticipate seeing sweet Baldeep and at the same time steel herself for another encounter with ever-sour Ruby. *Sweet and Sour* became her secret name for visits to her in-laws. Now Baldeep was gone, and the sweetness was no more. She turned into the curved crescent of a glorious Edwardian terrace where the tenants' association had successfully enforced a strict embargo on the internal rearrangement of grand homes into smaller flats. Which, at the very least, saved owners from the noisy parties and herbal smells associated with cursed bedsits. At the back of the building, the basement opened on to meticulously maintained gardens shaded by tall hedgerows, while at the front, a short flight of steps over the basement formed a bridge between pavement and main entrance.

A white marble button surrounded by polished brass set off an inner bell, a real brass one with a clanger on a metal post.

Arrivals on the crescent were never announced by electronic jingles.

Sheena kept one eye on the bay window of the living room. Sure enough, the curtain twitched for a split second. After sufficient time for Sheena to know she was being kept waiting, the sound of locks being disengaged was followed by the door opening far enough to snag on a stout security chain.

Through the gap, Ruby Kaur said: 'There was a time when you were welcome here.'

'Not that you ever expressed any welcome. Cut the bluster and let me in, Ruby. We need to talk.'

The door slammed shut. When Sheena was beginning to wonder if the old sourpuss wasn't going to let her in, she heard the security chain being slipped from its channel. Sheena opened the door to see Ruby moving towards the front room, the one she insisted on calling the "parlour". Sheena followed.

'I can't recall the last time I had a visitor and didn't offer them tea,' said Ruby. 'For you, I'll happily break a lifetime tradition.'

'Shut up and listen,' said Sheena. Nobody talked to Ruby Kaur with such disrespect. Sheena went on before she was interrupted.

'By coming here I am risking my career. Talking to you could see me in jail. If that holds some twisted appeal, be assured your beloved son would be in the next cell.'

Ruby sneered.

'And people have the cheek to call me a drama queen,' she said. 'What are you talking about?'

Sheena produced a photocopy of the faxed photograph showing an anguished Ashna in the Byres Road coffee bar. The photograph with Baldeep occupying much of the foreground.

'Look at this,' said Sheena. 'Tell me what you see.'

'What on earth? That's Ashna.'

'And who is she talking to?'

'How would I – wait –' she put on reading glasses from a chain around her neck. 'Oh no. Oh no!'

Sheena snatched back the photocopy and waved it in Ruby's face. 'You knew about this? You knew Baldeep and Ashna were spending time together. And for years you couldn't deal with whatever kind of shame you imagined you might have to suffer. Do you understand what your silence has done to hamper the investigation into Ashna's disappearance?'

'My Baldeep had nothing to do with whatever happened to the silly girl.'

'You knew they met up,' said Sheena. 'Why didn't you tell the police?'

'Because he was a sweet, sweet man who would never hurt a fly,' said Ruby. 'Why are you here? Do you want to destroy the good name of a dead man, a member of your own family, the beloved grandfather of your own children?'

'You treated me like dirt from the first day we met, but Baldeep was like a second father to me, and it is because of how much I loved him that I am here. Soon Inspector Malloy will knock on your door. Before he does, get one piece of advice into your thick head: cooperate fully and tell him everything you know, because if you lie to him now, he will find out and he will make your life hell. And if he even suspects you of lying, do you understand who will be next to fall under suspicion of engaging in some sort of cover-up? Do you understand?'

'I understand this is going to destroy me in the Indian community,' said Ruby.

'Me, me, me. I know you love your son, Ruby. Think of what this could do to him. This could wreck his career. And mine.'

Hen Henderson set the newspaper crossword to one side and removed the pencil from between his uneven teeth.

'Off to see Farty Caldwell?'

'Yes, sir,' said Constable Eric Young. 'He seems to expect a full investigative team to swarm over his house any minute.'

'Lord save us from a public happy to learn everything it knows about policing from the TV.'

'After we're finished there, I have to go to Glasgow,' said Rab.

'I take it you've already told the high heid yin?'

'How in God's name is that any of your business?' said Rab.

'I have no interest in what god your people worship,' said Hen, 'but I will thank you not to take the Lord's name in vain. I'm sure the Chief will be pleased as punch, his new CID man taking personal time on his second day.'

'Who said it was personal? Been tuned into the gossip, Hen?'

'Is it gossip when half the town is talking about you snuggling with a fifteen-year-old tearaway outside the school gates?'

Rab had had enough.

'No wonder the word is you don't have any friends,' he said.

'Says the man whose much more successful cop wife threw him out. Enjoy your day. I have work to do.' He went back to his crossword.

Eric Young drove. Rab knew he had to break the silence that lay over them like a fog.

'Farty?' he said.

'Mr Caldwell is head of the Art Department at the Grammar. Been there for twenty-odd years, everybody in town knows him. He could talk for Scotland, favourite subject anything to do with art. I think the nickname used to be Arty-farty.'

'First name?'

Eric had to think.

'Arthur. Might be where "Arty" comes from. Kids can be clever.'

'Cruel, you mean,' said Rab. 'It can't be nice having Farty for a nickname in a town this size.'

'Could be worse. There was a science teacher, Miss Anderson, she's dead now. A big woman, chest out to here.' He took both hands off the steering wheel to mimic a giant bust. 'Even shopkeepers in the town who were former pupils sometimes forgot themselves and called her Titsy.'

He drew to a halt in front of a row of identical detached 1950s bungalows differentiated mainly by paint schemes and tacked-on front porches. Cramped driveways led to a variety of lean-to car shelters and old garages constructed entirely of asbestos. In the nearest driveway sat the sorry sight of a Peugeot hatchback canted over on two flat tyres, side windows smashed, door panels dented, and big letters sprayed across the front windshield:

WE KNOW

A short, roly-poly man came out of the house to meet them. Fiftyish, he might have been attending a TV casting call for an aging hippy art teacher. Suspiciously black hair was swept back on both sides of a crown as bald as an egg. He had a precisely trimmed moustache and a basketball-sized stomach pushing at a tie-dyed T-shirt of the sort seen in photographs of Woodstock in 1969. The ensemble was completed by faded jeans, one knee torn, white threads dangling, and leather Jesus sandals. His face lit up at the sight of Constable Young.

'Eric! Nice to see you. How's your mum?'

'She's fine, Mr Caldwell. Your watercolour of me will always have pride of place on her sideboard. What happened here?'

Dismay swept aside the warmth in Caldwell's eyes.

'I wish I knew,' he said. 'I'm a bad sleeper and I sometimes take a wee pill the doctor prescribed. It knocks me out, dead to the world. I awoke this morning to find this.'

'Whoever did it had to have made a lot of noise,' said Rab. 'Didn't your neighbours hear anything?'

Caldwell took on the look of an indulgent teacher dealing with a slow pupil.

'You must be the new CID man,' he said. 'Most of these houses are owned by weekenders from Glasgow. Monday to Thursday nights, the street's like a cemetery.'

'Sorry Mr Caldwell,' said Rab. 'You're right. I'm the newcomer. Detective Sergeant Rab Singh.' They shook hands. Caldwell's felt like a handful of cold custard.

'We will still knock on every door on the street,' said Rab. 'What time did you take your sleeping tablet?'

'Not long before I went to bed, maybe eleven-thirty. I read for a while before putting out the light at roughly midnight. Even with the tablet I'm an early riser. When I opened the curtains at six o'clock I certainly didn't expect to see this.'

'But you didn't call the station until seventeen minutes past eight,' said Rab.

'I saw no point in dragging anyone out of bed.' He swept a podgy hand at the Peugeot. 'Let's face it. This wasn't going anywhere.'

'Have you made any enemies lately?'

'I'm a schoolteacher, Sergeant, I have no enemies. Or at least, I didn't think I had until now.'

Rab saw the poor man was on the verge of tears. Eric spotted it, too.

'Don't worry about it, Mr Caldwell,' he said. 'It's probably some kid acting out for the benefit of his pals.'

'Has anything like this ever happened before?' said Rab.

'Never,' said Caldwell.

Rab took a few steps until he peered directly in front of the message on the windscreen. '"WE KNOW", ' he said. 'Who knows, and what do they know?'

Caldwell looked uncomfortable.

'I only use it for weekend shopping or occasional visits to friends. I won't be in the least surprised if the insurance company writes it off and leaves me in the lurch.'

Chapter Thirteen

Gupta's Catering Cash & Carry was less than 200 yards from the Clyde, where, a century before, a third of all the world's ships were built. An industry that once supported thousands had all but disappeared, mostly swallowed by a network of roads supporting non-stop commuter traffic. The few industrial buildings not flattened to make way for retail giants and cramped starter homes had taken on new lives. Gupta's occupied an old, brick-and-steel-girder factory building whose paint-smothered beams soared above towers of metal shelving laden with pallets wrapped in plastic.

Instead of the roar of the forge or the metronomic clang of the steam hammer, the cavernous interior was filled with the nerve-shredding whine and safety-first beeps of fork-lifts juggling loaded pallets at dizzying heights. Brygida Kosofsky had never before contemplated death by tikka masala food colouring. In this place, it looked entirely plausible.

A wiry man with an unlit roll-up in the corner of his mouth and blurred sailor tattoos pointed them to a mezzanine floor surrounded by glass, affording management an all-seeing view of the warehouse floor. Malloy attacked the stairs first. After you, thought Brygida.

Dilip Gupta waited at the top of the stairs and silently led them into his office, where his wife Lala adopted an arms-folded stance, ready for battle.

'Thank you for seeing us,' said Malloy. 'I know you're busy—'

'Nothing you have done in years of investigation has helped us much,' said Lala, 'but do you think we will **ever** be too busy to talk to you if you think it might help?'

Malloy surprised Brygida by opting not to answer.

'Something has come up,' he said, 'and we would like to ask you a couple of questions.'

'Go ahead,' said Dilip before his wife could launch another attack.

'I know this is hard,' said Malloy, 'but can you think back to the weeks before your daughter disappeared?'

Brygida watched Lala Gupta's mouth harden. *Here we go.*

'We have never, not once in four years, stopped thinking about those weeks, Inspector.'

'I understand,' said Malloy, 'but if you think back, was there anyone who Ashna might have been seeing, for whatever reason, whom you haven't mentioned before now?'

'What do you mean "seeing"?' said Dilip. 'You know full well Ashna was fourteen years old, too young for boyfriends.'

Malloy reached for empathy and missed. 'Let me explain. We can now say with some certainty Ashna was in a coffee shop on Byres Road on Friday, March 17th, 1989.'

'A date branded in our memories,' said Lala Gupta. 'Wait. What coffee shop? What time was this supposed to be?'

With Malloy succeeding in pissing off the poor parents, Brygida picked her moment.

'It was in the afternoon sometime,' she said. 'A place called The Blue Parrot. She was not alone. A witness puts her in the company of a man he described as "Indian". An older man, possibly in his fifties.'

Lala and Dilip exchanged glances. Did they already have their suspicions?

'Who would that be?' said Lala.

'We were hoping you might be able to help us,' said Brygida. 'The witness said Ashna was visibly upset, perhaps even on the verge of tears, repeatedly asking the other man "What am I going to do?".' The man who saw them is an artist, and he took photographs. Kosofsky looked at Malloy. It took a moment, but he got the hint and reached into his pocket.

'This is a poor quality copy we received by fax,' he said, 'not as detailed as we would like. We should have the original in two or three days, but for now can you take a look and give us any idea who the other person might be?'

Both Dilip and Lala grabbed the paper, making Brygida think it might tear in half. They stared at it, desperate for something to fill the gaps in their knowledge, for any link to better days before their daughter disappeared from their lives

Mrs Gupta put a finger to the anguished face of Ashna and dropped into a seat, tears streaming. Mr Gupta's stare never left the blurred image on the paper, and after a few seconds his wife struggled from the seat to join him. Once more, the paper was clutched in the grip of parents whose grief saw no hope of waning.

Malloy pressed on. 'We found this after someone came into the station with a larger scale drawing of the same scene. In it, we could clearly see the headline on the newspaper on the nearby table. Combining this information with interview testimony from the man who took the photo and later made the drawing, we can be fairly certain this took place on the same day Ashna disappeared. As I mentioned, the photographer/artist says she was talking with an older Indian man. Unfortunately, there are no images showing the man's face.'

Finally, Dilip Gupta looked at Malloy. 'Perhaps you still hope we are going to surprise you with psychic powers. Much as we wish we had, we do not – and we cannot do your job for you. I suggest you get on with it and keep us informed.'

Kosofsky had to skip to stay alongside Malloy as he marched to where they had left the car. He was raging, a state she often ignored, but this time she knew he was right.

'What did you make of that?' she said.

'Obvious,' said Malloy. 'They couldn't get rid of us fast enough after they saw the fax. What do we learn from this, Sergeant?'

'They are holding something back,' said Kosofsky. 'And I don't mean the photocopy.'

'We will make a detective out of you yet,' said Malloy.

'Prick,' thought Kosofsky.

Zoe got home in the middle of the afternoon expecting to find the house empty, and she wasn't disappointed. Two of her dad's jackets hung from a coat stand in the entryway. It took a few seconds to go through the pockets and come away empty handed. The drawers of a desk in the living room gave up nothing, and she went upstairs to Archie's bedroom and straight to the bedside cabinet. Bingo. An opened pack of cigarettes in the top drawer. The drawer below was cluttered with junk including a disposable lighter which she tested to make sure it worked. She leaned down to close the drawer and, near the back, the corner of an envelope drew her eye. With her thumbnail she teased it free before getting a strong enough grip to pull it from the tangled mess. She could tell by feel it contained a few irregularly-shaped objects. A loud shout from the bottom of the stairs made her jump.

'Are you home already?' Her dad.

'Yep!'

'You're early.'

'I had sports this afternoon. I have a cold coming on.'

'Where are you?'

Zoe patted her skirt. No pockets. She pushed the envelope back in, plucked two cigarettes from the packet in the drawer above and returned it and the lighter to the same drawer.

'Coming!'

Fully an hour later, she stepped into the living room with a portfolio case over one shoulder. Archie was in his usual armchair. On a small table next to him, an ice bucket and a bottle a long way from full kept a whisky glass company.

'Where are you off to now?' he said, without looking away from the TV showing the news with the volume muted.

'You should know. You're always complaining about the cost of my art lessons.'

'Aye, gotcha now. Is what's-her-name going?'

'Sarah. Her name's Sarah. Yes, we always go together.'

'Good luck with that.'

He reached for his glass and Zoe left the room. What did he mean by *good luck*?

Chapter Fourteen

Ruby Kaur sat on the sofa, elbows on knees and head in hands. The empty armchair with the Baldeep-shaped dent where her husband used to sit and field her questions and debate her views, no matter how much at odds with his they were, served as another reminder of how solitary her life had become. And of how, in its later years, their marriage was loveless.

She had herself to blame for never getting close enough to Rabinder, and she knew she was at fault for the yawning gulf separating her from her daughter-in-law. When Ruby was a young bride being treated like a second-class citizen by her domineering mother-in-law, she resolved never to maltreat anyone who married into her family. But she had fallen into the same abusive mother-in-law role, and couldn't blame Sheena for hating her.

If she was to be honest, the blurry copy of the fax Sheena waved in her face had not been a shock. She had been married to Baldeep for nearly 30 years. Ruby ironed the shirt he wore in the photograph, and every morning she laid out a pair of what she laughed off as the Mississippi riverboat gambler armbands her husband donned every day of his working life. He swore they saved his cuffs from becoming smeared with ink and pencil marks from the old-fashioned hardbound accounts ledgers he maintained fastidiously.

She had known for years how he sought ways to escape the emptiness of life at home. Long strolls, cameras forever to hand, meetings of camera clubs and photographic societies and exhibitions, endless damned exhibitions, none of which she ever went to. Baldeep could ramble on for hours over the composition and depth of field and masterful exposure and printing of a black-and-white photograph of a bell pepper.

But she was certain her husband had never once indulged in what friends at the bridge circle called "hanky panky". This certainty made the meaning of the photograph of Baldeep and tearful Ashna on the day she disappeared all the more unfathomable.

The clang of the doorbell startled her enough to make her knock over the side table, launching the half-full cup of cold tea across a rug she had first cleaned the day she arrived in Glasgow, more than 20 years before. She lifted the cup and moved to the front window. Through a gap in the curtains she saw the Guptas, Lala leaning on the doorbell, face rigid with fury. What was it Rabinder liked to say? Her day had started off badly, but it was about to fall away. She briefly considered pretending not to be home, but Lala was wise to the possibility, her voice loud and shrill.

'Ruby Kaur, I know you're in there! Don't bother trying to hide. We are not going anywhere until we speak to you. If you don't open the door I am going to bawl and scream until the whole street is out here asking what you've done – and unless you let us in, I'm going to tell them.'

Ruby opened the door and was brushed aside as Lala and Dilip Gupta swept past. Shocked by their discourtesy, she followed them into the living room. She was no sooner there than Lala shoved an A4 photocopy literally into her face, sending her reeling.

'What do you have to say about THIS?' said Lala.

'What is it?'

Lala, expression dripping with scorn, looked at her husband.

'What is it, she asks! As if it's not as plain as the big nose on her face. It's our Ashna, on the day she disappeared, and who is she crying her eyes out to?'

Ruby glanced at the paper, still extended at Lala's arm's length.

'How should I know who it is?' she said. 'I can't see his face.'

Lala swerved round her to a corner of the room laid out as a miniature shrine to Baldeep. She roughly dug into a forest of framed photographs until she found what she wanted, spun around and waved it in front of Ruby. A photo of Baldeep wearing his business outfit, minus the jacket. He wore a neat, fitted shirt with sleeves made puffy by elasticated sleeve garters.

'Look at this!' said Lala. 'You used to say it yourself. Your shambling old fool of a husband was the only person we knew who dressed like an extra in a western movie with his stupid sleeve garter things. Come to think of it, you probably dressed him. It would be like you to make him look an idiot, thinking all the while you were adding a touch of class to your shopkeeper.'

Ruby rose to her full height of four feet ten-and-a-half and spoke at a pitch able to be heard streets away.

'This is how you reward me, after everything I have done for you and your family over the years? I lost my husband to a heart attack a few days after your daughter disappeared. Like you, I never had a chance to say goodbye. How dare you tarnish his memory in my own home. Is it my fault your Ashna disappeared? Why does one bad picture with a sleeve garter mean anything? She could be talking to anybody.'

96

Kosofsky and Malloy watched from a spot next to the double-parked unmarked car which blocked the crescent like a cork in a bottle. From fully 20 yards away, they could make out the entire shouting match coming from Ruby Kaur's front room.

'Do you think we should get in there?' said Brygida.

'Before someone gets their jaw skelped with a finely starched antimacassar?'

'The Malloys must be posh. My mum calls them doilies. Crochets her own, too.'

Malloy's head swivelled back to the flat.

'Jesus wept,' he said. 'What's he doing here?'

Kosofsky turned in time to see Rab Singh climb the last two steps to his mother's front door, where he seemed to contemplate ringing the bell before he fished a key ring from his jacket pocket and let himself in. The racket from the front room continued undisturbed.

When the living room door opened unexpectedly, all heads turned to see Rab.

'Oh, Rabinder!' said Ruby.

'*Oh, Rabinder!*' said Lala in a cruel parody of her old friend's dramatic tone. 'It's Glasgow's most useless policeman!' She snatched the photocopy from her husband's hand, took two strides towards Rab, and rammed it at his chest. He drew it out flat between two hands and examined it carefully.

'Well?' said Dilip Gupta. 'What do you have to say! The police are sure this photo was taken on the day we lost our Ashna. Maybe you can tell me why we have had to suffer years of misery before anyone told us about it?'

Rab sighed. 'This is the first time I've set eyes on it,' he said.

Dilip's firm grip of her arm prevented Lala from lunging at Rab. 'Liar!' she shouted.

'I understand your anger,' he said. 'I would be furious in your position. But at the moment this shows an unhappy Ashna talking to someone who might be Baldeep. It doesn't tell us anything about what made her upset, and certainly doesn't mean it was Baldeep who made her unhappy. I suspect the situation was quite the opposite. Knowing my father, I think he was probably trying to help a family friend.'

Dilip's face had gone a dangerous shade of red that made Rab think of his father's high blood pressure, and how it killed him.

'You call it helping, do you?' said Dilip. 'Helping a misguided fourteen-year-old turn herself out like a prostitute for secret photography sessions? He took that other photograph, did he not?' Dilip pointed at Ruby. 'Are you trying to tell us she knew nothing about whatever was going on? Ruby, the control freak who never let her pet shopkeeper out of her sight?' He stopped when Lala put her arm through his.

'Baldeep was photographing our daughter dressed like a whore, and he was involved in Ashna's disappearance,' she said. 'And now, years too late, the police can actually do their job and use these facts in their investigation. Why? Because you two kept it a secret. What kind of sick cover-up is going on? Whatever happened to Ashna, on your two heads be it.'

Rab answered the insistent knock at the front door. Finding Malloy and Kosofsky on the front step, on the verge of pushing their way in, was no surprise. He turned his back on them and returned to the living room.

The Guptas were making their way out when Rab came back, followed by Malloy and Kosofsky.

'Oh look!' said Lala. 'Darling Rabinder has brought reinforcements from Glasgow's own Keystone Cops!'

Beside her, Dilip's anger looked refreshed. 'Did you follow us from the warehouse? Are you treating us like common criminals?'

Kosofsky was quick. 'Certainly not, sir,' she said. 'When we left your business premises we had no idea you were coming here. However, we left there intending to speak with Mrs Kaur.'

'How convenient,' said Lala.

'Simply doing our job, ma'am,' said Malloy. 'We wanted to ask Mrs Kaur if she might have any theories on the identity of the gentleman in the photograph.' The blurry photograph on the sheet of paper Lala had snatched back from Rab, and held to her chest, close to her heart.

'Good luck getting a straight answer from that woman,' she said. 'I'll give you a tip. If her lips are moving, she's lying.'

Her husband took over:

'If you didn't already hear when you were outside eavesdropping, Detective Inspector, the man in the photograph with Ashna is Baldeep Singh, Ruby's late husband, your esteemed colleague Rabinder's father. He died a few days after Ashna disappeared. They said it was a heart attack, but the more we learn, the more likely it seems to have been a guilty conscience. Somehow these people chose to keep quiet about Baldeep meeting with Ashna for all the years you have been investigating Ashna's disappearance. I would love to see Ruby leave here handcuffed to her worthless son. But since he's one of you lot, I don't suppose it will ever happen.' He turned to Lala. 'Let's go, darling.'

Zoe McCusker and her friend Sarah McCrae took their time wandering through residential streets, the whole journey spent

99

chatting and giggling so constantly, they were almost surprised to find themselves at the front gate of Mr Caldwell's house, where Mr Caldwell stood waiting. Behind him in the driveway, his little car sat in ruins.

'I'm sorry, girls,' said Mr Caldwell.

'What happened to your car, Mr C.?' said Sarah.

'I'm afraid I can't do this anymore.'

'What do you mean?' said Zoe.

'The private lessons,' he said. Zoe realised his eyes were red, as if he had been crying.

'How come, Mr Caldwell?' said Sarah. 'We love your lessons.'

'You said we were doing so well,' said Zoe.

'You are,' he said. 'Were. But I can't. I simply can't. I'm sorry.'

Zoe stepped as near to the gate as possible, but Mr Caldwell backed off, maintaining a clear distance. He glanced from side to side as if fearful that someone was watching.

'Why does it say "WE KNOW" on your car?'

'It's not you, girls, you know I enjoy teaching you – you are the kind of students any teacher would be proud of. But people are spreading terrible rumours. To tell the truth I am scared. We have to stop the private lessons right away. I'm sorry, I really am.'

Zoe and Sarah looked on, speechless, as Mr Caldwell shuffled away, shoulders drooped, head down. Beside him, the stricken Peugeot leaned drunkenly on flattened tyres.

Chapter Fifteen

The sound of the door slamming said the Guptas had left, but Rab went to the window to make sure, and saw them descend the steps and turn to go past the front of the house. Dilip fired a look of hatred back at the window. Rab couldn't blame him.

Ruby faced off with Malloy and Kosofsky, all three crowding the middle of the living room. 'Identify yourselves,' she said. Never mind she had met with and talked with them both many times. They held out warrant cards for her to inspect. Rab knew she couldn't possibly make out a word of the small print without her reading glasses, and he also knew there was no chance she would put them on. Ruby never admitted to weakness of any form. Instead, she looked Malloy in the eye until he spoke.

'As you are well aware, Mrs Kaur, I am Detective Inspector Kenneth Malloy, and this is my colleague Detective Sergeant Brygida Kosofsky. This might be a good time for you to explain yourself.'

A light went on behind Ruby's eyes and transformed into a smile.

'You're the officer my son punched. I cannot normally condone violence, but in your case I am sure an exception could be made.'

Malloy dismissed her and turned to Rab.

'Tired of the sea air already? Or did someone tip you off about new evidence incriminating your father?'

'I take it you mean the photograph.'

'You admit you know about it? Who told you?'

'I came here because I received a call from my wife.'

'I might have known,' said Malloy. 'The Chief Super will be interested to learn about that conversation.'

'You don't know anything, but let's face it, there's nothing unusual about that. Sheena called to say she was worried for Ruby's health. I came to make sure she was alright.'

'See?' said Ruby. 'Rabinder might only be a policeman like you, but he's a good son. When was the last time you phoned your mother, Inspector?'

Malloy was stony-faced. Next to him, Brygida Kosofsky's eyes gave her away. She was enjoying this.

'I must say, Mrs Kaur,' said Malloy, 'you are an odd one to be giving lectures on social graces. You won't mind if Detective Sergeant Kosofsky and I take a look around?'

Ruby grinned at Rab. 'This clown thinks I am buttoned up the back,' she said, turning to Malloy: 'I'm sure you won't mind if I examine your search warrant?'

'Cooperating with us will do you no harm, Mrs Kaur,' said Kosofsky. Going through the motions for Malloy's benefit, thought Rab. In any case, Ruby was having none of it.

'Get out, both of you. Come back when your paperwork is in order. Ashna's mother got one thing right. Keystone Cops.'

'I must warn you,' said Malloy, 'we may return with an arrest warrant.'

'Ooooooh, he must warn me, Rabinder.'

'Arrest warrant?' said Rab. 'You're not serious.'

Malloy took a mobile telephone from his jacket pocket and left the room.

Brygida Kosofsky spoke in a rushed whisper.

'You know he's well within his rights to suspect you and your mum of attempting to pervert the course of justice and withholding evidence.'

Malloy shot her a dirty look as he came back into the room, reaching out towards Rab with the mobile phone.

'Detective Chief Superintendent Quigley would like a word,' he said.

Rab looked at the phone and said, as much for Quigley's benefit as Malloy's: 'Did he forget I am no longer under his command?'

He put the phone to his ear. 'Chief Superintendent. Singh here.'

'Sergeant. If you are not in my office inside thirty minutes, I can assure you there will be consequences.'

'Sorry sir, but I am afraid that is unlikely. I have been given time off from my duties in Dunoon to tend to my mother, who is unwell. Perhaps when I am certain everything is fine here, I might be able to drop by.'

'You devious black—'

'Sir, I am shocked,' said Rab.

'—blackmailer,' said Quigley. 'I'll give you three hours. Fail to appear, and I will have no option but to seek disciplinary action. With a record like yours, Sergeant, it might just be the end of your career.'

'Thank you, sir,' said Rab. 'My mother's health permitting, I will certainly do my best to be there within three hours.' Without checking to see if the call was disconnected, he lobbed the phone at Malloy, who fumbled the catch and rescued it two-fingered from the centre of what appeared to be a fresh stain in the carpet. Disgusted, he wiped it with a handkerchief from his trouser pocket.

'Three hours?' he said. 'More than enough time to organise a search warrant. In the meantime, officers will be posted front and back.'

Rab spoke to Brygida. 'Watch yourself, Sergeant. Nothing he likes better than trying to ruin fellow officers' careers.'

'You're on thin ice,' said Malloy.

Rab shook his head in wonder. 'The clichés never let up, do they? Don't you have paperwork to be getting on with, Kenny?'

Ruby put a precise measure of loose leaves in the pre-warmed teapot before adding boiling water. Rab sat at the little kitchen table where as a family they had eaten a thousand meals together.

'Malloy's not much of a detective, but he's no fool. Depending on what they find when they search the house, you could find yourself in court.'

Ruby reached for a long-handled spoon on a wall hook near the teapot and put it to its sole use, stirring the leaves in the pot.

'That is not going to happen,' she said.

'How can you be so certain? Perverting the course of justice is a serious offence.'

'They won't find a thing.' She put the lid on the pot and deftly filled two cups. Rab reached for one of them.

Ruby made the best tea Rab had ever tasted. It was deliciously aromatic, at precisely the correct temperature to bring out complex flavours, and very lightly sweetened. It was, of course, black. Ruby said only peasants on Indian trains and English building sites soiled good tea by adding milk.

'They'll tear apart Dad's workroom, look at every photograph, every negative, watch every second of Super8 or video,' he said.

'No they won't,' said Ruby.

Tea slopped over the rim of the cup when Rab returned it to the saucer much harder than intended.

'Please tell me you didn't get rid of Dad's stuff.'

Ruby warmed her hands on her cup. 'I can't.'

'You got rid of it? Do you have any idea what you've done? Even if Dad was spending time with Ashna, his photographs and videos could cast light on how innocent their relationship was. By getting rid of evidence, you put yourself in the frame for obstruction of justice. You could go to jail for this – and since nobody will believe I didn't help you, I'll go down with you. End of career. Are the Guptas right? Did you discover evidence that made you suspect Dad of something you can't face? Did you destroy that evidence to safeguard his reputation, or simply to protect your own standing in the community?'

'Nobody knew your father better than I did. I wasn't going to leave anything around to allow fools like Malloy and angry, sad people like the Guptas to cast a shadow on Baldeep's memory.'

Rab took a sip of tea to stop him saying something he might regret. Eventually he spoke:

'Ruby, you have just made things a hundred times worse.'

Chapter Sixteen

Archie McCusker sat back against the pillows and placed a heavy tumbler of whisky on the bedside cabinet. He used a remote to switch on the television and selected a cable channel with highlights of yesterday evening's football matches. Without taking his eyes off the TV, he reached with his left hand inside the top drawer of the bedside cabinet, but failed to find the packet of cigarettes he was certain would be there. Now frowning, he swung his legs off the bed and opened the second drawer. The cigarettes were there, with the disposable lighter placed neatly on top of the packet. Zoe. Doing what he used to imagine his own parents never noticed. As he pulled the lighter and cigarette packet from the drawer, something became snagged between them. An envelope.

Rab could feel the stare of every pair of eyes on the CID floor as he knocked on Chief Superintendent George Quigley's door.

'Come,' said the barely audible voice.

The Chief stared at Rab from behind his desk. He didn't offer Rab a seat.

'You do know, Sergeant, I could have you suspended,' he said.

'May I ask on what grounds, Chief?'

'Where do I begin? Suspicion of obstructing an ongoing investigation, suspicion of attempting to pervert the course of justice, suspicion of withholding evidence. Do I need to go on? Do I need to point out your appearance at your mother's home today also casts serious doubt on the professional conduct and judgement of Inspector Ferguson?'

'I understand, sir.'

'Do you want to be suspended? Because from where I sit, it looks as if you do.'

'Definitely not, sir.'

'Explain yourself, man.'

'Yes sir,' said Rab. 'You may not be aware my mother's angina has been a source of worry for months. The pressure she puts on herself as a spokesperson in the case of Ashna Gupta-'

'An unofficial, self-appointed spokesperson.'

'Sir, some see that as a measure of her commitment to the case. Never mind what anyone is hinting at now, she remains more determined than anyone to help solve it. And the stress she has put herself under, especially since the BBC programme, worried my wife enough to make her call me to say I should get over here.'

'You and your wife are separated.'

'But in regular contact, sir. 'And Sheena sees my mother almost every day because Ruby likes to stay involved with her grandsons.'

Quigley rocked from side to side in his chair, fingers steepled in front of his chin.

'Do you expect me to buy the notion of Inspector Ferguson failing to mention new developments in the Gupta case, and telling you nothing about a photograph sending the investigation in a new direction, one directly involving your father?'

'I do, sir. Only because it is true.'

'Sandy Woods is a friend of mine. We are meeting for dinner tonight, and this matter will be discussed. He already has doubts about your suitability to the Dunoon posting, and suspects we fobbed him off with an under-performing officer whose career is on a downward spiral.'

'If I may say so, sir, I think you are being harsh.'

'Frankly, Singh, what you think is irrelevant, because I call it accurate. A university graduate hired on the fast track should by now at least have reached Inspector level, as your wife has. But you have always rubbed colleagues up the wrong way, slowing your career in the process. Unless things change, even if you are not dismissed from the force because of this latest mess, you will spend the rest of your career as a sergeant. Is that how you envision your career playing itself out?'

'Not at all, sir.'

'Prove it to me. Start showing some responsibility. Interfere with the Gupta case again, and you will be suspended on the spot and out of a job inside twenty-four hours. And if we discover even a hint of collusion in efforts to hide or destroy evidence, your career and your wife's career are over, and you will both leave here in handcuffs. Are we clear?'

'Perfectly clear, sir.'

'Get out of here.'

Ruby entered the gurdwara wearing traditional dress and with her head covered by a dark purple scarf. She crossed the entrance hall towards a room where informal meetings could be held without disturbing activities elsewhere in the busy temple. She opened the door to find chairs arranged in a circle, every one occupied.

The Guptas and about ten others turned towards the door, expressions varying from mildly aggressive to filled with venom. Ruby spun on the spot and left, indignant murmurs following her through the closing door. Footsteps caught and passed her, but she kept walking. It was the gurdwara Granthi. Out of respect for her pastor and out of fear for the wellbeing of the much older man who was gasping for breath, she stopped to hear him out.

'Ruby, I am glad you came. We are all desperately sorry to hear about your recent troubles.'

Ruby cast a backward glance at the door to a room where she had spent countless hours with fellow members of the community who valued the gurdwara so highly.

'Some of our mutual friends don't appear to share your sympathy for what I have suffered in the last day or so.'

'Which is exactly why we must talk,' said Granthi Singh.

'I have never once missed a meeting of the support group.'

'You know better than anyone how things are changing, by the day.'

'I founded the group because I knew Baldeep would want me to. Before his death he was a great friend to the Guptas, as was I.'

'And nobody appreciates your friendship more than I do. But these are difficult times for the family. Because of the new evidence the police have, your presence here is simply too upsetting. Time will heal, and when the truth emerges, I am certain you will be welcomed back with open arms. The gurdwara would never have prospered as it has without you and Baldeep. Nobody is going to forget our debt to you both.'

The bedroom door was slightly ajar. The lights were off, but the room flickered from the light of the television that must have been on when Archie fell asleep, its volume dialled down to a murmur. Archie was fully clothed on top of the duvet, lying on his back, mouth open. Now she could hear him snoring gently. She put one finger to the door, opening the gap as softly as she could. A low creak from the hinges made her freeze when the snoring stopped. She slipped back out of sight and listened patiently. When snoring resumed, a little deeper and more regular, she toed off her shoes and ghosted into the room. The strong smell of whisky pleased her. The more drunk Archie was, the less chance of him waking up. She moved like a cat towards the bedside cabinet.

As she reached out to apply fingertips to the handle of the second drawer, Archie abruptly rolled onto one side, his face coming to rest so close to her hand she felt the warmth of his whisky breath. She teased the drawer open and dipped her fingers inside. They came back out with the envelope pinched precariously between fingertips. She paused long enough to take a look in the flickering glow from the TV at the other end of the bed. It was the envelope from a greetings card, its outside decorated in childish drawings and bearing the letters 'I Love You MuMmy'. But something was different. It was empty. She slipped out of the room as quietly as she came in. As the door closed, Archie's eyes flicked open. He was wide awake.

Rab tiptoed gingerly to the bedroom door and gently pushed it wide. Neither of the boys saw him. Stuart was studiously attending to homework while Ronnie was engrossed in the din of a Nintendo game.

'Boo!' said Rab. Ronnie's eyes didn't even move from the video screen. 'Hi Dad,' he said, his thumbs a blur on the controller.

Stuart hit Rab at full tilt, little arms reaching around his middle, tugging unwittingly at his dad's emotions.

'Sorry I didn't call when I promised,' Rab said, 'but things at the new job are a bit crazy.'

Ronnie put the controller on the desk. 'My pal Billy says moving to Dunoon would be like getting locked in an old folks' home.'

'He's not far off,' said Rab. 'It's quieter than most old folks' homes.'

Ronnie was still clinging to Rab's midriff. 'Why did you have to go? Who's going to take us to the football?'

'Sometimes you have to do what your bosses tell you to do. I'll still be able to take you to most of the home games,' said Rab.

'Hear that?' said Ronnie. 'Most of the home games. It used to be all of them, Dad.'

Stuart backed off to make eye contact. 'Mum says you were sent to Dunoon because you don't have any friends left in Glasgow.'

'It's true,' said Ronnie. 'Mum said. And she says she's an inspector and you're a sergeant because you spend all your time at work picking fights.'

'Face it, lads,' said Rab. 'Mum's usually right.'

'Is that why you never win arguments with Mum?' said Stuart.

'I think I won an argument one time,' said Rab.

'When?' the boys yelled in perfect unison.

'Can't remember,' said Rab.

'What was it about?' said Ronnie.

'Maybe I only imagined it,' said Rab. It bought him the laughs he yearned for, and he had his younger son's attention. 'Your brother and I need to have a word. Can you go and watch TV with Mum for a few minutes?' Stuart didn't have to be asked twice.

As the door closed behind his brother, Ronnie looked away, refusing to lock eyes with Rab.

'Mum showed me the letter you brought home from the headmaster,' said Rab. Ronnie kept his eyes averted.

111

'Want to tell me about it?' Silence.

'Who did you punch?'

'Robert Cooperwhite.'

'I've never heard of him. No friend of yours, then?'

'He's in the year above me,' said Ronnie. 'He's a Rangers supporter.'

'That's a black mark for a start,' said Rab. 'Did he deserve it?'

Ronnie shrugged.

Rab changed tack. 'Can I tell you a secret?' For the first time in the exchange, Ronnie's gaze locked on Rab.

'That thing Mum said about me always picking fights. It's at least partly true. I've been transferred to Dunoon for taking a swing at one of my colleagues.' Ronnie's eyes widened and Rab went on: 'Lucky for me I missed, or I'd be out of a job. And you know what? I'm not sorry. He deserved a thumping for what he said. Something really nasty. About Mum.'

Ronnie thought for a moment. 'Cooperwhite deserved it.'

'Tell me why,' said Rab.

Ronnie pointed to a shelf that was reserved for Stuart's prize collection of Power Ranger figures. The *Famous Five*, Rab called them, to great confusion. Except now there were only four. Ronnie pulled open a drawer of the desk where Stuart had been doing his homework and his hand came out holding multiple pieces of broken Power Ranger. Even from where Rab sat, he could see footprints from when someone had stomped Stuart's toy to pieces.

'Cooperwhite did that?'

Ronnie nodded.

'And you punched his nose for him?'

Ronnie nodded, and reached around to pull a school shirt from the boys' laundry basket. One sleeve end was soaked in blood. Ronnie waited, fearful of what might come next.

'Do you know what you have to do now?' said Rab.

112

'No.'

'Get that soaked in cold water quickly or we'll never get the blood out of it.'

Rab came back to the living room and flopped onto the sofa. Stuart ran the other way, doubtless to grill his big brother for information on what all that had been about. Sheena pushed a glass of wine across the coffee table.

'Cheers. What a day,' he said.

'For you and me both,' said Sheena.

'Sorry if the Quiet Man hauled you over the coals.'

'Lucky we talked before he called me into his office, but even that nearly backfired. He said he was always suspicious whenever suspects' stories were too closely matched.'

'He accused you of hatching a cover story with me?'

'Isn't that what we did?'

'I know, but he had the cheek to accuse you of it?'

'Not quite.'

Rab took a small sip of wine. 'How did you wriggle your way out of that?'

'I fluttered my eyelashes and assured him I valued and respected his authority far too highly to ever try and deceive him.'

'And he bought it.'

'Beneath the holier-than-thou exterior is a conceited sexist. Did Ruby destroy your dad's beloved photography collection?'

'That's her story, and she's sticking to it. Even when I tell her not having it around makes it harder to prove Dad had nothing to do with Ashna's disappearance.'

'But?'

'I don't believe her. Not even threats to Baldeep's sainthood would make her destroy the fruits of his beloved hobby.'

'And you don't believe he had anything to do with Ashna's disappearance.' She raised her glass to find it was empty.

'There's not a chance my dad was involved,' said Rab. He leaned over and transferred most of the wine from his glass into Sheena's.

'Do I hear the cop thinking, or the son who loved his father and never really saw eye to eye with his mother?'

'Maybe both.'

'What's next?'

'Quigley said if I am caught meddling in the case he'll fire me on the spot.'

'I'm sure that scared you off.'

'It gets worse. Any proof of you doing the same, and you will be fired as well.'

'Maybe I didn't flutter my eyelashes convincingly enough.'

'We have to be careful. But without Baldeep's photo collection there is no chance of clearing his name. If Ruby's hidden it, finding it will be tough. You know she still has property all over the West End. Apartments, shops, offices and who-knows-what else. When Malloy requisitions a full list of Ruby's assets he'll burst into tears because it could take weeks to search them all. And it still wouldn't take into account the homes and workplaces of every friend she ever made in the city.'

'You'll find it,' said Sheena.

'I have to,' said Rab. He looked at his watch. 'I better get going if I'm to catch the last ferry. I promised the boys I'd say goodnight.'

Sheena sat with what was left of her wine while in the background was the murmur of conversation between Rab and their sons. In a home central to your existence, sounds came in recognisable sequences. Now came the click of a bedroom

114

door before Rab's footsteps padded downstairs to the living room.

He headed for the door, Sheena close behind. She saw him waver and gave him time to say what was bothering him.

'I'm sorry Sheena.'

'You're not to blame for everything your stubborn mother does.'

'I'm sorry for everything. I'm sorry for the madness with Jane Ross that destroyed what we had here. And I'm sorry for being a complete idiot at work. The boys said you were making excuses for me. You shouldn't have to do that.'

'Not excuses. If you'd done things differently, people like Ken Malloy would be taking orders from you.'

'What about "Dad was sent to Dunoon because he doesn't have any friends left in Glasgow"?'

'Maybe I was being unfair.'

'It was the truth. The kids are lucky to have you.'

They were still on the edge of an embrace when a wee voice came from the stairs.

'Can't Dad stay tonight and take us to school in the morning?'

They had no idea how long Stuart had been there.

'Isn't your Gran doing that?' said Rab.

'I want you to take us.'

Rab held out his arms. The three-way hug was lopsided, and sincere enough to make Rab cry, but he still had to go. He hurried out, head lowered to hide his tears as Sheena held Stuart tightly with one arm while with the other hand she surreptitiously dried her eyes.

Chapter Seventeen

Zoe McCusker sat on the floor, leaned back against her bed and hugged her knees. On the bedside cabinet next to her sat a framed copy of the same photograph she showed Sergeant Singh, the close-up of her mum proudly holding the necklace with the letters Z-O-E in fine gold.

Between her hands Zoe clasped the envelope, which she brought to her face and sniffed as if she might catch the scent of her mother. She patted it between her palms to confirm for the umpteenth time it was indeed empty.

Something made her stop, and with thumb and forefinger she caressed the outside of one corner of the envelope. The sound of a toilet flushing nearby made her jump with fright. She got to her feet and gently closed the bedroom door.

Rab arrived at the Crest exhausted, couldn't find his key and had to press the bell. Within seconds, as if she was waiting in the hallway like a worried parent, Mags Henderson opened the door.

'Somebody left the key in his room,' she said. 'And forgot to check the front door. I put it on the snib for you.'

'Sorry, Mags.'

'No need to apologise.'

'I don't know how people manage to do the round trip to work in Glasgow every day. I'm jiggered.'

'Probably peckish, too.'

Rab was faint with hunger. 'I don't want to bother you,' he said.

'So you're starving,' said Mags.

'Is mind-reading another prerequisite for people in the B&B trade?'

'I always keep a few things in reserve. Do you mind having shepherd's pie again?'

When he returned from washing his face to try and waken himself up, he met Mags coming out of the kitchen with her saltire tray.

'You are a magician,' he said.

'A magician highly dependent on her freezer and microwave,' she said over her shoulder as they made for the dining room, where the tray went straight to the table.

Rab sat. The pie smelled amazing.

'There was a telephone call for you,' said Mags.

'Who was it?'

'A young female, definitely not your wife. Whoever she was, she didn't want to leave a message. Oh, and she had a local accent.'

'Not many people know I am here.'

'Unless it was the McCusker lass.'

'You recognised her this morning?'

'Everybody knows Archie McCusker, and young Zoe's antics draw a lot of attention. The poor girl's at a difficult age.'

Rab put his knife through the slight crust on the top of the mashed potato, releasing steam from the meat below. Keeping it waiting was torture.

'The caller said nothing at all?'

'All I remember is her saying: "Is Sergeant Singh there?".
I said you were out and would she like to leave a message, but
all I got was "No thank you." A lot more polite than her
reputation makes her out to be. Assuming it was Zoe
McCusker.'

Rab looked wistfully at the pie. 'Can I make a quick call?
I'll get back to this in a moment, I promise.'

From the phone in the hallway he surprised himself by
remembering the switchboard number for the police station.
He got another surprise when Eric Young answered.

'Dunoon police, how can I help you?'

'What are you doing there?'

'Sergeant Singh? I'm pulling a double shift to help one of
the lads get to a stag night he didn't want to miss. I clock off in
about an hour.'

'Anything happening?'

'Nothing, sir. It's quiet as Ibrox when Rangers go two
goals down.'

'I got back from Glasgow a few minutes ago, and Zoe
McCusker might have called the B&B looking for me. She
didn't leave her name or a message.'

'I drove past their place a wee while ago. There were some
lights on, but nothing else I could make out. Because we used
to be called out there often, I still pay attention.'

'Who do you hand over to when you clock off?'

'Barn Owl Andy's on permanent night shift. Constable
Andy Barnes.'

'Do me a favour please. Tell him what I said about Zoe,
and ask him to watch the phones and drive past the McCusker
house once in a while.'

'Will do, sir.'

Not wanting to sleep through another attack by vandals, Arthur
Caldwell left the sleeping pills in the bottle, and a few hours

later was startled from uneasy slumber by the sound of bottles clinking. The digital clock on the side cabinet said 03:47. He went to the edge of the front window, where he could look out on the street without being seen. A strange car was parked by the kerb about three doors away, and a shadow fiddled with Arthur's gate before entering his front garden. He was dressed all in dark colours, wearing some kind of balaclava, and the clinking had come from whatever was in one of two plastic bags. Arthur watched in disbelief as the intruder turned one bag inside out and bricks fell to the lawn; a gloved hand came out of the other bag clamped around the necks of two bottles. Frozen by fear, Caldwell watched the man use a cigarette lighter to set fire to the necks of the bottles before he casually selected bricks from the grass at his feet and launched them through downstairs windows, followed by the bottles. Apparently satisfied by the WHOOSH from inside the house that Caldwell heard clearly from his bedroom, the intruder hurried in the direction of the parked car.

Blue flames climbing the stair carpet cut off his escape route. He slammed the bedroom door shut and reached for the telephone next to the bed. His hands shook uncontrollably and it took him three attempts to dial 999.

Rab was keeping his eyes half-shut in a daft attempt to maintain a state of near-sleep while he urinated, when the frosted bathroom window flickered with blue light. He hurriedly finished what he was doing and went through to the bedroom in time to hear a single wake-up siren blast. Rab opened the window and a uniformed constable called to him.

'DS Singh!'

'What's going on?'

'You're needed, sir. Right away.'

Two minutes later he was in the car beside PC Andy Barnes, who thrashed the panda car along narrow suburban streets at a rate that made Rab twice check to ensure his seat belt was securely fastened.

'Sorry for the rude awakening, sir, but it was quicker than knocking on the door or trying to get Mrs Henderson on the telephone.'

'You did the right thing. What's going on?'

'A fire, sir. The fire station gaffer took one look at it and requested police attendance. Suspicious circumstances, he said.'

'Where is it?'

'Dhailling Crescent, number 17. A two-storey detached home belonging to a teacher at the Grammar, name of—'

'Arthur Caldwell,' said Rab.

'Yes sir. Farty Caldwell himself.'

The man's house was on fire and still they called him Farty.

'Is he hurt?'

'They brought him out alive, but in bad shape. Ambulance took him to Cowal hospital, where A&E straight away called in the Coastguard helicopter. Right now he's in the air on his way to the Southern General in Glasgow.'

Barnes pulled to a halt close to where crew worked to stow gear in a fire engine parked behind the vandalised Peugeot. Beyond them, the house was in a sorry state, much of the ground floor black with soot, all of the windows blown out. One fire crew member doused wreckage with water to eliminate any remaining source of smoke from causing a secondary flare-up. Barnes led the way to the officer in charge.

Rab held all of the emergency services in high esteem, and this was a man who had doubtless seen more tragedy than most folk could deal with. He was a powerhouse of a figure with a Kirk Douglas dimple on a chiselled face that somehow, at four o'clock in the morning, was perfectly clean-shaven.

'Detective Sergeant Rabinder Singh, our new CID man, transferred from Glasgow this week. Meet the gaffer, Station Officer Angus Ross.'

They didn't shake hands because Ross's glove was soaked and covered in soot.

'Good to meet you, Sergeant. I wish the circumstances were less grim. Call me Gus.'

'I'm Rab. Was Arthur Caldwell the only victim?'

'He was known to live alone, but we still carried out a careful search. Anything bigger than a budgie, we would have found it.'

'How badly injured is he?'

'I'm no doctor, but I've seen a lot of burns victims and it wasn't pretty.'

'I learned from talking to Mr Caldwell after his car was vandalised there's hardly anyone at home in this street midweek,' said Rab. 'Do we know who called it in?'

'Mr Caldwell had a phone extension in his bedroom, probably saved his life. If we'd got here even a few minutes later, he would have been gone. If the flames hadn't got him, the smoke would have killed him.'

Rab looked at the house. Most of downstairs was gutted, meaning the flames must have trapped Arthur upstairs. The nice wee man he had spoken to the day before was lucky to be alive.

'Constable Barnes says you suspect foul play.'

'I'd bet my pension on it being arson,' said Ross. 'When we pulled up, two downstairs windows were already broken from the outside. We found a single brick in each of the living room and the hallway, as well as bottle fragments smelling of petrol.'

'Molotov cocktails?' said Rab.

'Crude but effective.'

'Have you been in Dunoon for a while? Do you remember any similar cases?'

'Been here nineteen years. Never once came across a Molotov. We had one dodgy fire at a wee engineering business about five years back and suspected arson for insurance purposes. But there wasn't enough evidence to prove anything, and the insurance company paid out. Normally I'd be asking if Farty had any enemies, but from the look of his car, that question has already been answered.'

'I was here about that yesterday,' said Rab. 'One day malicious vandalism, the next attempted murder. After Glasgow, I expected this place to be so quiet it would be sleepy.'

'It's the quiet places you have to watch out for,' said Ross. 'Around here when things blow, they really blow.'

Chapter Eighteen

Rab trudged wearily into the police station, still wearing the clothes he'd pulled on in a hurry when Andy Barnes arrived outside the Crest with blues flashing to interrupt his pee. Chief Inspector Sandy Woods got up from a chair next to Rab's desk.

'My office please, Sergeant.'

Rab followed him into the office. When he turned from closing the door behind him, the gaffer was already sitting behind his desk. Rab remained standing.

'Terrible bloody thing to happen,' said Woods.

'Yes, sir.'

'What's the latest from the Southern General?'

'Mr Caldwell is under intensive care in the burns unit. Nobody knows when he'll be fit enough to answer questions.'

'Angus Ross is certain it was arson?'

'He says it's as clear cut a case as you'll ever see, sir. Bricks lying in two front rooms - thrown through the windows to clear the path for Molotov cocktails made from Irn Bru bottles. Ross's men found bottle fragments smelling of petrol in both rooms.'

'The most common soft drink bottle in the country,' said Woods.

'Yes, sir. Even in the unlikely case of getting fingerprints from glass fragments, they'd probably belong to a shop assistant or an innocent punter who dropped the bottle in a bin somewhere.'

'Which leaves us with what, exactly?'

'The vandalism of Mr Caldwell's car about twenty-four hours earlier,' said Rab. 'Two words spray-painted on the windshield: WE KNOW.' When I asked Mr Caldwell what it might mean, he clammed up. Something was bothering him, but he wasn't prepared to tell me. Perhaps now, or whenever he is fit to answer questions, he might give us something to work with.'

'Farty has no criminal record of any sort, or he wouldn't be in his job. I'm not aware of any nasty rumours, but you will have to look into the possibility of them circulating without us knowing. Do it gently. He's the victim here, a well-known and liked figure in the town. We can't be seen to tramp over a professional reputation thirty years in the making.'

'Understood, sir.'

'I take it you've considered the forensic value of the spray paint used on his car?'

'We are calling around the local retailers, but it could easily be from a shop in Glasgow or Greenock or from an aerosol sitting in someone's shed for years.'

'Chase down every possibility, Sergeant. Now, what the hell happened in Glasgow yesterday?'

'I think I mentioned to you, sir, I was worried about my mother. Since I'm her only child, she has nobody else to look out for her.'

'George Quigley is an old friend of mine. He's too nice a bloke to be a CID chief, and when I had dinner with him last night he couldn't bring himself to say he had a good idea you were lying through your teeth.'

'But he didn't say that.'

'Put yourself in his shoes, son. After the Gupta disappearance featured on *Crimewatch*, your father was suddenly linked to the case by new evidence. And the next thing, you were high-tailing it to Glasgow to see your mother.'

'I see, sir.'

'We're short-handed, Sergeant. You being posted here was meant to help us, not add to our human resources problems. George Quigley assures me you're a good detective, despite having a reputation for letting things get in the way of doing your job. I'm not pleased even by the possibility that Glasgow fobbed you off on us, but right now I'd still be happy to prove your doubters wrong.'

'Thank you, sir.'

'When was the last time you tried on your uniform?'

'Sir?'

'If you let the side down, here or anywhere else, you'll be hoping it still fits you.'

A loud knock at the door announced the arrival of Hen Henderson.

'Sorry, sir, but Archie McCusker is here, and making a fuss.'

'Show him in,' said Woods.

McCusker blew into the room.

'What's wrong, Archie?' said Woods.

'Bloody Zoe's done a bunk again.'

'Are you sure?'

'Someone at the school called my office. She hasn't turned up.'

'When did you last see her?' said Rab.

Archie scowled at him. 'Yesterday,' he said. 'Early evening.'

'How about this morning?' said Woods.

'I slept in. Far too much to drink last night. This morning I hurried out to the office without checking her room. Assumed she was already off to school, since she usually gets herself out on school days. When the school phoned, I went home and there was no sign of her.'

'Did you check with her friend Sarah,' said Rab. 'The one she stayed with the other night?'

'I asked the school to check with her. She hasn't seen Zoe. The kid's gone, I tell you. Are you going to take this seriously?'

'Easy, Archie,' said Woods. 'This is the second time in three days you've been in here to report her missing.'

'Beg your pardon, sir,' said Rab. 'In the absence of proof otherwise, I think we have to treat this as urgent.' Looking at Archie, he said: 'I need permission to search your house.'

'You won't find anything.'

'I still have to look.'

'It's still unlocked.'

'Boss,' said Rab. 'I need a constable to go to Mr McCusker's home and secure the scene. And I need a car.'

While he waited for the head teacher to arrive with Sarah McCrae, Rab browsed the shelves of the school library. When he was in secondary school the library was his favourite room in the building, probably because it was a place where his identity and his background and the colour of his skin were irrelevant. The school librarian, Miss Wilson, ran a tight ship, encouraged exploration of anything in print that took a student's fancy and tolerated no noise louder than a whisper.

Rab knew his fondness for Miss Wilson's workplace had a lot to do with the pretty girl who, one lunchtime, sat across from him and opened a heavy hardback on the technical aspects of photography.

'I couldn't care less about cameras,' she volunteered in a murmur barely audible to Rab and quiet enough that not even Miss Wilson detected it, 'but I love looking at the photographs. Odd, eh?'

Rab knew she was one or two years below him; he had seen her with a group of girls who occupied the same spot every breaktime on steps under the shelter of a cantilevered roof. Glasgow's climate made good spots worth hanging on to. Rab looked across the table and found her eyes locked on his. Intelligent, self-confident hazel eyes. She had straight dark brown hair worn with a fringe in what might be a page boy style. Her skin was pale and the faintest of freckles danced on her cheekbones. She was gorgeous, and she was happy to talk to the brown kid wearing the patka. This was something entirely new.

He blushed when it dawned on him she might be waiting for a response.

'My dad's crazy about photography,' he said. 'Has his own darkroom.'

'Maybe he wouldn't think I was odd.'

'I bet he could cure your lack of interest in cameras,' said Rab. 'He has cupboards full of the things. Always trying to get me to use them.'

'Sounds like a nice dad.'

'He is. I don't think you're odd.'

'You are sweet. My name's Sheena.'

'Rabinder. Call me Rab.'

He was brought back to today when the door opened and in came Sarah McCrae and the head teacher, Mrs Jackson, who made the introductions even before Sarah sat at a table opposite Rab. Sarah had to be about the same age as Sheena was that day. She too had an intelligent, friendly face, but her eyes were Paul Newman blue and her face round and cherubic.

She had the regulation school uniform of skirt, white blouse and tie, the latter worn so short it curled at the end. When she rested her hands on the table he saw they were small and chubby with nails gnawed to nothing. As she waited to find out why she had been called by the head teacher to the library to meet a policeman, she angled the tip of a forefinger between incisors in a vain attempt to get some nail to chew on. A little nervous.

Rab spoke to the head teacher.

'In the absence of Sarah's parents, I need you to be here, Mrs Jackson. 'But if you don't mind, I would like you to give us a little space. For Sarah's sake.'

Mrs Jackson nodded silently and went over to the door, where she rocked from one foot to the other with a face like fizz. Rab knew he had dispatched the head teacher to stand in a corner like an errant pupil, but he had other things to worry about.

'Thanks for coming to talk to me, Sarah,' he said. 'Mrs Jackson gave me your dad's mobile number, and I called him. He told me he and your mum are in Glasgow, and will be back as soon as they can, but not for another hour or two. When I assured him you are not in any trouble, he and your mum gave me permission to talk to you. Is that OK?'

'I suppose,' said Sarah.

'Any time you want to stop talking, tell me.'

'It's alright. I don't mind.'

'You know Zoe didn't come to school today?'

'We're in the same classes for French and History, and she wasn't there.'

'Do you have any idea why?'

'No.'

'Zoe's dad is worried because he has no idea where she is. Do you know anything to help me find her?'

128

While Sarah considered the question, Rab wondered if he had seen her flinch at the mention of Archie McCusker.

'I don't want to get anyone into trouble,' she said.

'You won't. I promise. Mr McCusker says you and Zoe went to your art lesson with Mr Caldwell yesterday afternoon, but Zoe came home early because it was cancelled.'

'We were shocked,' said Sarah. 'Zoe and I both love our lessons with Mr Caldwell.'

'Can you remember how Mr Caldwell seemed when he told you the classes were cancelled?'

'Sorry. And frightened.'

'What exactly did he say?'

'People were spreading rumours and he couldn't do any more private lessons.'

'Do you know there was a fire at his house last night?'

'Everybody's talking about it. Is Mr Caldwell OK?'

'He's in hospital in Glasgow. Where did you two go after Mr Caldwell sent you away?'

'My house is on the way to Zoe's. She always walks me home.'

'Did she come in with you?'

'I asked, but she said she wanted to get home for something.'

'To get something? To do something?'

'I don't know. She was acting a bit weird, even for Zoe.'

Rab wanted to keep her talking.

'The last you saw of her was when you said goodbye outside your house?'

'Right. But we spoke later. She called me at home. She's got a mobile. My old dears say I'm too young to get one. Zoe phoned me last night. About eight o'clock.'

'To talk about anything in particular?'

'She was excited about something, but wouldn't tell me what it was. She said she would show me at school today. It had to be important, because Zoe doesn't often get excited, and this morning I was looking forward to hearing what it was all about. What could she want to show me?'

Exactly.

'You weren't just looking forward to finding out about it, you were worried what it might be,' said Rab. 'Friends look out for their pals, don't they?'

'What do you mean?' said Sarah.

'I'm staying at the Crest B&B. Maybe you know it?'

'Everybody knows the Crest.' For the first time since she arrived, she looked worried.

Rab kept his voice calm. 'Yesterday when I was in Glasgow someone called the Crest asking for me. A girl's voice with a local accent, Mrs Henderson says. She remembered the voice was quiet and shy. I don't think it was Zoe.'

Sarah managed to get her teeth around a tiny corner of thumbnail.

'Am I in trouble?'

'Absolutely not,' said Rab. 'You were worried about a friend.' Sarah didn't respond, and he went on, speaking softly.

'You were scared for Zoe, and you tried to get me on the phone.'

Sarah looked Rab in the eye for the first time.

'She likes you. I hoped you might talk with her, stop her doing something silly.'

Chapter Nineteen

Eric Young struggled with latex gloves as he and Rab approached the front door of the McCusker home, an imposing structure on Alexandra Parade with unbroken views over the Firth of Clyde.

'Not had much practice with these things?' said Rab.

Eric waved one hand, latex fingers flapping.

'I've never done this before,' he said.

'Never searched a private home?'

'There's not much of it goes on around here. Whenever some minor drug dealer gets nailed, I always seem to be somewhere else.'

'We need to remember,' said Rab, 'this is not yet a crime scene, so the idea is to be methodical without turning the place upside down.'

'What exactly are we looking for?'

'Evidence of a crime, or anything hinting at Zoe's disappearance.' He nodded his thanks to a constable he had never seen before who opened the front door for them. Eric and the constable exchanged a few quiet words. In the hallway, he had a question:

'Shouldn't we be talking to the ferry company and trying to identify anyone who drove out of town yesterday or last night?'

'I already asked Sandy Woods to take care of that,' said Rab.

'The chief would love taking orders from a sergeant.'

'Suggestions. Requests for professional assistance in an investigation involving the daughter of his good friend. You start with the kitchen and living room. I'll take the bedrooms.'

Half an hour later, Rab sat on Zoe's slightly rumpled bed in her slightly rumpled room. He sighed when Young came in, the younger man's face telling him he had nothing to report. Rab pointed to a kiddy chair in front of a small desk. Young looked ridiculous, long legs bent like paper clips, knees against his chest. He waited politely for Rab to speak.

'I found next to nothing,' said Rab.

'Same here. Apart from a few gaps in the wardrobe and clothes drawers,' said Eric. 'And her make-up bag and toothbrush being missing - along with a backpack Archie says used to be in the bottom of her wardrobe.'

'Her friend Sarah said Zoe was excited last night, and talked about showing her something today. Some time after that, she disappears. I'm bothered by this, not least because running off in the night has to be much more difficult than during the day, when there are buses and ferries. If she ran off during the night, did someone help her? Maybe a car driver or a truck driver?'

Hen Henderson's voice barked from Eric Young's radio, which was turned loud enough to wake the dead.

'Dunoon control calling Eric Young, over.'

'Constable Young receiving you, over.'

'Are you with DS Singh?'

'Yes, sir. He is right beside me.'

'There's a message from Glasgow. His mother was arrested three hours ago.'

Rab gestured for the radio handset.

'Singh here, Hen. Who did the message come from?'

'A telephone call from a woman, Glasgow accent, probably a cop. Didn't want to leave a name.'

'The number she called from is in the system?' Rab was ashamed of asking. Of course it would be.

'Hold on.' Rab listened to a keyboard being attacked by big meaty fingers before Hen came back on the radio with a number Rab didn't even have to write down. Before he could thank Hen, the sergeant urged him to turn on McCusker's television.

Eric Young held out a mobile phone. The number barely began to ring before being answered.

'Bistro Ahmed,' said the voice with the thickest Glasgow accent Rab had ever heard. Mohammed Ahmed ran a coffee and sandwich bar that wasn't the closest takeaway to Pitt St HQ, but was definitely the most popular among Rab's ex-colleagues.

'Rab Singh here.'

'DS Singh! Haven't seen you for a few days. You want the usual? Two rolls and sausage, a large Americano and one of Noor's finest Empire biscuits?'

'I wish I could, Ahmed, but sorry, I'm out of town. Is DS Kosofsky there? She's not at her desk and she left her mobile behind when she stepped out.'

'Och you're out of luck, pal. You missed her by minutes. I know she forgot her mobile, 'cos she had to borrow my landline for a minute.'

They made small talk for a few seconds before Ahmed had to get back to the serious business of taking phone orders. Rab returned the mobile to Eric Young.

'Do me a favour,' he said.

133

'Yes sir,' said Young.

'I didn't make that call.'

'What call?'

Rab went through to Archie's bedroom and used the remote control to switch on the TV at the foot of the bed.

Claire Christie gave her cameraman the "give me a moment" signal and used a hand mirror to go through the last-minute check of her neckline, jewellery, hair and make-up. When she was certain everything was satisfactory, she ran her tongue across gleaming TV-presenter's front teeth that had been the biggest investment in her career so far. Going live with lipstick on your teeth was a rookie error they all made, though usually only once. Claire had done it four times already, and colleagues had taken to calling her "lippy Claire".

The reflection in the mirror also gave her an idea of how she would look on camera, framed by the setting and the crowd. The backdrop featured local faces filled with tension and emotion, which suited her needs well. She checked her teeth one more time while her cameraman grinned behind the shelter of his viewfinder.

Glaswegians holding home-made signs saying PROTECT OUR KIDS and KEEP GLASGOW SAFE made for good TV. Less appealing were the ones saying THIS IS OUR HOME and GO BACK WHERE YOU BELONG. Some of the throng held the front page from a red-top tabloid desperate to show its concern for the local community. Over a much-run photo of Ashna Gupta was the banner headline: JUSTICE FOR ASHNA.

Claire was on the verge of speaking when the camera swung away from her to follow a skinhead who pushed through the crowd yelling: 'PAKIS GO HOME! PAKIS GO HOME!'

Fellow demonstrators surrounded him and forced him to lower the volume. He continued to remonstrate, but fell silent when Inspector Sheena Ferguson, in full uniform, used a squeaky bullhorn to address the crowd.

'Everybody, please be calm. There is nothing you can do here. Anyone who resorts to force will be arrested and charged with obstructing officers in the execution of their duty.'

If she was expecting Glaswegians to bow meekly to authority, she was rapidly disillusioned.

'Aat's the game, hen,' drawled a thin man wearing a shrunken hand-knitted sweater showing off his bare midriff. 'Protect yer plods. What happened to lookin' efter Glasgow's weans? How come the bitch in there isnae locked up?'

'Ah'll tell ye,' said a woman wearing curlers under a head scarf. 'The bitch's son is a cop, that's how.'

A well-dressed woman standing alone waved a gloved fist emphatically at Ruby's front window and shouted:

'These people are ruining a perfectly respectable neighbourhood!'

Claire Christie's cameraman gave her the three-finger countdown. Three, two one – go.

'We are in the respectable West End neighbourhood of Dowanhill, where dramatic newspaper reports have brought residents out in protest. Behind me is the home of Ruby Kaur, wife of the late Baldeep Singh, who reportedly has become a subject of interest in the four-year-long investigation into the disappearance of fourteen-year-old Ashna Gupta. Ashna's family live a short distance away – and were known to be close friends of Mrs Kaur and Mr Singh.

'We understand that early this morning Mrs Kaur was placed under arrest and removed from her home in handcuffs. Sources tell us she was taken straight to Glasgow Sheriff Court, where she appeared in private at a special session of the court. Following her appearance, she was released on bail pending further enquiries. We understand bail terms included the surrender of Mrs Kaur's Indian and British passports and compulsory daily reports to a local police station.

'Mrs Kaur's present whereabouts are unknown, but throughout yesterday evening and today her home has been a hive of activity, with police teams carrying out a thorough search of the premises. Earlier today, in a shocking development, a mechanical excavator was brought in to aid the search; police have sealed off the lane leading to the back garden and blocked all access. From a camera position in the upper floor of a nearby property, George Frampton filed this exclusive report a few minutes ago.'

Viewers in homes all over Scotland saw the picture cut to reporter George Frampton looking earnest, microphone held rigidly in line with a square jaw he liked to think was reminiscent of Superman in the DC Comics. He occupied a carefully selected location at a window overlooking back gardens between parallel curving lines of homes and split along the middle by a narrow lane. Beside George was an elderly woman wearing her Sunday best and beaming as if there was nowhere else in the world she would rather be.

'I am in the flat of Mrs Stella Davies,' said George. 'Stella's back window overlooks the rear gardens of Ruby Kaur's home. Mrs Davies has lived here for more than thirty—'

'Thirty-seven years,' said Stella. 'My late husband William and I bought it on our tenth anniversary. He—'

'And Stella kindly invited us to take a look at what is going on in the Kaur garden.'

The camera moved to look out of the open sash window and zoomed into activity in the back garden of the Kaur house, where a backhoe was noisily tearing up a cement patio. The camera returned to the reporter and his interviewee.

'Mrs Davies,' said George Frampton.

136

'Please call me Stella, George.'

'Stella, can you tell us when you first become aware of police activity inside Ruby Kaur's house?'

'Yesterday evening when I was looking out over the gardens. I like to watch the birds. The ones who haven't been eaten by cats. Some people think it's strange, a woman of my age enjoying bird-watching—'

'What did you see yesterday to give you pause?' said George. This old biddy was a tricky interviewee.

Stella looked put out by the unwanted direction.

'I know she had a few visitors in the afternoon: if her kitchen door's open you can see all the way to the front hallway from here – it went quiet for a while before the police arrived mob-handed. A search party. They all wore those rubber gloves and bootees. Like something off the TV.'

'And you were able to see that from here?'

'I have binoculars. For the birds.'

'Very handy,' said George. 'Can you tell us anything more about what went on after the search team arrived?'

Stella certainly could, and she was warming to the task.

'The house was lit like a Christmas tree well into the night – I'd hate to pay her electric bill. About midnight everything calmed down, but they left two big burly policemen on guard in the back garden. Not one, two. As if our taxes aren't stretched enough. They never stopped blethering all night. I hardly got a moment's sleep, but I did learn two or three sweary words I never heard before.'

'And this morning,' said George. 'I believe things took a macabre turn?'

'You mean when they brought in the digger? Never saw such a thing here, never in all my years. They had to tow cars out of the lane and cut down two lovely big sycamore trees. I'll be dead and buried before this place ever sees trees as grand as those.'

'And why do you think they brought in the excavator?'

Stella squinted at him like she smelled a trick question.

'To dig holes,' she said. 'They've went and made the garden look like a bomb site, and now they're going at the cement patio. The Indians didn't keep the place nice, but—'

'As a long-time neighbour of theirs, do you have any theories as to what might have made the police concentrate on the back garden?'

'Probably because of the phone calls,' said Stella.

'What calls?'

'The ones I made to tell them these folk did an awful lot of digging about four years ago, about the time her man dropped dead.'

'Are you friendly with Mrs Kaur, and were you acquainted with the late Mr Singh?'

'I'd see them on the street sometimes. My mother always said it costs nothing to be nice, God rest her soul. Her man always had a neighbourly nod for me, but I don't think the Kaur woman would smile if she won the lottery. She never had a kind word for anyone. I'm not racist, but sometimes the smells from that wumman's kitchen! Curry this, curry that, always curr—'

'Thank you, Stella. 'This is George Frampton in the Davies household overlooking the back garden of Ruby Kaur's home, where police activity since shortly after dawn can only be described as intense. Now back to Claire Christie, outside the Kaur home.'

Claire was primed by a producer to take over the live broadcast from George.

'I have been joined by Inspector Sheena Ferguson, who has taken some time out from controlling the police operation today. Inspector, following the broadcast of *Crimewatch* this week, we have been told that new evidence has emerged: the

138

late Baldeep Singh, who was Mrs Kaur's husband, has seemingly become implicated in the disappearance of Ashna Gupta – and developments here at their home yesterday and today are directly linked to this break in the case. What do you have to say?'

Sheena wasn't going to let the reporter ruffle her.

'Uniform branch is here in a supervisory role. Supervision of the scene to prevent any escalation of demonstrations has been ongoing since early this morning. People are understandably upset, and my officers are here to ensure nothing gets out of hand.'

Now Claire was ruffled.

'What about Baldeep Singh?' she said. 'What can you tell us about the latest developments in the Ashna Gupta case, a case that has gripped the country, and which now sees such an outpouring of emotion on the streets of Glasgow?'

Sheena shook her head dismissively.

'It is well-established police policy not to discuss details of ongoing investigations,' she said. Her body language screamed *Interview over.* She turned in time to see a demonstrator launch something at the front of the Kaur house. A half-brick bounced harmlessly off the house wall as two big constables took down the offender, hard. Sheena winced. It was a clip made for endless TV repeat showings, often with broadcasters conveniently ignoring the half-brick that came within two feet of destroying one of Ruby's windows. The offender, the same man who had been yelling about sending Pakis home, was marched in handcuffs towards a police van while, in living rooms all over the country, news presenters in the studio moved on to the latest exciting developments in the worlds of sports and entertainment.

Chapter Twenty

Mags backed into the dining room holding the saltire tea tray looking empty with only a mug of coffee, a cheese omelette and two slices of toast.

'If you change your mind, shout and I'll get you a fry-up.'

'Thanks,' said Rab. 'Sorry about last night. I was feeling anti-social. And knackered.'

'When you came back with a take-away pizza under your arm and a bottle of fizz in your jacket pocket, I got the hint. Did you sleep OK?'

'Eventually. When I've got a lot on my mind I can lie awake for hours.'

'You saw what went on in Glasgow?'

'Hen radioed and told me to turn on a TV. I caught the whole show.'

Mags reached out to a shelf and made a microscopic adjustment to the placement of a glass figurine that might have been a rabbit eating a carrot.

'The Inspector Ferguson they interviewed was your wife?' Rab nodded as he took a sip of coffee. 'But Ruby Kaur is your mum. Should your wife be anywhere near the case?'

'Uniform branch was only there to keep the peace.'

'While I'm being nosey, shouldn't you be there for your mum's sake?'

'Ruby wouldn't accept help from me if it came gift-wrapped. And there's the complication that the moment I show my face in Glasgow, my old boss will have me fired. And anyway, I've a job to do here,' he said.

'Do you think Zoe has run away again?'

'Again?'

'She's done it before, at least once that I've heard of. Things get around.'

Especially in a small town with a blabbermouth cop for an ex-husband.

'I knew Zoe was unhappy, but nobody mentioned any previous attempts to run away.'

'Maybe you didn't ask the right questions. What about the press? The Glasgow press. They'll be onto you before long.'

'Nothing surer,' said Rab.

'I already fielded two calls this morning, asking if a Rabinder Singh was staying at the Crest.'

Rab put down his coffee. 'And?'

'They got my best Pride of Miss Jean Brodie voice. I told them Rabinder Singh sounded awfully foreign to me, and the Crest prided itself in being a place where good Christians needn't worry about sharing the breakfast table with non-believers.'

'You did not.'

'Even worse, they believed me,' said Mags. 'I'll be in trouble if they report me to the Tourist Board.'

'I'll put in a good word for you,' said Rab.

'And I'll keep my eyes open and the door locked.'

Mags headed off to the kitchen. She was right. He wanted to get back to Glasgow, but first he had to worry about Zoe, and the media vultures would doubtless arrive soon, desperate for bones to pick through. If Zoe wasn't found quickly, it

141

would not be long before the press linked Ashna to Zoe through Rab, and from that point on, it wouldn't be just Ruby who was deep in shit.

The canteen table served as the war room. Chief Inspector Sandy Woods fidgeted with a teaspoon while Rab Singh and Eric Young awaited instructions. The spoon flew into the sink with an almighty clatter and Woods spoke to Rab:

'For the time being Constable Young is going to work directly with you. Since everyone within twenty miles of the station already knows him as a police officer, he will remain in uniform.'

'Understood, sir,' said Rab.

'The chances are Zoe will turn up full of lies and excuses, but if not, maybe we're lucky to have you at a time like this.'

'I don't quite understand, sir.'

'Too modest, Sergeant. The Ashna Gupta case gave you experience of a serious missing person investigation, experience nobody here can match.'

'To be frank, sir, I was barely involved in the Gupta investigation,' said Rab. And it had so far been a failed investigation, hardly a badge of honour worth presenting at the canteen table.

'You were the liaison officer for the Gupta family, which means there's not much about it you won't know. The decision is made. What's the next step here?' He looked between Rab and Eric Young. Rab answered with a question.

'Is it true Zoe tried to run away to London at least once before?'

Eric seemed relieved to be able to contribute.

'She did a bunk late one night about a year ago,' he said. 'Archie was in a lather until Zoe came back before breakfast with her tail between her legs. She tried to hitch-hike out of town, but everybody here knows her, and no tourist in his right

142

mind would give a lift to a girl her age in the middle of the night. She eventually admitted defeat and trudged back home.'

'Where I'm sure she was met with compassion and understanding from Dunoon's favourite parent,' said Rab.

'It was the first time Zoe stayed out all night,' said Woods. 'Archie was raging.'

'You know what bothers me? The rage, the anger. Twice this week she has seemingly done a bunk, and twice Archie has been more pissed off than anything. What kind of parent of a missing teenage daughter blows a gasket instead of crying his eyes out with worry?'

Nobody had an answer to that.

'From what little we know,' said Rab, 'we still have to treat the runaway possibility seriously. We need to speak with everyone who works on or near the ferries. Talk to bus drivers and truck drivers – especially anybody who works for Archie, since she might have asked for a favour – and residents along the roads out of town in case she set off on foot hoping to hitch a ride. I have to talk to her pal Sarah again.' He knew the next bit was going to raise an eyebrow or two.:

'We also need to ask Glasgow for some help.'

Woods was doubtful. 'I thought Glasgow would be the last place you'd seek help right now.'

'Arthur Caldwell saw Zoe shortly before she disappeared. He's in intensive care at the Southern General. If he's able to talk, he needs to be interviewed.'

'George Quigley says if you go anywhere near his case, he'll have you thrown off the job.'

'I have enough to do here,' said Rab.

The CID floor at Pitt Street HQ always lacked enough space for a decent-sized meeting. Officers, plain-clothed and in uniform, leaned on desks and on the backs of occupied chairs in order to keep eye contact with the gaffer as he spoke.

Detective Chief Superintendent George Quigley was no fan of such gatherings. The Quiet Man simply didn't have the right manner to take command of a room, but this was important, and he did his best.

Detective Inspector Ken Malloy, who surely spent all his school years sooking up to teachers, occupied a spot directly in front of Quigley. Next to him was Detective Sergeant Brygida Kosofsky. Unlike Malloy, her natural presence made Quigley certain she was there to take everything in, not to seek opportunities to impress.

Behind Quigley was a white board with photographs of Ashna Gupta, Ruby Kaur and her late husband Baldeep Singh, as well as an enlarged and rather blurry version of one of the photographs faxed from Tasmania showing an anguished Ashna talking to a man suspected to be Baldeep Singh. Quigley quietly praised the Lord Rab Singh was no longer working there, though the presence of his estranged wife made him uncomfortable.

Notes scrawled on the boards provided details of the people in the photographs, and links connected them in different shades of ink. He took a deep breath and spoke in what, for him, was a loud voice. People more than two desks away struggled to hear a word.

'It's the usual story, I'm afraid. Years of painstaking work gets us nowhere until a TV show throws a spanner in the works and everything moves into fast-forward. Ken, where are we with the photographs from Australia?'

Malloy liked being the centre of attention.

'Sir, the courier company says they are being fast-tracked, and we should have them by this time tomorrow. The negatives are coming with them, and we have a photo lab on standby to rush poster-size enlargements.'

Quigley politely aimed a finger at Brygida. 'Sergeant Kosofsky. What about warrants?'

144

'The people at the bank where Ruby holds all her money have been sticklers for legal protocol, sir. But later today we should get our hands on full financial records, including those of credit cards for both Ruby and her husband, going back ten years.'

Malloy didn't like Kosofsky getting too much attention. He butted in with some less positive news.

'Unfortunately, we are still drawing a blank on the whereabouts of Baldeep Singh's photography equipment and files. Everyone we talk to says he never went anywhere without a camera. Often he would carry a video camera and a stills camera at the same time. A well-equipped darkroom remains in the loft office of Ruby Kaur's house, but other than family snaps on display in the living room, we haven't been able to find a single photograph or strip of negatives. Same with home movie films or videos.'

'The survival of family snaps in the living room maybe tells us how much they were valued,' said Kosofsky. 'The big question must be: Why would they get rid of all the other photos and videos when some of them must also be of great sentimental value?'

'Probably because a clean-out was done in a hurry,' said Quigley. 'Which suggests to me they might be hidden away, safe somewhere.'

'If there was a clean-out, my guess is it must have happened in the last thirty-six hours, sir,' said Brygida.

'Instead of guessing, explain your reasoning, Sergeant,' said Quigley.

'Sir, Simran Gupta sprung the burlesque studio photograph on us earlier in the week. It drew endless attention from the public, as a result of which we got the pencil sketch from the coffee shop alerting us to the existence of photographs in Tasmania. That was thirty-six hours ago. Mrs Kaur knew nothing about it until yesterday morning when the Guptas confronted her with a copy of one of the faxed photos.'

Quigley tried and failed not to look at Sheena Ferguson. She looked straight back, eyes blank. He shifted his gaze back to Malloy and Kosofsky.

'You conveniently left the photocopy with the Guptas, which I'll grant you was clever, and they took it straight to Ruby Kaur. She had no idea of the possibility of a search warrant being served until you spoke with her yesterday. How did she know to empty the house of evidence? Do you think someone in the force tipped her off?'

'That is a possibility we must consider, sir,' said Malloy. He couldn't resist firing a dark glare at Sheena, who remained impassive.

Quigley knew he had to keep an eye on the ongoing friction. He didn't fancy Malloy's chances if Ferguson ever cornered him in a dark alley.

'While we are on the subject of leaks,' he said, 'it's obvious from the sensationalist rubbish in the press that someone here has shared information with the newspapers. Hence the mob that besieged Ruby Kaur's house before we were even ready to make a statement about the latest developments. For the time being I'll concede it may have been the result of some fool talking too loudly in the pub. But if the leaks continue and I find out the source, I will not have to think twice before I tear someone's career out from under them. Is that clear?'

To Quigley's experienced ear, the chorus of "Yes, sir!" was loud but unconvincing.

Brygida Kosofsky was startled by a voice in her ear. It was a constable in uniform. She knew the face but couldn't put a name to it.

'Phone call for you, sergeant. Insists on speaking to you and won't take no for an answer. Strong Indian accent. I put him on hold. Line Seven.'

She did the *telephone call* hand mime to the Chief Inspector, who nodded his assent. Investigations didn't grind completely to a halt just because the gaffer called a meeting.

At a desk phone at the back of the room she punched the button for line seven. 'This is Detective Sergeant Kosofsky.'

'Brygida,' said a familiar voice with no trace of the heavy Indian accent put on for the constable. 'Thanks for the call yesterday from Ahmed's shop. Can you talk?' Kosofsky saw Malloy stare at her. She gave him a *nothing important* shake of the head and turned her back on the room.

'What the fuck are you doing calling me here?'

'Take it easy.'

She lowered her voice to a hiss. 'Take it easy? We're all under strict instructions not to touch you with a twenty-foot pole, and you call me at work when the whole department is being briefed on how to deal with your mother and your dead dad.'

'Thanks for the update.'

'You've got five seconds.'

'I need a couple of favours.'

'Not a chance. The Quiet Man is already furious about leaks in the investigation—'

'I get it,' said Rab. 'You're pissed off, but I need your help precisely because the gaffer will soil his tighty whites if I show my face in Glasgow.'

Chapter Twenty-one

Rab was amused by the circuitous route his thoughts took before they eventually led to his sons. It began as he strolled prosperous Dunoon streets bathed in the last of the morning light glinting off the Firth of Clyde, when he spotted in the distance the Inverkip power station chimney. At nearly 800 feet, it was the tallest free-standing structure in Scotland. Intended for a new oil-fired power station, even before it was complete, it fell victim to the 1973 oil crisis. In America, record numbers of gas guzzler cars went to the scrap yard to be crushed. In Scotland, a new power station was moth-balled before it went into service.

While it was being built, Rab appeared in Scotland straight from the Punjab and struggled to make friends in an almost exclusively white secondary school in Partick. One classmate, Stephen Storrie, seemed to empathise with his state of isolation, took him under his wing, and later took him home to meet his dad. Stephen and his dad James were the first Scots Rab knew who looked at him and saw a kid, maybe even a nice kid, not a Mowgli with a funny headdress, whom they were happy to befriend. From the moment they were introduced, Stephen's dad insisted Rab called him "James".

'There'll be none of your Mister Storrie shite here, son,' he said. James was also, without a doubt, the funniest man Rab ever met.

Twenty-five years later, "Uncle James" was the funniest man Rab's sons had ever encountered, and they, like Rab a quarter century before, liked nothing more than to be retold yet again the stories of how Uncle James had worked on the construction of the Inverkip chimney. In Scottish parlance, James had always "liked a drink", and he openly confessed to needing a dram to stop his knees knocking at 700 feet above the Clyde coast. Somehow, because it was James telling the story, instead of inspiring horror, it and many other stories like it made them laugh until they cried.

Now Stephen was a senior paramedic whose work meant he occasionally bumped into Rab, often at scenes involving carnage, sometimes accidental, but depressingly often of the man-made variety. James, a lifelong St Mirren fan who had passed his love of the Buddies to Stephen, still made fun of Rab and the boys for sticking with Partick Thistle. Since neither Rab nor Sheena had siblings, the boys lacked uncles. Despite the best efforts of well-meaning friends in the Indian community, somehow it fell to Uncle James to fill the void, and nothing raised spirits more dependably than time spent in his company.

Eyes drawn as ever to the redundant chimney tower, Rab resolved to get the boys to see Uncle James as soon as he was back in Glasgow.

He enjoyed the fresh air, eyed appreciatively the orderly clean streets with their obsessively neat gardens, and was coming to look forward to encounters with other strollers. On the streets of an impersonal city the size of Glasgow, strangers rarely exchanged greetings. In cosy wee Dunoon, even a brown-skinned man in a turban inspired a welcoming smile and a "lovely morning" from anyone he nodded to. It occurred to him how much the boys would enjoy it here.

He watched a slender gent in a faded green anorak wait patiently while a chubby black Labrador voided its bowels on a grass verge. The man surprised Rab by using a plastic bag from his jacket pocket to pick up the mess. As he tied a neat knot in the plastic, he saw Rab watching.

'You'd be the new officer at the police station,' he said.

'Yes, sir. I'm Rab Singh.'

Dog mess in one hand and dog lead in the other, the man shrugged an apology for being unable to shake hands.

'Davie,' he said. 'Davie Bowie. Spare me the jokes. It was my name long before that singer bloke decided he wanted it, but at least I got my own back.' He waved the bag at the Labrador. 'Meet Ziggy.'

Rab smiled and Davie spoke again, holding up the bag.

'Do you know what this is?'

'I'll take a wild guess,' said Rab. 'Ziggy stardust?'

'Ooh, that's good. I might have to use that. No, this is a package for Maggie Thatcher. But before you arrest me, Officer, it's a metaphor.'

'Not a bad one, either,' said Rab. Baldeep would have got on well with this chap.

So far, it seemed as if nowhere in Dunoon was more than two or three turnings away from Argyll Street. Today he followed Argyll all the way to the police station before branching onto Argyll Road.

Hunter Street felt like a modern afterthought, a twisting lane, barely wide enough for two cars and at times without sufficient breadth for any kind of footpath. It clung to sloped terrain that tumbled towards the coast. Houses, no two the same, were designed to exploit sea views from upper floors. Sarah McCrae's father had given Rab directions that, going by the way he waited in his front doorway, perhaps he didn't have

150

much faith in. After an exchange of introductions, John McCrae led Rab into an open plan kitchen where Sarah and her mother perched on high stools at a breakfast bar. John introduced Hilary and, while Rab took to a stool, got them both steaming hot mugs of coffee from a fancy espresso machine.

'You'll be sick of the sight of me, Sarah,' said Rab.

'Mum and Dad said you need more help to find Zoe.'

'You don't mind me asking a few more questions?'

'I want to help if I can.'

'Have you had a think since we talked at the school? Are you sure Zoe never hinted about running away?'

'Like I said yesterday, it was the opposite. She was excited about showing me something at school.'

Rab had a sip of coffee. As well as being delicious, it was hot enough to weld his tongue to the inside of his mouth.

'Do you see how that makes us worry for her even more?' he said, with difficulty.

'I get it. It means either she's hiding or something bad has happened.'

'Can we talk a little more about Mr Caldwell?'

'What about him? He's a lovely wee man. He talks to us like we aren't stupid. He appreciates our art, even when it's rubbish.'

'Sounds like a great teacher,' said Rab.

'The best in our school.'

'Sorry, Mr and Mrs McCrae, but I have to ask this. Sarah, do you know what grooming means?'

Sarah gave him a blank look. Beside her, Hilary McCrae turned white. Rab had to push on:

'It's when an adult tries to gain the trust of a child to help persuade them to have an improper relationship with them.'

Sarah laughed out loud.

'Are you kidding? Don't you know anything about Mr Caldwell? He's gay. He has a boyfriend in Edinburgh called Samuel and they spend weekends together. He told us in confidence, said there were too many bible thumpers in this town who can't handle the idea homosexuals even exist. Anyway, he never once laid a finger on us and simply wanted to teach us art. Anyone who says anything else is lying.' Next to her, Hilary McCrae managed to look both relieved and proud of her daughter.

'What about the rumours he mentioned,' said Rab. 'The rumours that made him too scared to continue your lessons. Have you heard anything?'

'Nothing. But we felt sorry for him, because he was frightened. They teach us about bullying at school, but nobody ever told us teachers could be the victims.'

Rab took a cautious sip of coffee, which by now was only mildly scalding. 'Zoe told me she had adult male friends,' he said. 'She hinted to me she was having sex with them.'

Hilary McCrae's face returned to fear of where this might be going, but Sarah didn't appear at all bothered by the change of topic. She had nothing to hide, thought Rab, who felt glad for her parents.

'Zoe enjoys the attention she gets from guys,' said Sarah. She likes to lead them on, give the impression she's easy to get into bed. But she's not like that.'

'Can you name any of the older men who might have got such an impression from her? It's important.'

Sarah looked to her mum and dad. Their expressions matched. *Tell him.*

'Two of them have been hanging around. A guy from Glasgow, somebody Baxter, I think he works on building sites. And a taxi driver who works for Zoe's Dad, Iain McDonald. Big guy, yellow teeth and horrible tattoos. They've both been trying to get into her knickers. Sorry Mum. But honest, it's all

152

a show from Zoe. She likes the attention, she likes to shock people who spend every free moment gossiping about her, but no way she's having sex with those losers.'

'That's good,' said Rab. 'Does that mean, as far as you know, Zoe's a virgin?'

Sarah's face fell and her eyes brimmed with tears her mum spotted right away.

'The other day,' Hilary said, 'I was surprised when you and Zoe came back early, and even more surprised when Zoe didn't come in with you. I could see from the living room window Zoe was crying her heart out. What was that all about?'

Sarah took a moment to compose herself.

'Zoe never mentioned it before. She told me about it for the first time when we were coming back from Mr Caldwell's. I promised not to tell anyone – she made me swear to keep it to myself "Give me a couple of days," she said. "I'll speak to Sergeant Singh when I'm ready."'

'Speak to me about what?' said Rab.

'It started before her mum went away,' said Sarah, her voice not much more than a whisper.

'What did, pet?' said John McCrae. 'You can tell us.'

Sarah waited a couple of seconds before blurting:

'Zoe's dad has been sneaking into her bed for years.'

Brygida Kosofsky entered the intensive care unit respectfully and slowly. The one bed in the unit was occupied, by a middle-aged man with both arms and much of his head and torso encased in bandages that in places, made way for wires and pipes connecting points on his body to an array of monitors. One eye was visible, but closed. A man in an armchair next to the patient used his finger to keep his place in a book on his lap.

Brygida arrived with her ears ringing from the warning delivered by the steely-eyed ward sister. 'You can have a few minutes,' she told her. 'No more. The patient is in extreme pain and his medication is devised to let him sleep in order to promote healing.'

The man occupying the bedside vigil still kept his place in the book with one finger. He looked at Brygida expectantly.

'I'm Detective Sergeant Kosofsky. The staff nurse said I might talk to Mr Caldwell for a moment.'

'Samuel Jennings,' he said. 'He's in a state of extreme exhaustion, but can't sleep for more than a few minutes at a time because of the pain. Please don't wake him.'

Brygida spoke softly. 'My colleagues in Dunoon asked me to find out if Arthur can tell them anything about the fire. Has he spoken about it?'

'Nothing yet. We speak on the phone every day – I live in Edinburgh – and on Tuesday Art said something about ugly rumours going around town. Then this happened. Do you think there's a connection?'

'What kind of rumours?'

'The sort that destroy careers. I am not even sure he wants to discuss them with you or anyone else.'

'The thing is,' said Kosofsky, 'my Dunoon colleagues have asked around, and nobody seems aware of any rumours about Arthur.'

Arthur's voice, little more than a dry croak, startled them both.

'Not just rumours,' he said. 'Threats. Blackmail.'

'Art, this is Sergeant Kosofsky,' said Jennings. 'She wants to ask you a couple of questions.'

Kosofsky stepped closer to the bed and lowered her voice. She didn't want the ward sister throwing her out.

'Can you tell us anything to help my colleagues in Dunoon find who did this?'

'I received phone calls at home. From a public phone box – I could hear the beeps as the money went in. Accusing me of sexually abusing kids who come for private lessons. And I only had two private students.'

'Zoe McCusker and Sarah McCrae,' said Kosofsky.

'Lovely girls, good students. I would never, ever—'

Samuel Jennings put himself between Kosofsky and Caldwell. 'Remember the doctors told you not to get upset, Art.'

Kosofsky moved enough to one side to regain contact with the one unbandaged eye. 'How many calls did you receive, Mr Caldwell?'

He waited while Samuel held a glass of water with a straw to his lips. When he answered, his voice was relieved of much of its hoarseness. 'Two,' he said. 'I was hardly in the door from work when the phone rang the first time, and the girls were due for their lesson about an hour later. About twenty minutes after the first one, he called again. Same message, same vague threats.'

'Same voice?'

'I think so. Yes, I'm sure.'

'Did you recognise the voice?'

'I can't say.'

She was losing his cooperation. *Can't or won't* was what she wanted to ask.

'Look what happened to my house and my car,' said Caldwell. 'And to me.'

'Are you aware Zoe McCusker is missing?'

The poor man twisted in shock and winced in pain. 'No!' he said. 'Since when?'

'Since a few hours after you told her and Sarah you couldn't teach them anymore.'

Even with only one eye visible, Arthur looked confused. 'Wait,' he said. 'What day are we talking about?'

'Today is Friday,' said Kosofsky. 'You saw the girls on Wednesday and the fire was in the wee hours of Thursday morning.'

'The caller on Wednesday warned me to stop the private classes. I told the girls I couldn't do any more lessons and sent them away. I did what he said, but Zoe went missing the same night and a few hours later my house was set on fire?'

'You can't expect to make any sense of this,' said Kosofsky. 'But what happened that night could be related to Zoe's disappearance. Do you see why we need to know who was making the threatening calls? Did you recognise the voice?'

Arthur Caldwell's one visible eye closed. 'I want to rest now.'

'Sergeant Kosofsky,' said Samuel Jennings, 'please.'

The door opened and the ward sister came in. They were done here.

Chapter Twenty-two

Brygida's mother hated sausage. "Butcher's profit," she called it. Brygida and her Polish father disagreed, and the smell of bread rolls with thick, salty butter pouring from fried square sausage made her mouth water.

She was astonished when Ken Malloy came back from the counter to their rickety table carrying a tray. In a year of working under him, she had never known Malloy to dip into his own pocket to pay for anything, and here he was with big mugs of tea, two fat floury white rolls and square sausage, and even a couple of Tunnock's tea cakes for afters.

If Kosofsky had been allowed to choose, they would be along the street at the University Café, but this greasy spoon, a favourite among taxi drivers and construction workers and university students, was one of the last of its type in the area. Maybe Malloy was determined to enjoy it before it was erased by gentrification changing the face of Glasgow's West End forever, though Brygida thought it more likely he was attracted by its low prices.

He sat down, used the heavy glass jar with the peculiar chrome funnel to add an unquantifiable cascade of white sugar to his tea, took a bite from a roll that left his mouth rimmed with flour, and at last got to what was bothering him. Their inability to locate Baldeep Singh's missing photography materials was making him look silly. Sillier than a man with half his face covered in flour.

'How much stuff do you think we are looking for?' he said, as he examined the roll appreciatively.

Brygida took a cautious bite. The bread was doughy to the point of being sponge-like and the sausage gritty-crisp on the outside and chewy-greasy inside. Perfect.

'In Baldeep's photography files? About thirty years' worth. Boxes and boxes of prints, negatives, Super8 films and old video camera tapes. If Ruby moved it, she would have needed help.'

Malloy wiped his face with the back of his hand and managed to shift some of the flour to one cheekbone.

'More haystacks to pick apart looking for needles. Where did you disappear to earlier?'

'I had to do someone a favour.'

'What kind of favour takes precedence over the biggest investigation of your career?'

'It was during my lunch break. I helped Dunoon with a quick interview of an assault victim who's in the Southern General.'

'Dunoon? You mean you helped Singh?'

Kosofsky put her roll back on the plate. Malloy's presence threatened to spoil it for her.

'It's an active case and, like him or not, sir, he's still one of us. Things have gone bad over there. As well as the assault, there's a missing girl. Fifteen years old.'

Kosofsky could hardly believe it when she saw in Malloy's reaction a mixture of amusement and satisfaction.

'Christ,' he said. 'Déjà vu all over again. What did you get for him?'

None of your bloody business. 'Nothing,' she said. 'The assault victim, more like attempted murder victim, was too scared to name names.'

'That means you've spoken to Singh. What did he say about us investigating his dad?'

'Nothing.'

'You expect me to believe that?'

'He didn't ask, and I volunteered nothing.'

Malloy made another assault on the roll while he considered what this meant.

'Maybe that tells us something,' he said.

'Such as?'

'If he doesn't want to talk about it, it might be because he has something to hide.' Malloy popped the rest of the roll in his mouth and reached for a napkin to wipe his hands. Kosofsky didn't tell him he had flour all over his face. Nor did she tell him what else Rab had asked her about.

Rab showed Eric Young the search warrant. 'It's time to give the McCusker home the fine-toothcomb treatment,' he said.

'When do we do that, sir?'

'I need you to take care of it.'

The constable looked doubtful. 'On my own?'

Rab patted his arm. 'I'll join you as soon as I can,' he said. 'Take another officer for corroboration in case anything turns up. Be methodical and thorough. Now we have the warrant, we don't need to worry about making a mess. Turn over furniture, lift carpets, check for loose skirting board hidey-holes, empty every pocket in the drawers and wardrobes. Remember when you were a teenager, how hard you tried to hide porn magazines and condoms from your mum?'

'And still she found them,' said Young.

159

'Put your teenager's thinking cap back on. If Zoe hid anything from Archie, we need to find it. Likewise anything Archie has salted out of sight.'

'Do you have any tips on getting into the mindset of a middle-aged alcoholic child molester? Sorry: **alleged** child molester.'

'Do your best,' said Rab. 'I don't expect Dunoon's got a Dog Branch?'

Young's head swivelled like a spectator at a tennis match. 'Do you see any kennels around here?'

Sergeant Henderson drove the panda car with Rab in the back seat. Beside Hen sat a shaggy-haired German Shepherd the size of a small bear which panted continuously, its lolling tongue leaving an ever-expanding puddle of drool on the seat.

Henderson used the rear-view mirror to look at Rab. 'Are you going to tell me why you need Luther?'

'He's my ace tactical card,' said Rab.

'The sweetest, gentlest hound on the Cowal Peninsula?'

'Can you make him bark?'

'Nothing makes him happier,' said Henderson, rubbing Luther's back with one hand while he called out in a special, talk-to-doggy voice.

'Luther! Where's your lead? Where's your lead, Luther?'

Luther barked loud enough to disturb the occupants of nearby cemeteries.

'Perfect,' said Rab. 'James Baxter will fold into a steaming heap.'

'Are you going to tell me how you know this?'

'He was one of my first ever arrests, in Glasgow more than ten years ago. We got a tip-off about a nutter who was lifting women's knickers and bras from washing lines all over the East End. But when we got to his mother's flat he legged it, out the window and down a drainpipe. He hid in a derelict

160

tenement and we'd never have found him without the Dog Branch. Two minutes after the dog and his handler began their search, Baxter was begging to be placed under arrest, in the paddy wagon, in the jail – anywhere to get him away from the dog.'

'Isn't it funny,' said Henderson, 'how we can forget an event from years ago, then suddenly something brings it all back?'

Dunoon police station's interview room was no different from most. Unlike on TV shows, there was no two-way mirror for observers to lurk behind. Some rooms had a CCTV feed that could be viewed elsewhere, but not Dunoon's. It was small, windowless and musty-smelling. James Baxter sweated copiously, a mix of stale tobacco and partially processed alcohol marking his light blue T-shirt. He was not a happy man

'No way you didn't break the rules there,' he said. 'I'm going to sue youse lot.'

From the other side of the table, Rab smiled. 'Sergeant Henderson took the call to collect you when he was driving his dog Luther home from the park.'

'Aye right,' said Baxter. 'And you happened to be along for the ride.'

'You've got your knickers in a knot,' said Rab. 'Answer a few questions and you can run away and get changed. Y-fronts, boxers or frilly ladies' lace-wear, it's all the same to me. Do you understand you are not under arrest, and you can leave at any time?'

'And if I leave right now?'

'You might want to hold off on changing your underwear, for the lovely Luther will be back in your life within the hour. How well do you know Zoe McCusker?'

'I know her Dad better. Bastard stiffed me on a job I did on one of his properties. McCusker. What kind of name is that? Sounds like a drunk choking on a kebab.'

'I'll bow to your expertise,' said Rab. 'What about Zoe? I hear you've been hanging around like a bad smell, trying to make friends.'

'Bullshit. It's a wee town. We bump into each other, it's natural we talk once in a while. But only talk, nothing else.'

'Do you know she's missing?'

'Finally, we get to the point. Since when?'

'Miss McCusker disappeared on Wednesday night,' said Rab. 'It's possible she ran away from her dad. Is she hiding out with you?'

'I wish.'

'She's fifteen years old, Baxter.'

'Campbeltown,' said Baxter.

'What about it?'

'The new dentist's surgery at the harbour end of the Esplanade.'

'What are you on about?'

Baxter crossed his arms. On safe ground now, smug and content. 'I was in Campbeltown, all day Wednesday and yesterday. Got back late last night. A work crew, at least two dentists and god knows how many folk with toothache will give me an alibi. I don't know anything about what happened to Zoe McCusker.'

'We will check.'

'Do I look worried?'

He didn't, thought Rab.

'If you're in the clear, who else should I talk to?'

Baxter gave him the gravely offended look. 'Do you take me for a grass?' he said.

'Call it an appeal to your civic-mindedness, the response to which could avoid the need for Luther to bump into you at the

162

most inopportune moments. Zoe's a nice kid and she is in some kind of trouble. Who would you look at first?'

'There is one weirdo,' said Baxter.

'Coming from you, that's something. Does he have a name?'

'Private hire taxi driver, works for Zoe's father. Iain McDonald. He's never been done for it, but take it from me, he's yer classic short-eyes.'

'You are telling me Iain McDonald is a paedophile.'

'In Barlinnie they have to lock folk like him in their own wing. If they were in with the rest of the cons, they'd form a queue to cut his balls off. Prison justice is rough.'

All the rougher when you consider the scum who dish it out. 'Have you seen McDonald with Zoe?'

'I've seen her getting into his cab,' said Baxter. 'I bet the meter never gets switched on.' He put his fist to his face and with his tongue pushing at the inside of his cheek, mimicked something going in and out of his mouth.

'This is an informal chat,' said Rab. 'There's no video camera, not even a tape recorder. Nobody watching.'

'So?'

'Where are the witnesses if I come over the table and knock your teeth down your neck?'

Brygida looked at Malloy's face and wondered if anyone else would spot his rage. Grumpy was his default look, after all. They left the interview room with Ruby Kaur and her solicitor a few paces ahead. Malloy slammed the door behind him, making Ruby and the lawyer jump.

'I can't believe what happened in there,' said Malloy. 'Unbelievable.'

Brygida agreed with him, but wasn't about to say so.

'In what way, sir?'

'I'm used to being lied to, it's part of the job,' he said, 'but usually when we get that kind of treatment, it's from a career criminal with a face like a bag of spanners sitting next to a crook in a lawyer's suit that cost more than we make in a month. Who were we lined up against just now? A wee Indian granny and a real estate solicitor who's never worked a criminal case in his life. How many times in a row do you think she said "no comment"?'

Brygida was tempted to tell him if it was important, they could check the video tape.

Malloy changed direction. 'I'm going to have a word with the gaffer,' he said before he stomped off.

Thanks for inviting me along, thought Brygida.

The last time he was in Zoe McCusker's bedroom, Rab felt guilty for leaving it slightly rumpled. Now, along with the rest of the house, it looked like a hurricane had passed through. Eric Young sat on the bed, head in hands.

'It happens sometimes,' said Rab.

'Finding not a single thing?'

'Maybe it's the information you needed, but didn't know you were looking for.'

'Is this when you call me Grasshopper?'

'We still didn't locate Zoe's mobile phone, nor the diary Sarah says Zoe updates every day.'

'Folk would argue those are the things you'd expect a runaway to make sure she took with her.'

'Smart thinking, Constable. But I keep coming back to something Archie said when I told him we'd have to search the house. What would we expect a frantic parent to say when his daughter's gone missing and we ask to take a look at the family home? Maybe something like "be my guest, what can I do to help?" You know what Archie said? "You won't find anything."'

164

'What do you make of that?' said Eric.

'It could mean he was innocent, certain there was nothing here to find.'

'Or cocky because he had already looked, made sure there was nothing here.'

'And if he did, isn't it possible he missed something?'

Rab's eye fell on the bedside cabinet, to a framed photo lying on its back. He pulled a wrinkled photograph from his pocket, the one Zoe gave him with notes about her mum written on the back. The two photographs were identical.

He turned the frame over. One of the metal tangs to secure the plywood back plate was broken and the plate was seated unevenly. Furrows appeared in Eric's forehead as he watched.

Rab put on fresh latex gloves, worked the remaining tangs loose and extracted the plywood plate. There was nothing in there except the back of the photograph. Bugger. Another avenue closed. He put it on the cabinet.

He watched Eric examine it closely. There was something caught in the corner, snagged between the edge of the glass and the wood of the frame. Rab took the frame back and picked at the fragment. It was the corner of an envelope. Eric held an evidence bag beneath the fragment as Rab gently squeezed at two points of the paper triangle. Something fell out and when Rab raised the evidence bag to the light from the bedside lamp they saw a flicker of gold.

It was a short length, no more than an inch of fine gold chain linked at one end to two, stylised letters. Z-O.

Eric examined the complete photo Zoe had given Rab and pointed to what they were both thinking about. The photo was a close-up of Zoe's mum proudly showing off a gold necklace with Zoe's name spelled out in individual letters. The broken fragment in the evidence bag matched the necklace in the photograph.

165

'I have no idea what this means,' said Eric, 'but it gives me a bad feeling.'

'Where's Archie now?'

'Waiting in the station, no doubt with his solicitor threatening lawsuits.'

'Do you know a taxi driver who works for McCusker by the name of Iain McDonald?'

Again, the change of subject failed to fluster Young. Rab liked this kid.

'Everybody knows Iain,' said Eric. 'He's an old pal of Archie's.'

'Sarah McCrae says McDonald was hanging around trying to impress Zoe. Her actual words were "hoping to get into her knickers". The other name Sarah gave me was James Baxter, but he has a solid alibi for when Zoe went missing. When I brought Baxter in, he claimed McDonald was a paedophile. I need you to find out where McDonald is. On the quiet. No scaring him off or giving him a chance to get his story in order.'

Chapter Twenty-three

Detective Chief Inspector George Quigley gazed at Ken Malloy and Brygida Kosofsky as if to say *where do we start?* In front of them were whiteboards covered in photographs, drawings and hand-written notes in different colours of marker pen. A blurry image from an old newspaper cutting showed Ruby Kaur standing next to her late husband Baldeep. It was connected by a red line to a box with MISSING PHOTO EVIDENCE? in bold letters.

Malloy finally took the hint.

'Sir, I am sorry to say questioning Ruby Kaur and searching her house and garden got us absolutely nowhere, but we switched focus to the paperwork we got from the bank and telephone company and came across something interesting. Ruby's house has just the one telephone line now, but when Baldeep was running his business from a home office in the loft – alongside his darkroom and photo stuff – he had a separate line. He could receive and make calls from there without Ruby knowing, and Ruby's such a nosy woman I suspect the arrangement suited him fine. We never had any reason to look into their phone records until now, or we would have known a number of calls – seven in all, spread out over the month before Ashna Gupta's disappearance – took place between Baldeep's office phone and the Guptas' home telephone.'

Quigley was not impressed. 'Seven calls? Why on earth did they not raise any red flags four years ago when you spotted them on the Gupta phone records?'

Malloy was embarrassed enough to glance hopefully at Kosofsky, but she wasn't about to take the rap, and he had to go on.

'Those seven calls were noted, sir, and marked as calls to a number registered to Baldeep and Ruby's house. They were known as close friends of the Guptas who frequently socialised with them. Unfortunately, the junior officer assigned to the task failed to register there was another phone line registered at the same address.'

'The other number being the main home telephone,' said Quigley.

'Correct, sir,' said Malloy.

'What about calls between the two homes on that line?'

'We checked again this morning,' said Malloy. 'A sprinkling of irregularly placed calls in both directions over the course of the previous three years, but none in the month before Ashna disappeared.'

'We checked all the interview logs, sir,' said Brygida Kosofsky, 'and there's no indication from either the Guptas or Baldeep Singh or Ruby Kaur of any reason for them not to be talking.'

'One theory is they fell out with Ruby. God—sorry, sir – goodness knows it would be easy enough, and perhaps after the falling out, all calls went through Baldeep.'

'Another possibility, sir, is Mr and Mrs Gupta were not involved in those seven calls,' said Kosofsky. 'We have evidence supporting that possibility. All seven calls took place during business hours.'

168

'And the Guptas keep regular hours at their cash & carry?'

'Exactly, sir.'

'Wouldn't Ashna and her brother be at school?'

'Their house is five minutes away from the school, and the calls took place either at lunchtime, or between four and five pm, outside school hours.'

'We have to talk with the brother, Simran,' said Quigley.

'Yes, sir, but can I suggest we should question someone else?'

'Go on.'

'DS Singh.'

Quigley looked disappointed. 'If I think for a minute you are letting a personal grudge get in the way of an investigation,' he said, 'it won't fail to be noted in your next PDR.'

Kosofsky actually saw Malloy flinch. The grade given in an officer's annual Personal Development Review could make the difference between continued promotion and professional stagnation.

Malloy recovered impressively:

'Sir, if we don't question Singh now, we could look like mugs – or worse, be accused of extending favouritism to a colleague. The press would have a field day.'

The chief inspector winced at the mention of the press. Malloy knew he was back to pushing the right buttons.

'DS Kosofsky?' said Quigley. 'What do you think?'

'I don't like having to question DS Singh, sir, but I agree with DI Malloy – we should have a word with him. At the very least we have to address the possibility of a cover-up to protect either or both of his parents. And as DI Malloy says, if we don't do it now, the blowback later could be rough.'

'We are stuck between pillar and post,' said Quigley. 'If word gets out, how will the newspapers react to us questioning an officer who was on the fringe of the Gupta investigation from day one? And doesn't Singh have his hands full across the water?'

'We could be in for a beating from the press no matter what, sir,' said Kosofsky. 'DS Singh currently has an attempted murder and a missing fifteen-year-old to worry about.'

'Good Lord,' said Quigley. 'Imagine what happens if we question Singh and the press get a whiff of him being around when two different teenagers go missing. We have to hold fire for now. When the time is right we will invite DS Singh over for a chat, but not yet. For the time being, this conversation never took place.'

Rab Singh let go of the handle of the interview room door when he spotted Chief Inspector Sandy Woods gesturing to him from the end of the corridor. He and Eric Young went to find out what the gaffer had to say.

'Because he's an old friend, I can't be seen anywhere near this. But remember he hasn't been charged with anything.'

'Understood, sir,' said Rab. 'This is strictly a fishing exercise.'

Archie McCusker was sitting at the table when they went in. Pacing the room behind him was a fat man in a suit whom Rab had not yet met, though he knew he had to be Archie's lawyer.

The fat man stopped pacing long enough to shake Rab's hand. It was like having his hand wrapped in a loaf of soggy bread. 'Graeme Brown,' he said. 'I represent Mr McCusker. You must be Detective Sergeant Singh.'

As soon as they were seated, Brown spoke first in a predictable attempt at setting boundaries.

'You do know my client is under considerable strain as a result of his daughter being missing.'

'I am aware of that,' said Rab.

'Shouldn't you be out there looking for her?'

'Your advice is gratefully noted. There are a couple of things we would like to discuss with Mr McCusker, matters directly related to the investigation.'

'He is not under arrest, nor has he been cautioned.'

'Correct,' said Rab. The guy was trying to piss him off, put him off guard, cause him to let something slip. But rent-a-mouth wasn't finished yet.

'Is this interview being taped?'

'If you would give me a chance to speak,' said Rab, 'I was about to request your client's permission to make an audio record of our talk.'

'The answer to which is a non-negotiable "no",' said Brown. Beside him, Archie looked pleased.

Eric Young was taking notes by hand. Rab put a finger on his notebook.

'Note, constable, Mr McCusker is being uncooperative. Under the urgent circumstances, Mr Brown, don't you find such an attitude a little odd?'

Brown smirked. 'Are you here to question me, or my client?'

Touché, you bastard.

'Mr McCusker,' said Rab, 'when you came in to report Zoe missing, I told you I would need to search your house. Why did you reply telling me I would "find nothing there"?'

'What kind of question is that?' said Brown.

'Didn't we already establish I wasn't here to ask you questions?' said Rab. 'Why are you doing all the talking? Does your client have something to hide?'

'When I said that about you searching my house,' said Archie, 'it was a, whadyoucallit ... figure of speech.'

'It sounded to me like a declaration your house would be clear of evidence that could aid us in the investigation of the disappearance of your daughter. Why would you say so?'

171

'Don't answer,' said Brown.

Rab placed on the table an evidence bag containing a fragment of Archie's wife's necklace. 'In fact, Mr McCusker, we did find something,' he said. 'Do you recognise this?'

Archie tried to play it calm. Rab thought he failed.

'No.'

'You've never seen it before,' said Rab.

'My client already answered,' said Brown.

Rab produced the photograph of Archie's wife proudly showing the camera a "ZOE" necklace.

'Do you see the necklace your wife is wearing in this photo?'

'I'm not blind,' said Archie. 'I never saw it before.'

'You never saw your wife wearing it?'

'Again, Sergeant,' said Brown. 'Asked and answered.'

'She had so much fuckin' jewellery,' said Archie, 'I couldn't keep track of it.'

'And yet, when we searched your house, there was no sign of any jewellery belonging to your wife.'

'She must have taken it with her.'

'One possible explanation,' said Rab, 'however unlikely. Do you agree, Mr McCusker, that the piece of jewellery in the evidence bag looks like it comes from the necklace in the photo of your wife?'

'Where is this going?' said Brown. 'What are you trying to establish here?'

'Mr McCusker, this photo held pride of place on the bedside cabinet in Zoe's bedroom. But you never saw the necklace before?'

'Never.'

'Not even in the photograph?'

'I don't go into Zoe's bedroom.'

'That's not what people tell me,' said Rab.

It took a couple of seconds for Brown to jump to his feet.

'You are way out of line, Sergeant. My client came here in good faith to help the investigation into the disappearance of his daughter. You thank him by making baseless insinuations threatening his good name. I will speak to your boss about this. Repeat such a smear under any circumstances and we will see you in civil court. Come on, Archie. We are finished here.'

Ruby approached the ringing telephone warily. Eventually she lifted the receiver from its cradle.

'If I don't know you personally, I will not utter another word.'

'It's me,' said Rab. 'Have you been getting a lot of calls from the newspapers?'

'The demonstrators and press hyenas have left us alone, so I thought it would be safe to come back to my own house. But I forgot about the phone. I don't suppose my only son is calling to offer long distance support to his mother in her moment of need?'

'Come on, Ruby. If I show my face in Glasgow and my old boss even thinks I am interfering in the Ashna investigation, I'll be fired.'

'I would be delighted.'

'Do you want me jobless and unable to support your grandsons?'

'You could do what your father always wanted, and come to work for the family business, safeguard and build on the inheritance for my grandsons.'

'And how would that protect Baldeep's reputation?'

'Don't try to lecture me, Rabinder. Nobody is more conscious than I am of the need to protect your father's good name.'

'You are trying too hard,' said Rab. 'Was Baldeep somehow involved with Ashna and you can't bear anyone finding out?'

'Your father was the sweetest man alive. He would never harm a hair on the poor girl's head.'

'Another question avoided. You knew something was going on?'

'Your awful friend Malloy came to see me again.'

'He's no friend of mine, and you know it. What did he want?'

'They've been going through your father's bank records. They found a cash withdrawal a week before Ashna disappeared. Four thousand pounds.'

'And you knew nothing about this?'

'I assured the snivelling Malloy it was news to me. Your father ran the business while I looked after the home and the family. Old-fashioned but traditional, the way we liked it. I told Malloy your father probably needed money to bribe corrupt policemen. It wouldn't have been the first time.'

'I'm sure that got him on your side,' said Rab.

'The calls from the media.'

'What about them?'

'Some of them don't want to talk about Baldeep.'

'What do they want to talk about?'

'You.'

Chapter Twenty-four

The crowd at the entrance to the school hall in Dunoon made Rab think of one of the happiest times of his life, when he and his father spent two weeks together in India. With Ruby remaining in Glasgow to take care of the family business, Baldeep took the opportunity to show his teenage son how proud of his roots he ought to be. Rab remembered the shock on the faces of relations in the Punjab when, after two days with them, Baldeep announced he and Rabinder were going off on a trip for the rest of their time in India.

The days became a blur of train journeys, sometimes in the pristine luxury of First Class, but often mired in the delightful chaos of Second or Third, where Rab would wake on his bunk with his knees to his chest because fellow passengers had somehow managed to fall asleep where his legs used to be.

He had never seen his father so *alive*. As they rushed from one artistic or architectural wonder to the next, Baldeep waxed endlessly about the culture and heritage and art they should be proud of.

Visits to the Taj Mahal and New Delhi's Red Fort were fleeting, and represented the ticking of boxes for what the tourist brochures insisted on calling "must-see" attractions.

From the Taj Mahal in Agra to the city of Aurangabad in Maharashtra province involved a twenty-hour rail journey, an adventure etched indelibly in Rab's memory. Aurangabad was the setting off point for day trips to the wonders of Ajanta and Ellora's caves and cave temples, some of whose origins stretched back over fifteen hundred years.

For two solid days Baldeep was beside himself with joy at being surrounded by astonishing creativity, whether in the form of Buddhist murals at Ajanta showing artistic techniques the Europeans failed to master until centuries later, or in the Ellora temples carved out of single pieces of basalt. The dedication and toil involved in their creation was Sysiphean. Baldeep spent hours waiting for the perfect light to photograph ancient creations by people of different faiths from his own – Buddhist, Jain and Hindu – and one of Rab's favourite possessions was a photograph of himself, a gangly acne-ravaged teenager, at the Kailasa Hindu temple, the largest structure at Ellora, multiple floors and ceilings and pillars and artwork hewn from a single piece of rock.

Another memory from the trip was having to queue for a train ticket out of Aurangabad and listening to Baldeep, who for two solid days had described all things Indian in flowing streams of superlatives, pour scorn on his fellow Indians as they scrambled for access to the ticket office window. A hundred or more would-be ticket purchasers, packed like tinned fish with their chests pressed on the backs of those ahead, spilled sideways, creating an ever-expanding mushroom of humanity going nowhere. Sounding awfully British, Baldeep heaped upon them looks of scorn and said:

'Like sheep at a bloody gate.'

Tonight, the sheep were journalists, local and national, desperate to get good spots at the event Sandy Woods had organised at Dunoon Grammar School.

The twin odours of curtain hems filled with mothballs and the machine-polished wooden floor striped with multi-coloured markings for basketball, volleyball and badminton took him back to another set of memories – annual school dances in the 1970s, eagerly anticipated evenings of hormone-fueled chaos and romantic failure and fulfillment. On nights organised around ballroom dancing, kids who had made long-distance eyes at one another for months finally had a chance to rub bodies while doing their best to recall the steps involved in a Dashing White Sergeant, Veleta Waltz or Canadian Barn Dance.

There would be no dancing in the Dunoon hall tonight, which was laid out as if for a concert. On the stage a table with three chairs faced a hall so filled with seating it made Rab wonder if Sandy Woods had over-estimated the likely turnout, a theory that was blown out of the water the moment the doors opened. Soon, every seat was taken and the passageways around the edges of the hall were filled with Dunoonites shifting from foot to foot as if concerned they might have missed something, even though the event was yet to get under way.

Before long, a space cordoned off near the back of the hall for the grumbling media was filled to overflowing, its command of the event hampered by yet more Dunoonites in need of somewhere to stand. TV crews set their equipment on tall tripods, camera operators on step-ladders. Stills photographers appeared from outside carrying spindly chairs commandeered from elsewhere in the school.

Finally it was time for Sandy Woods to address the expectant crowd. He sat between Archie McCusker on one side and Rab on the other. Rab had tried to gauge McCusker's mood, but could only detect a strong smell of whisky.

Chief Inspector Woods waited for the noise to drop, which did not take long. This was the moment everyone came for, and as he stood to the whir of camera motor-drives, he soon had the attention of every curious soul in the building.

'Ladies and gentlemen, thank you for coming. As you know, fifteen-year-old Zoe McCusker has been missing for just short of forty-eight hours. My officers, led by Detective Sergeant Rabinder Singh, have worked tirelessly to try and find out everything we possibly can to help us locate Zoe.

'Having spoken to almost everyone we want to talk to, it is now time to ask for your help. Dunoon people are proud of a friendly community where we all know each other. Now we need you to share anything you know which could help us find Zoe.

'Any suspicions or concerns or incidents overheard or witnessed, no matter how minor you think they are, may be vital. If you are reluctant to discuss anything in public, officers can take confidential statements after the meeting comes to a close.'

He paused to let his words sink in. The room was tense, and parents exchanged looks flickering between anxious, fearful – or thankful this was happening to someone else. Inspector Woods went on:

'You all know Zoe's father, Archie McCusker. Mr McCusker would like to make a statement.' He extended one hand to McCusker. 'Archie?'

Archie McCusker got to his feet, a little unsteadily. His forehead was moist with perspiration and a droplet ran from one temple to his jawline before splashing onto a sheet of A4 paper held in a shaky grip. He looked at the paper for a few seconds before speaking in an unsteady voice, eyes fixed on the silent crowd.

'As Sandy said, everyone in Dunoon knows me, and everyone knows my Zoe, so you understand how much she means to me. I am here because I would do anything to get Zoe back home safely. If anybody in this room is in contact

178

with my daughter, or knows someone who can get in touch with her, I beg you to pass on this message from me: I love you Zoe, and I want you to come home. I am not angry, only worried for your safety. Come home please. If anyone has any information to help the police investigation, I beg you to come forward.'

A sympathetic murmur passed through the audience as Archie dropped the piece of paper and glared at Woods and Singh.

'There's something I don't understand. Why are the press hemmed in at the back of the hall, instead of near the stage, where they can properly give the story of Zoe's disappearance the coverage it needs?'

He reached sideways and prodded Sandy Woods on the shoulder. 'Is it true you kept them away from the front? Why? Are you ashamed of how you've done next to nothing to find my daughter?'

The reaction he got from the floor told him he had the crowd on his side. He stepped around the table to the edge of the stage.

'Do you know what the cops were wasting their time doing this afternoon? Asking me about Zoe. They've run out of ideas so now I'm a suspect in my own daughter's disappearance.'

Shouts of disgust from the audience prompted the media corral to disintegrate and send journalists past Sergeant Henderson as if he were not there. They battled their way to the front, cameras flashing and microphones and tape recorders at the ready. One audience member, a middle-aged man wearing a leather jacket and a baseball cap drew a forest of microphones.

'I want to know something,' he said. 'Has anyone questioned you?' He jabbed one finger at the table on the stage. Every pair of eyes in the hall fell upon Rab.

'Aye, **YOU**!,' he said, 'the Pakistani guy, whatever your name is. 'Ahm a news junky, I read the Record and The Sun every day, cover to cover – and they are full of stories about your mother and father. They're prime suspects in another disappearance of another teenager. Ashna sumbody – she was a family friend – and as of today your mammy and your dead daddy are the main suspects. How come **you** aren't being questioned about Zoe?' His chest puffed out with pride. He had hit a mark, and he knew it. Locals' eyes shot daggers at Rab, and the crowd exploded in anger.

Sandy Woods jumped to his feet, yelling at the top of his voice.

'Please! Everyone, quiet please! If you could calm down a moment—'

'Bugger off,' shouted an older man with spectacles as thick as beer bottle bottoms. 'It's a serious question. Your so-called detective was hardly off the boat before he was cuddling up to Zoe at the Cowal Café.'

Rumbles of agreement and growing outrage subsided when a woman Rab had seen outside the school raised her voice.

'I saw them holding hands and kissing outside the school gate! Zoe's only fifteen! How come the predator isn't under arrest, instead of heading the investigation into her disappearance? Answer me, Sandy Woods!'

Rab found himself looking at a microphone held by a journalist who pushed against the stage and stretched to get it as close to Rab as he could reach. When he realised he needed to use it first, the journalist pulled the microphone back abruptly, coming within an inch of hitting himself on the face.

'I have a question for Sergeant Singh,' he said. 'Sergeant, is it true in 1976 you were arrested at an Oban campsite on suspicion of having sex with an underage girl?'

Rab had been wondering if this could get any worse. At least Sandy Woods was game enough to divert the line of discussion.

'Sergeant Singh is not the subject of this meeting,' he yelled.

'Maybe he bloody should be,' shouted a member of the public.

The reporter timed his next question to perfection to catch the next dip in crowd volume as people struggled not to miss what was said next.

'Sergeant Singh is closely connected to two cases of underage girls going missing, and was once detained on suspicion of having sex with a minor. Why isn't he a suspect?'

'Exactly!' shouted Archie McCusker. 'There's a poacher turned bloody gamekeeper in charge of finding Zoe, and we're not supposed to ask questions? What are your priorities, Sandy? Who are you protecting?'

Sandy Woods stepped to the edge of the stage and held both hands high until at last everyone shut up. He spoke in a low voice.

'The meeting is over. Anyone who wishes to make a report in strictest confidence can speak to Sergeant Henderson or Constable Young.'

Woods took Rab's arm and spirited him off towards a backstage door, but even before they got to his car, journalists were in pursuit, shouting questions neither of them was about to answer. They bundled themselves into a car and Woods took off, tyres squealing.

He zig-zagged through the streets as if he had been patrolling them all his life before he surprised Rab by taking a sharp turn into an empty car park behind a bankrupt Chinese takeaway.

The dust was still rising from the car skidding to a halt when Woods spoke.

'Now might be a good time, Sergeant, to tell me why I was blindsided by a story about you being arrested for a sexual offence in an Oban campsite in 1976.'

Rab took a deep breath. He needed his boss to remain on his side.

'You can thank Hen Henderson for that. From the moment I got here, he has been asking if we'd met before. Now he's remembered where, and rather than informing you of something he deemed relevant to the investigation, he chose to leak it to the press.'

'It's Henderson's fault you were accused of having sex with a minor?'

'Can I explain, sir?'

Woods gestured with one hand. *Go on.*

'It's true I was briefly detained, on suspicion of an offence I was never charged with,' he said. 'My girlfriend and I went camping, and her parents, who weren't exactly filled with joy by their middle-class Scottish daughter having an Indian boyfriend, reported me because she was underage. But only by a couple of days. When Constable Hen barged into our tent a few days later she had already turned sixteen.'

'Is this an admission of you having sex with a minor?'

'When we set off on our trip – against the wishes of her parents – I was seventeen and she was days shy of sixteen. Nothing was going on to merit police involvement except her dad is a Sheriff Court Judge and a control freak who made some calls accusing me of sexually abusing his daughter. In the end, nothing was proven and no charges were filed. Four years later we were married; we're still married and she's the mother of my two boys. Her dad dotes on his grandsons, and nowadays will even give me an occasional dram from his collection of stupidly expensive Single Malts. The Oban thing was water under the bridge for more than fifteen years.

Nobody gave it a moment's consideration until holier-than-thou Henderson chose to drop a fellow officer in the shit.'

Rab wondered at first if he had overstated his case, but at least he appeared to have given his boss time to take a breath.

'What a mess,' said Woods. 'Moving on. I knew your mother was under investigation in Glasgow and I had heard there was suspicion your father was somehow involved, but nobody told me your name had come up.'

'Because it hasn't really, Sir. 'DI Ken Malloy is desperate to be the cop who cracks the impossible case. He has no evidence because there is no way my dad had anything to do with Ashna's disappearance. Because Malloy can't prove anything, he's punting wildly at anything and anyone close to my dad. Including me.'

'Item three on the charge sheet: cuddling up to Zoe McCusker at the Cowal Café? Kissing at the school gates? You're not making this easy, Singh.'

'I know how it looks, sir, but Zoe is a show-off, an attention-seeker, a troubled kid. You know we suspect her dad of raping her repeatedly; her mum ran away and left her; and she's got a reputation for being a tearaway I don't think she deserves. I sat with her at the Cowal Café for five minutes. Eric Young was with me the whole time. **She** came to **our** table. She was showing off to her pals, but the accusation I was cuddling up to her is nowhere near accurate, not in the slightest bit true.'

'What about the episode at the school gates?'

'Your regular mountain out a molehill, sir. I came out of Mags Henderson's B&B to find Zoe waiting for me. She asked me to walk her to school. The day before she had hinted men were taking advantage of her, and because I had told her if she needed to talk she could trust me, I agreed to accompany her in the hope of gathering information. Outside the school gates she took me by surprise by kissing me on the cheek. She did it to shock the nosey parkers who were watching, and they got the wrong end of the stick.'

Without taking his eyes off Rab, Woods shook his head as if to say *what the hell did I do to deserve this*, turned the ignition and drove.

It took minutes to get to the police station, where a press phalanx including at least one TV crew did their best to block the doorway. Andy Barnes appeared from within and helped Woods and Singh get through the reporters without acknowledging them. Rab knew it would look bad on the late news.

The front desk was empty, but there was a reception committee waiting.

'What are you doing here, Malloy?' said Rab.

'Detective Inspector Malloy to you, Detective Sergeant Singh.' Malloy reached out and shook Sandy Woods's hand while at the same time introducing Detective Sergeant Brygida Kosofsky.

'To hell with this,' said Rab, and took off for the back offices.

'Take it easy Rab,' said Brygida Kosofsky. 'The Chief Super wants a word with you.'

'George Quigley?' said Sandy Woods. 'I'll talk to him.' He looked at Malloy and Kosofsky as if one of them might hand over a telephone.

'Sorry sir,' said Malloy, 'but DCS Quigley was most specific. He wants DS Singh to accompany us to Glasgow. For questioning in the matter of Ashna Gupta.'

'So George Quigley instructed you to arrest me?' said Rab.

'With the latest developments in the Gupta case,' said Kosofsky, 'obviously we need to talk with you. And no, you're not under arrest.'

'You're wasting your time and mine,' said Rab. 'I have a job to do, a teenager missing for forty-eight hours.'

Sandy Woods took a half-step forwards.

'Sorry, Singh,' he said, 'but after what happened tonight, my hands are tied. I am placing you under immediate suspension from all duties.'

Ken Malloy smirked like he had won a prize.

'You heard your boss, Singh,' he said. 'You either come with us willingly, or you go out the front door past the press in handcuffs.'

'Kenny boy, you are a moron. I will meet with DCS Quigley when I'm good and ready.' With a dismissive wave, Rab headed towards the offices.

Chapter Twenty-five

Before Rab took two steps, the front doors of the police station blew inwards under the power of Sergeant Henderson and Constable Young, who pivoted and slammed them shut to stop baying journalists from following. Sandy Woods was first to react:

'What's going on, Sergeant?'

'A crowd from the school hall collected folk along the way and is coming here mob-handed, sir. They're calling for the arrest of DS Singh for whatever happened to Zoe McCusker. The press are egging them on.'

'I understand we have you to thank for at least some of this fuss, Hen. We **will** have a talk later.' said Woods. Henderson looked like he wanted to be somewhere else. Anywhere else.

'I still bet the daft girl's in London, snuggled up on her mum's sofa,' said Woods.

Malloy took a symbolic step towards Rab.

'This changes things, Sergeant Singh,' he said. 'Now it's a safety issue. Our car is outside. We had better get you out of here.'

Rab did nothing to hide his sneer. 'Do you think I'm leaving here in the back of a police car? Past a horde putting on a special show for the ten o'clock news?'

'It's for the best,' said Malloy.

'We already established I am not under arrest,' said Rab. 'I will leave in my own car.'

'Then I will come with you.'

'Trust me, Kenny, that is never going to happen.'

The crowd numbered over a hundred, many of them united by chants of "Arrest Singh! Paedo Paki bastard! Lock him up!" A collective roar met the doors opening as Sergeant Henderson and Constable Andy Barnes emerged protecting Sandy Woods and another officer who each held the arm of a figure whose head and shoulders were covered in a blanket.

'They've arrested him,' cried one protester. 'They're trying to get away with the bastard,' yelled another, as the throng surged forward.

The prisoner was bundled into the back of a car as Sandy Woods raised a megaphone and faced the mob.

'We'll have no vigilante nonsense here!'

The car nudged through the crowd, bonnet and roof ringing to irate thumps, Constable Andy Barnes and the prisoner, head still covered, in the back seat. Demonstrators took to rocking the car while others ran for their own vehicles.

'The ferry leaves in twenty minutes,' shouted one.

'Best thing for the pervert,' yelled another. 'He wouldnae last long here.'

Malloy's car was the last to drive onto the ferry before the ramp was raised. Behind them, protesters' car horns blared and citizens took to the waterfront to vent their rage. Two minutes later, Constable Barnes and Eric Young, the latter out of uniform and his hair dishevelled, were the last to cross the pedestrian bridge to pierside before the boat and harbour crews set about casting off. The two men slipped out to a waiting taxi without drawing attention from a mob whose fury was focused entirely on the departing ferry.

Brygida looked around the cramped interior of the Datsun while it took Rab three attempts to engage third gear. The noise of cogs thrashing against one another would have made her engineer father weep.

'Nice car,' she said.

'Go ahead and mock it,' said Rab.

'Did you have to visit a lot of scrapyards to find one this bad?' She fingered the wires dangling from the mangled hole in the middle of the dash.

'I'll have you know the Datsun 120Y is the car of choice among taxi drivers all over Asia,' said Rab.

'Don't tell me. They love its spacious interior, or perhaps in some cultures they savour not knowing when the next gear will engage?'

'The 120Y is indestructible,' said Rab. 'Japanese functional engineering at its most effective. Engines can do half a million miles with maintenance from a shifting spanner and a couple of screwdrivers.'

'Is having no two wheels pointing in the same direction an optional extra?'

Brygida looked around at streets she had never seen before. She had a feeling Singh was equally lost.

'Do you think it worked?' she said, as they slowed for an intersection and two men leaning against a wall pointed at Rab's turban.

'Hey!' said one. 'That's him, Singh!'

An empty beer can clattered against the back windscreen.

'Lucky the can wasn't full,' said Brygida.

'Lucky it wasn't a bottle,' said Rab.

'How far to Glasgow?'

'I've never driven it. Maybe eighty, ninety miles, a lot of it narrow winding roads. In the dark. Three or four hours?'

'You and I need to talk,' said Kosofsky.

Rab tried not to show his delight when this time third gear engaged without complaint.

'Off the record?' he said.

'If you insist. Did your parents and the Guptas have a falling out a few weeks before Ashna disappeared?'

He looked directly at Brygida. The road in front was straight and empty of traffic. At last he spoke.

'Where did such a notion come from?'

'Phone records. Calls between the two houses went from nearly every day to virtually never. Any particular reason?'

'I never could work it out,' said Rab.

'Aw come on.'

'I'm serious. The Guptas were good friends, but there was always an undercurrent of competitiveness between them and my folks. Correction – between them and Ruby. Remember Ruby can start a fight in an empty room. They were always falling out over trivial nonsense, much of it a result of Ashna's mother being a notorious gasbag. If you want the whole of the Indian community to know anything, talk about it within earshot of Lala Gupta.'

'Everyone we speak to describes your mother in exactly the same way.'

'Then you can imagine how their relationship had its rough moments,' said Rab. 'I knew they weren't talking, but I never knew why. These rifts usually blew over in a few weeks.'

'But this time their daughter vanished,' said Brygida. 'What about your dad? The evidence points to some kind of involvement with Ashna, no matter how innocent. Like we tell punters: there is a need to eliminate him from our enquiries.'

They left behind the town's street lighting and the road became lit only by the Datsun's weak headlamps and infrequent glimpses of the moon. Occasional buildings from the days before fast-moving traffic clung uncomfortably close the edge of the road. One or two had signs to draw travellers towards hot drinks, cold snacks or tourist knick-knacks, while others perched roadside in anonymous darkness.

'You're thinking of the studio portrait of Ashna,' said Rab.

'Of course we bloody are. But with your dad dead and Ashna vanished into thin air and your father's photo files conveniently gone, what can we do but speculate about possible connections between the two of them?'

'You don't think Baldeep did it,' said Rab. Not a question, a statement.

'What I think is irrelevant.'

'Malloy's obsessed with my dad and won't entertain anyone else as a suspect.'

'You're wrong there. He does have someone else in mind,' said Kosofsky.

'And you're dying to tell me.'

'If "off the record" works both ways.'

Rab nodded his agreement, and she went on: 'Ken thinks you were in on it with your dad, and won't rule out the possibility the plot involved your mum. Imagine what the press will make of that. The psycho Paki family from hell.'

'It's bad enough having a complete thicko like Malloy casting misplaced suspicion on my family, but I've had it up to here with this Paki shit. My mum is Indian. My dad was Indian. And I might have been born in India, but I'm Scottish.'

'If you were Transylvanian, Malloy would still have you as a Paki and a suspect, and the press would be delighted to go along with him.'

'Listen,' said Rab. 'You didn't tell me any of this. It wasn't off the record, it didn't happen.'

Brygida didn't understand.

'You didn't tell me Malloy pegged me as a suspect,' said Rab. 'Being considerate of my feelings, you never even mentioned Pakis, psycho or otherwise.' He pulled sharply to the side, braking hard and throwing them forward against their seat belts. They came to an abrupt halt in front of a lochside hotel with lights still burning and a sprinkling of vehicles nosed into a small car park.

'Don't know if your mobile will work here,' he said, 'but they will have a land line you can use. You can get yourself a drink while someone comes from Glasgow to pick you up.'

Before pulling away and while Brygida watched from the car park in silent disbelief, Rab scissored a cassette from the hidey hole and savoured the surprise on her face when the stereo erupted at a deafening volume: Springsteen playing *Born To Run*.

A few minutes later, the Datsun picked its way through near total darkness beneath low cloud that blocked all trace of light in the sky. Rab could only take Springsteen in small doses, and when he went to Radio Two in search of something to cheer him up, he was met with the gravelly croak of Dylan singing *Don't Think Twice, It's Alright*. Baldeep loved pre-electric Dylan, never drove anywhere without a greatest hits selection of his musical hero's 60s songs on cassette tape.

Rab found himself thinking of how there wasn't much alright about life at the moment. The mess he was in had so much to do with Baldeep and was putting yet more strain on an already fractured relationship with the only woman he had ever loved. He was estranged from Sheena, but needed her help to rescue his career, and the Quiet Man had made something very clear. *If we discover even a hint of collusion in efforts to hide or destroy evidence, you and your wife's careers are over, and*

191

you will leave here in handcuffs. Even when he spoke quietly, the gaffer didn't leave much room for misunderstanding.

If there had been an arrest warrant out for him, Malloy would have been more than happy to put it to good use in Dunoon. Rab knew that could change within hours, and what he needed to do now couldn't be done from a police cell. He had careers to save and his family's good name to preserve. In that order, never mind what Ruby said.

Police called their truncheons "sticks". Sheena Ferguson kept an old stick of Rab's next to her bedside cabinet, since the one she was issued as a WPC in the early 1980s was a force-wide source of embarrassment and derision. Female constables carried a miniature truncheon sized to fit in their police-issue leather handbag. It was ridiculously short, had a ribbed handle with a leather thong, and could easily be mistaken for a dildo.

When a strange noise woke her in the middle of the night, she padded soundlessly to her bedroom door, Rab's old stick held in the raised ready position. Someone much bigger than either of her sons was climbing the stairs with great care not to make any noise. She switched on the lights behind her, wrenched the door open and charged.

'It's me, it's me!' said Rab, words pouring out in a rush. 'I let myself in because I didn't want to ring the bell and wake the boys. I was trying to let you know I was here without giving you a fright.'

'I nearly knocked your brains in.'

'I know. And with my stick.'

'If you recall, mine wouldn't put the frighteners up many burglars.'

The tension evaporated and they giggled together. Rab gently put his hand over Sheena's mouth to help not wake the boys. The smile left her eyes when she remembered the question she had yet to ask.

192

'Something's wrong,' said Sheena. 'Why are you here?'

'Sorry to interrupt your beauty sleep.'

Downstairs, Rab turned on the kettle and popped tea bags in two mugs. When they were sitting at the kitchen table, he explained. About the community meeting where no light whatsoever was shed on the Zoe investigation, and which went on to demonise Rab, prompting his escape from Dunoon and from surprise visitors Malloy and Kosofsky, one at a time.

The last part of the story raised a grin.

'You dropped Kosofsky off in the middle of nowhere?' she said.

'It was a hotel in the middle of nowhere. There were lights on and two Land Rovers and a tractor in the car park.'

'Imagine the shit she'll have to take from a colleague who isn't known for being supportive or understanding.'

'Brygida can handle him.'

'He'll push for your arrest,' said Sheena.

'He will,' said Rab, 'but so far at least, he has no evidence to support an arrest.'

Sheena shook her head again. 'And people wonder how you never got past sergeant,' she said. 'You've added to Malloy's tally of grievances, and he will find a way to bring you in.'

'Maybe I'll deny him the pleasure, and go in myself when the time is right,' said Rab.

'And in the meantime, skulk around working the Ashna case? The one case the Quiet Man told you to avoid if you want to keep your job?'

'There are things I have to do.'

'While hiding from Malloy and company, without being able to show your warrant card, with no authority whatsoever?'

'Malloy couldn't find his own backside with both hands.'

'And meanwhile you'll be deep undercover?' Sheena did more head-shaking while she sipped tea. 'Have you looked in a mirror lately? You're a brown-skinned man in a turban. How are you going to investigate anything on the QT without finding yourself in an interview room sitting across from Malloy and George Quigley? And what about the missing girl in Dunoon?'

'Sandy Woods means well, but he has an old pals' act going on with Zoe's father, and instead of turning Dunoon upside down, he's telling anyone who will listen she is probably safe and sound at her mother's place in London.'

'What if he's right?'

'I hope he is, but I doubt it.'

'So you're going to be the Secret Squirrel investigator in two cases, both of which you've been warned away from?'

Little feet thundered down the stairs and in bounded a young lad wearing Partick Thistle F.C. pyjamas.

'Dad! When did you come? Are we going to the football next Saturday?'

'We certainly are,' said Rab. 'Who are we playing?'

'See! Ronnie said you'd forget. St Mirren. The Buddies.'

'The Buddies are in for a tanking,' said Rab.

'The Jags are going to tear the Paisley numpties a new—'

'Now might be a good time to go back to bed, Stuart,' said Sheena.

'Will Dad have breakfast with us? Can you take us to school, Dad? Are you sure about going to the St Mirren game? Will Uncle James come?'

Rab counted off the answers on his fingers. 'Yes. Yes. Yes. And I don't know about Uncle James coming to Firhill. If he got too excited I might have to arrest him. Now, young man – bed!'

The smile on Sheena's face would melt any dad's heart. Rab looked at his watch. Past two o'clock. 'Is it alright if I kip on the sofa?'

Rab woke when Sheena brought him a cup of tea. He was shocked to see it was nearly nine o'clock, and only relaxed when Sheena pointed out today was Saturday. Which meant no school for the boys, though they did have football training at ten, and needed to be fed in a hurry.

Rab made breakfast for all four of them while the boys did a lot of giggling. When they set about tucking into toast and scrambled eggs, he slipped out to use the telephone. He dialled the number from memory and Mags Henderson answered before the second ring.

'The Crest B&B, good morning.'

'Hello Mags, this is Rab.'

'Good morning. The whole of Dunoon is talking about you. They say you escaped to Glasgow by sending a ringer onto the ferry.'

'The attention was getting a bit too much for me,' said Rab.

'Plus all the nonsense folk were spouting,' said Mags, 'my idiot ex-husband included. Nobody seemed to worry what might happen to the Zoe investigation if you were hung out to dry, did they?'

'Could you possibly do me a favour? I'm afraid it'll have to be quick.'

'Under pressure?'

'I have to take the boys to football practice in a few minutes,' said Rab.

'The right sort of pressure for a change,' said Mags. 'What do you need?'

Rab was up to his elbows in soap suds, washing the breakfast dishes. The boys teased and bothered each other the way only siblings can and Sheena warmed her hands on a fresh mug of coffee and relished the rare freedom from morning chores.

'Dad's taking us to the game next Saturday,' said Stuart.

Ronnie looked doubtful. 'Are you, Dad?' he said.

'Can't possibly miss playing the Buddies at home,' he said as he grabbed a dishcloth. 'It's like a real local derby, but without all the shi— the bullshi— I mean all the nonsense when Rangers or Celtic turn up.'

'You nearly said shit' said Stuart

'Twice!' said Ronnie.

Rab consigned the last dish to the drying tray. 'Do you have everything ready for football practice?'

The phone in the living room rang and Rab put the dishcloth back on the towel rack. He made a show of looking at his watch before declaring:

'Estimated time of departure, three minutes and counting. Two minutes and fifty-nine seconds, fifty-eight, fifty-seven … ' The boys dashed from the room in fits of laughter.

Rab answered the phone.

'Eric?'

'Yes, DS Singh.'

'Let's drop the formalities, Eric. I'm suspended, remember. You got my message from Mags Henderson?'

'She told my mum we needed to talk.'

'I hope it's not a problem,' said Rab.

'Why would it be?'

'Your mum might not be happy about her boy keeping in touch with the Paki pariah.'

'Didn't you tell me you were Indian? I told her what happened at the school hall last night. She's on your side.'

'Tell her I appreciate it. Did you find Iain McDonald?'

196

'He was out of town all day yesterday. Took a fare to Edinburgh and back, an older couple going to a family funeral. He's coming in to the station later this morning. I'm about to jump on my bike and get over there. Do you have any advice on how to handle him?'

'I do,' said Rab.

Chapter Twenty-six

Baldeep's successes in West End real estate dealings were the envy of his friends. After Rab came to Scotland, it seemed like his dad could do no wrong buying, renovating, renting and selling dozens of properties, mostly in ever-more desirable Dowanhill and other districts close to Glasgow University. Instead of resorting to the standard developer's vandalism transforming spacious old flats into cramped multi-roomed student bedsits, Baldeep restored flats, retaining their period character, and rented them to students or to visiting professionals employed by the university. He bought from bankruptcy estates and from families desperate to turn grandma's run-down home into hard cash in order to fight over the money among themselves, and he sold when the price was right. The frequency of his purchases made him his bank's most coveted mortgage client. He played the market like a maestro who never hit a bum note.

Despite being justifiably proud of what he achieved, only once did a property purchase mean more to him than any measure of capital gain. It was also the time he put one over on a Glasgow crime lord.

The Victorian-era bank building had been empty for 25 years and was falling prey to vandals and internal fires set by homeless squatters hiding from the winter chill. Baldeep knew about it, but hadn't given it a moment's consideration until he received strictly-off-the-record calls from his own bank manager and from a friend at Glasgow City Council whose job was to protect listed buildings. The word from the banker and the civil servant was the same: their worst nightmare wanted the old bank building – a notorious mobster from Glasgow's East End had put in a lowball offer. The whisper going around was property developers were being warned away from bidding against him because he wanted the prime site to build luxury flats, something that would only happen if the listed building mysteriously burned to the ground. It was a ploy the crime lord had made work before.

Baldeep and some friends took no more than a few minutes to be certain this was the perfect place for a new gurdwara to serve the West End's growing Sikh population. Within 48 hours, and one day before the close of bidding, Baldeep's makeshift syndicate put in an offer precisely one thousand pounds higher than the mobster's. More importantly to the council, the bid came with fully-costed plans to preserve its Category B listed status while renovating it and turning it into the West End's first Sikh gurdwara.

Work on the refurbishment commenced within days of their winning bid being approved, and sure enough, a few weeks later the building was visited late at night by six East End hard men who broke the lock on a side door and swaggered in carrying five-gallon containers of petrol.

A powerful spotlight froze them on the spot. The door swung closed behind them as every light in the building came on, adding to their look of rabbits caught in car headlights. The initial spotlight came from a video camera on the shoulder of an older Sikh man. Spread out on either side of Baldeep were some of the biggest "Pakis" the wannabe fire-raisers had ever seen, all standing with their hands behind their backs. A loud bang from behind made the neds jump when the door blew inwards, opened by the face of the friend they had left waiting at the wheel of a stolen Transit van. Nose broken by the impact, blood streaming over the front of his shiny white Adidas tracksuit, the driver shrugged as best he could with his arms hauled high up his back by two more burly Sikhs.

Baldeep spoke without taking his eye from the viewfinder.

'Please put down the petrol cans,' he said.

The neds looked to one another until their leader took a half step forward. He had red hair cropped short, sideburns hanging below earlobes studded with gold baubles. Grey blue eyes stared malevolently at the camera lens, a look ruined by the rash of freckles speckling his entire face.

'What the fuck do youse think ye're doing,' he said.

'We might ask you the same, with far more justification,' said Baldeep.

Freckle-face rocked his head from side to side like a cartoon Indian, earning sniggers from nervous hangers-on. 'Oh my golly gosh. More justification, indeed!' he said. His attempt at an Indian accent broadened the smiles and boosted his confidence. Baldeep was having none of it:

'We have you on video, leaving your van, approaching via the side lane and breaking your way into our building,' said Baldeep. 'All of your faces are recorded for evidence and your fingerprints are all over the petrol cans.'

The eyes of every one of the intruders except Freckle Face swept downwards to the cans. Nobody was wearing gloves.

'Put the cans on the floor and you will be allowed to leave,' said Baldeep.

Something clicked and flashed in the spotlight. A flick-knife with a long narrow blade honed to a deadly point.

'Fuck you, ya Paki bastart,' the thug said. 'You'll gie me the camera or …' he rushed Baldeep, knife point aiming for the older man's throat.

A field hockey stick descended on his wrist with sufficient force to make the knife fly from his hand. With a thud it buried itself deep in the wooden floor after first passing through an expensive Nike shoe and the foot inside it.

Baldeep watched the thug's face turn pale enough for freckles to disappear in the viewfinder. Hockey sticks materialised in the hands of the entire makeshift security crew, held at the ready, each with a target clearly defined. The wannabe fire-raisers froze like they all had their feet nailed to the floor.

'Last chance,' said Baldeep. 'Cans on the floor.'

It was an event Rab was too young to have witnessed, but one he had often heard discussed, though never by Baldeep, whose pride in the part he played in the establishment of the West End's gurdwara was deep, but unexpressed.

Rab arrived early, anticipating the buzz his appearance in the langar hall was sure to create. Every Sikh gurdwara has a langar hall, the room where volunteers work, year-round, to ensure the temple can offer free vegetarian meals to any visitor. It was through such customs that Rab, an infrequent visitor, drew joy from Sikhism, from the way it embraced all comers, no matter their personal beliefs. Followers of other faiths would never be turned away from the temple, but it was in the fundamental generosity of spirit of the langar hall, from which nobody could leave hungry, that Rab saw a community worthy of admiration. And the love of authentic Indian cuisine brought by the langar to thousands of Glasgow's homeless over the years was a stroke of public relations genius on behalf of the gurdwara and the community who called it their own.

The three women working in the langar had been volunteering there since Rab was a teenager, and they still treated him like a kid, palming his face with flour-covered hands and admiring how tall and handsome he was. Exactly like a young Baldeep, was the phrase he heard over and over again. He left the door open a crack while freshly-prepared chapatis and mouth-watering curries were forced on him. Refusal was not an option.

When he saw first his mother and later Dilip and Lala Gupta being led into a meeting room by Granthi Singh, the temple priest, he thanked everyone profusely, patted his stomach to emphasise how full they had made him, and slipped across the hallway. He opened the door to find exactly what he expected: Ruby and the Guptas competing to see who would be first to leave in the greater state of high dudgeon while Granthi Singh did his determined best to keep the peace.

'Why are they here?' said Ruby. 'Do you have any idea the lies about me they are spreading all over town?'

'I am sorry, Giani-ji,' said Lala Gupta, 'but we refuse to be anywhere near this woman.' They spun resolutely towards the door, to be confronted by Rab.

'What's this?' said Dilip Gupta, 'an ambush?'

Palms out in a symbolic attempt at appeasement, Rab spoke quietly.

'We have to talk,' he said. 'Hiding in the trenches swapping insults isn't helping. I asked Giani-ji to help. We can trust him to help keep this civil. We need to find something new to assist the investigation.'

Lala put hands to hips in moral outrage. 'It's not your investigation. They sent you off to some place on the coast where you couldn't mess anything up. Except you are all over the news again, and now people say you are a suspect in Ashna's disappearance. And here you are, still meddling. We trusted you!'

'My Rabinder is not a suspect – never has been, never will be,' said Ruby.

'Which is more than can be said for your husband,' said Dilip.

'Let's all take a deep breath,' said Granthi Singh. 'Cups of tea for everyone?' He looked to the door, where two of the aunties from the langar hall held trays. Summoned ahead of time, and in no hurry to leave in case they could pick up on a little chatter to share in the langar hall.

Cups of tea were served and distributed, and they all sat on chairs with nowhere to put the teacups. A brilliant move from Granthi Singh, thought Rab. Hot tea held in laps was one sure way to reduce the waving of arms.

'We all want the same thing,' said Granthi Singh. 'To find out what happened to Ashna.'

Lala Gupta couldn't possibly show disrespect for the priest. Others in the room failed to command any such consideration.

'Some of us seem to want to hide what happened to our daughter,' she said.

'I'm sorry you feel this way, Lala,' said Rab, 'but it's simply not true. We want to help.'

Dilip got the dig in first. 'Why? And why you? On the news last night they said you are suspended, not even a police officer now. Detective Inspector Malloy warned us about you.'

'Malloy is a fool,' said Ruby. 'He thinks my Baldeep made your daughter disappear.'

Lala shot Ruby a withering look. 'Baldeep was up to something with Ashna. Or were you too blind to see it?'

Rab spoke to avert a full-on cat fight.

'I need to know why you and my parents had a falling out a few weeks before Ashna disappeared,' he said. 'What did my dad do to deserve that? Falling out with Ruby I can understand—'

'Rabinder!' said Ruby. What kind of—'

'For once in your life, mother, be quiet,' said Rab.

Ruby started to get up, but Rab wasn't finished.

'Stay where you are!' He looked between Ruby and the Guptas. 'What caused the falling out?'

'You know perfectly well,' said Dilip. 'The disgusting photographs.'

Rab shook his head. 'No. It was something else. You knew nothing about any photographs until a few days ago. I'm talking about whatever it was caused you and my parents to stop talking shortly before Ashna disappeared.'

'Ashna was spending time with your father and coming back to us full of rebellion,' said Dilip. 'Baldeep was driving a wedge between us and our daughter. What kind of man would—'

'What kind of family smothers a daughter's ambitions?' said Ruby.

Lala Gupta laughed out loud. 'Did that really come from the lips of the most interfering woman in Glasgow?'

Her husband's anger was instantaneous.

'You knew!' he said.

Ruby crossed her arms across her chest. 'I knew Baldeep offered support to Ashna. Support she couldn't get from her own parents.'

'We were protecting our daughter's future!' said Dilip. 'Every child goes through a phase of wanting to be a pop star or a footballer. Ashna was one of the brightest in her school. We couldn't stand by and watch her throw her life away acting or dancing. We told Detective Inspector Malloy about Ashna and Baldeep spending time together, but by then Baldeep was dead and Malloy said they could find nothing whatsoever to connect them. Notch up another failure by Glasgow's finest. Four years later, and they only made the link with the help of an artist in Australia.'

'In any case, what are you two getting at?' said Lala. 'Our Ashna didn't run away. She would never have run away, and if she did, she would have come back, or at least let us know she was safe. Our little girl is surely dead – and you bloody Singhs were involved in whatever killed her.'

By now all the teacups were on the floor, forgotten. 'She's right,' said Dilip, gathering his wife's arm in his and bringing her to her feet. With the other hand he pointed at Rab and Ruby. 'We numbered you among our closest friends. Lala and I are heartbroken, but Simran suffers more than any of us. He is a shadow of the cheerful young man he once was, barely able to talk to his own parents. All thanks to you.'

They stomped from the room. Rab and Ruby were speechless, and Granthi Singh looked heartbroken. Ruby surprised Rab with a tight embrace.

'Look at you,' she said. 'A face like your dear old Aunty Ajay's, shrivelled like a prune.' Looking pleased with herself, and clearly in no particular hurry, she followed in the footsteps of Dilip and Lala.

Chapter Twenty-seven

Constable Eric Young drove the panda car with his boss, Chief Inspector Sandy Woods in the passenger seat.

'You know where we're going?' said Woods.

'Every kid who ever rode a dirt bike knows Peninsula View,' said Young.

'I hope you are not referring to illegal off-roading on unlicensed and uninsured two-wheeled vehicles.'

'Well ...'

'Relax, constable. At least we should be in plenty of time to catch him before he heads out,' said Woods.

'Exactly, sir,' said Young. 'He won't be able to turn us away without looking suspicious. But don't you think we might still be taking a bit of a chance?'

Woods encouraged his junior officers to speak out, and Young was thinking along the right lines.

'An informal chat to save him making the trip in to see us later this morning, not under caution, nothing admissible in court. But he'll be on his own, which could be important. At the station the chat would turn into a formal interview, he would quickly demand a lawyer, and we'd get bugger all.'

The short drive followed the coast to a cut-off with a rusty sign that pointed uphill to Peninsula View. Despite having been signposted for more than 50 years, Peninsula View had never come into existence. A tight lane flanked closely by neat woodland with Forestry Commission signage eventually popped out next to a clearing with an unobstructed view across to the mainland.

A sagging chain link fence with a broken gate ran around the plot, which sloped downhill towards its eastern boundary, where a weather-bleached static caravan sat, partly shaded by pine trees. Parked next to it were an old tractor with a grader blade attachment, a rust-ridden backhoe and an American station wagon slightly smaller than the caravan.

Everyone knew the story of Peninsula View because it was regularly rehashed in The Standard, Argyll & Bute's weekly newspaper. Shortly before the end of World War II, 300 acres of prime Forestry Commission land was sequestered by the War Office for the construction of heavy artillery emplacements to protect air and sea approaches to the Scottish economy's Clydeside engine room. By the time the land was cleared of trees, the war was over, and the site remained untouched for nearly 20 years before it was sold off to a mystery London developer and surprisingly rezoned for residential development. Lawsuits from angry locals alleging corruption in high places and from the Forestry Commission demanding the return of its property slowed things to a crawl. But when the US Navy saw a threat posed by direct line of sight between Peninsula View and a military base hosting nuclear weapons, the development ground to a halt, apparently for good.

Shortly before the Americans announced the closure of their base, Archie McCusker somehow arranged to buy the site for a pittance. Now all he needed was to prevail over legal action from the Forestry Commission. Elevated uninterrupted coastal outlooks from a sloped site surrounded by forest, protected from the elements and within commuting distance of Glasgow. It was a potential gold mine.

Young took the panda car along the pitted gravel track from fallen gates to ageing caravan.

Iain McDonald had closed the caravan door at the same moment a police car pulled into the site. He hurriedly peeled off his waterproof jacket, outdoor boots and woollen hat and tossed them in a closet, taking care to close the cupboard door securely. When a heavy-handed knock rattled the caravan, he took his time before opening up. At the bottom of the two steps was Sandy Woods, with the young constable standing a couple of paces behind, one hand on the bonnet of his pride and joy, the Chrysler New Yorker Fifth Avenue.

'Good morning, Iain,' said Woods. 'Didn't wake you, did we?'

'I'm not long up,' said McDonald. 'About to fix myself a cup of tea.'

'We're here to save you a trip into town,' said Woods. 'Hope that's OK with you?' He moved onto the first step, crowding McDonald. It made him take a backwards step, and Woods and Young didn't wait for a formal invitation. Woods gestured at the spectacular view from the caravan's bay windows.

'You've got a million-pound vista there,' he said.

Eric Young made a show of looking around the dingy interior, all smiles.

'My mother's scared stiff of me fleeing the nest, but if I could get myself a bachelor pad like this,' he said, 'I'd take my chances with breaking her heart.' He put fingers to interior doors, which swung wide enough for him to peer into the rooms.

'What's he doing,' said McDonald, jerking a thumb at Young. 'I don't see a search warrant. Do I need a lawyer?'

'Relax, son,' said Woods. 'We only want a friendly chat. If you'd rather, we can take this to the station, where you can call your solicitor and the friendly chat will become a statement taken under caution. If that's what you want ...'

'I wasn't born yesterday. If I think you're trying to frame me for something, you two are out of here.'

'And fair enough too, if I may say so. Now did somebody mention of a cup of tea?'

From an uncomfortable park bench bathed in sunlight in the Botanic Gardens, Sheena Ferguson watched Rab pause on the way from the main gate to purchase coffees from a stall where they made what he ranked as the best cappuccino in the West End.

She would never completely forgive his crazy one-night stand with the young constable, but at least she could begin to understand it. Jane Ross's fondness for casual sexual episodes had marked the careers and personal lives of half a dozen officers in HQ; and on the night it happened, friends told her Rab was steaming drunk.

Rab was what an Australian she met at a conference in London called a "two pot screamer". After a couple of glasses of beer he was anybody's. On the night in question he was picked off by a colleague with a love of uncomplicated sex and who, if she were a male, would be admired as "a bit of a lad". Sheena's coming to terms with it, reluctant though it was, owed something to the painful memory of waking up with a thumping hangover, next to the Australian cop in his London hotel room.

Rab handed over a cappuccino and took a spot on the bench next to her. He looked drained.

'Bad?' she said, as she prised the lid from the drink and took in the welcome aroma.

'Worse,' said Rab. He tried to get a sip from the cup's tiny aperture, supposedly devised for drinking on the move.

'You must have got something out of it.'

He abandoned the silly wee gap, cautiously removed the lid and sipped foam. 'A couple of things,' he said. 'Dilip and Lala seem obsessed with how all this has affected Simran; they as good as said Simran is unravelling.'

'Which doesn't tie in with my memory of how he and Ashna got on.'

'Precisely. They didn't get on. They had virtually nothing in common and no time for each other.'

'Grief affects us in different ways,' said Sheena, 'but it might be time to talk to him. What was the other thing?'

'Eh?'

'You said "a couple of things".'

'Ruby came out with something weird.'

'When is Ruby anything other than weird?'

'She remarked on me having a face like a dried prune, like Auntie Ajay's.'

'The old dear who never married, died a couple of months back?'

Rab's eyes softened at a memory. 'Do you remember a couple of years ago we brought the boys to her flat on Dumbarton Road? She must have spent the whole night baking Indian sweets. Took us ages to persuade them to try anything, but as soon as they got a taste, they couldn't stop eating the stuff.'

'I remember they were on a sugar high for days. Why did Ruby drop her name into conversation?'

Rab sampled the coffee again. It was worthy of the stall's reputation.

'The weirdest bit is still to come,' he said. 'For the first time in my life, she wrapped me in a bear hug.'

'Ruby? An outward show of affection? What was she after?' She saw something dawn in Rab's eyes. He set the cup at the end of the bench and dipped into his jacket pockets. One pocket dealt a handkerchief long overdue for the wash. From the other emerged a Hindu deity key ring with two well-worn keys.

He and Sheena spoke as one: 'Auntie Ajay's flat.'

Rab dropped his coffee in a waste bin. 'I have to get over there.'

'Hang on,' said Sheena. 'Debbie McCusker. I did some digging.'

Rab was impatient to leave. 'You found something?'

'Not a thing. The National Insurance number you gave me is correct for a Deborah McCusker, born Deborah Anne Wilkins in Leeds in March 1962. She doesn't appear in any records after February 1991. She hasn't paid income tax or National Insurance since she drew a salary from her position as a director of Archie McCusker's company, ending a little over two years ago. She appears on no electoral register anywhere in Britain. Her last passport expired before she left Dunoon, and has never been renewed. Wait. You're not surprised by any of this.'

'It's what I feared most,' said Rab. He surprised Sheena with a kiss on the cheek and hurried off towards where the Datsun sat resting against a kerb on Queen Margaret Drive.

Chapter Twenty-eight

The kitchen area in Iain McDonald's caravan was filthy enough to make Eric Young steer well clear of tea delivered in a chipped mug with multiple tannin tide marks. Sandy Woods didn't seem to share his worries, and after adding two sugars straight from a bag and milk from the carton, he slurped at the mug happily. If the old pro was working at putting a suspect at ease, his performance deserved an award.

'Nice drop of tea, Iain,' he said. 'We were looking for you yesterday.'

'You were wasting your time. I took the McGonigles to Edinburgh for a funeral.'

'Yes, we eventually worked that out. What time did you get back?'

'About seven.'

'Didn't make the big meeting at the school hall?'

'Too knackered.'

'You're good pals with Archie McCusker,' said Woods.

'The last I heard, it wasn't a crime. I seem to remember you and Archie are pretty thick, too.'

Woods nodded. He'd lost the exchange, and they both knew it.

'And now you work for his private hire firm.'

'You're doing a grand job of telling me things I already know.' McDonald pushed his mug across the table hard enough to spill tea. Woods plucked a handkerchief from his pocket and made a little dam to stop a mixture of stewed tea and food crumbs dripping onto his trousers.

'A couple of years ago you went through a rough patch, and Archie helped you get back on your feet,' he said. 'And here you are, with the best view on the peninsula, and a second line of work as caretaker.'

'Are you going to get to the point?'

'There's probably nobody in town knows him better than you.'

'When you opened the door to us, you said you were not long up,' said Eric.

McDonald gave him a goofy look. 'Is it your turn to talk in riddles?'

'You told us, not long up, about to make some tea.'

'And here I am, uninvited guests drinking my tea.'

Eric looked to his boss, who gave him the slightest of nods. Go on.

'That's some car you've got,' said Eric. 'Did you get it when the Yanks left town?'

'All paid for and receipted, registered, road taxed, tested and insured. Or is there something else you're wondering about?'

'Not apart from how many gallons it does to the mile,' said Eric. 'When we pulled up, the bonnet was roasting. You must have got back a minute or two before we arrived.'

'Aye,' said McDonald. 'I forgot. Last night it was running rough. As soon as I surfaced I took it for a spin to see if I needed to get it checked out. Must have been dirty fuel, 'cos it was running fine this morning.'

Sandy Woods drained his tea and clattered the mug onto the table. 'Where were you on Wednesday night?' The noise of the mug and the change of subject had the desired effect. McDonald was spooked.

'Eh? Wednesday night?' he said, fingers fumbling with a loose tassel on a cushion next to him. 'My shift ended about nine o'clock and I got a pizza and rented a video and came back here.'

'Good video?' said Eric Young.

'The best. Al Pacino. Scarface. Seen it that many times I should have bought my own copy years ago.'

He reached for a VHS tape next to the TV and flicked it into Young's lap. Scarface, with a *24 Hour Rental Special* label from a video shop in town.

'That'll be overdue by now,' said Sandy Woods.

'You'll have the cuffs on me in a minute.'

'So you ate your pizza, watched Al Pacino – and stayed home?'

'I'm beginning to think there's an echo in here.'

'You heard about Farty Caldwell's house being fire-bombed? In the wee hours of Thursday.'

'Same as hundreds of Dunoon folk, I was here doing a Macauley Culkin, home alone. How many other folk do you expect to make you a cup of tea while you check where they were on Wednesday night?'

'Barn Owl Andy was working,' said Young.

'I drive private hire cabs for a living. I see him most nights if I'm on late,' said McDonald.

'He's got a couple of spots where he likes to park out of sight and watch the world go by. Says it's interesting what he sees when nobody knows he's watching.' Young ignored the puzzled glance from his boss.

'Folk must envy the fascinating life he leads,' said McDonald.

214

'If you were dreaming of Al Pacino and digesting pizza in the early hours of Thursday morning, how come he saw you twice?'

'Not possible. I was here.'

Sandy Woods saw what his constable was doing.

'Are you sure about that, Iain?' he said.

McDonald made a poor show of pretending he was thinking hard. He made an even less convincing show of remembering something.

'I might have gone out for a few minutes,' he said. 'I get insomnia. Sometimes a wee drive helps.' He looked pleadingly at Sandy Woods, whose gaze gave him no comfort.

'Let's run by what we've got so far. You were out somewhere this morning, but you lied to us. You were out in the wee hours of Thursday, but you lied to us.' He looked first at Eric Young before returning his gaze to McDonald. 'I think we'll continue this discussion at the station. You're not under arrest, but you are being invited to come into the station at your convenience later today; when you do come in, you will be asked to make a statement. You may bring a solicitor if you wish.'

McDonald didn't show them out.

Eric Young got into the police car first and put on his seat belt. Sandy Woods sat with the passenger door open, one foot on the ground. They watched the curtain twitch. Woods spoke in a low voice.

'Explain to me if you can, Constable, why I heard nothing about Andy Barnes seeing McDonald in the wee hours of Thursday morning?'

'I made it up, sir. And it worked. His home alone alibi is blown.'

Woods scowled at the caravan as if he couldn't bring himself to look at Young. 'Do you even remember the procedure for detention on suspicion of willful fire-raising?'

215

'Yes, sir,' said Young. 'A suspect would need to be cautioned under section 2 of the Criminal Procedure (Scotland) Act, 1980, sir.'

'Not bad, son. And, prior to the cautioning and detention of a suspect, what is required?'

Eric saw where this was going. He had jumped the gun.

'Evidence, sir.'

'Exactly,' said Woods. 'Evidence. Evidence that we don't have, which forces us to request that he comes in at his leisure. Meanwhile any evidence, if it even exists, will disappear.'

'Sorry, sir,' said Young. 'I messed up.'

His boss pointed towards the underside of the caravan.

'What do you see over there, Constable?'

'I see a crate, sir. 'Empty bottles. Irn Bru bottles.'

'The same kind of bottles used in the arson attack at Farty Caldwell's.'

'Yes, sir, but with respect, it's one of the most popular drinks in the country.'

Woods climbed out of the car, knelt next to the crate and explored the gap between it and the underside of the caravan. Young, who had struggled for a moment with his seat belt, stood by, awaiting instructions.

'Constable Young,' said Woods. 'Can you smell petrol?'

Rab admired the ornate tiles that marked the tenement as a "Wally Close" serving residential flats that a century before were a socio-economic cut above "single-end" slums where working people squeezed out an existence, as many as 15 to a room with no toilet. The tiles in Ajay's close were immaculate, the well-worn but spotless sandstone steps testimony to a hundred years of weary footfall and meticulous care by generations of houseproud tenants. He got to the third floor, where the landing was bracketed by doors at each end. The

216

first was neat and brown and plain, its sole decoration a gleaming brass plate reading R T McMillan.

The other was a riot of colour, symbolism and Indian iconography. Its entire centre panel was a garish painting of the Hindu God Ganesha, elephantine features rendered in shining gold. The hardware was heavy wrought iron: a tiger's head door handle, a king cobra door-knocker and other Indian-inspired extravagances. The name plate looked like it came from Carnaby Street, *circa* 1966. In rainbow-striped raised enamel it said: Agila Jayashankar – 'Ajay'.

Rab paused in mid-landing to catch his breath and smiled at a hundred happy memories of Auntie Ajay. From his pocket he took out the key ring and immediately worked out the Yale lock was not engaged. The other lock, in the door handle cluster, was a clunky 1940s lever device requiring the second key, which was heavy enough to serve as a weapon. He recalled from one of Auntie Ajay's many stories there was a trick to this lock, but he could not remember it. When nothing he tried worked, he levered the sturdy handle away from the door jamb and hit the door with his shoulder. Metal parts tinkled across the inner hallway as Rab crossed the threshold and engaged the Yale behind him.

He dipped into the living room and the kitchen, untouched since Auntie Ajay died. Her bedroom, overlooking washing greens on the quiet side of the building, was the same. He moved to the spare bedroom on the Dumbarton Road side of the flat and found it filled with boxes and files hastily taped closed. When he prised them open, they overflowed with envelopes and folders and smaller boxes bearing the fading emblems of Kodak and Ilford and Fuji. He put one box on the floor, sat cross-legged on the Persian rug and set about making some sense of the mess.

Half an hour later he was still on the floor, surrounded by materials dug from boxes. Piles of Super 8 movie films and

VHS cassettes. 8×10-inch and 11×14-inch black-and-white prints of a young Ruby, with and without Rab; later shots documenting Rab's school years, his marriage to Sheena, and his sons Stuart and Ronnie growing up; contact sheets of medium-format negatives of landscapes, cityscapes and documentary images going back to when Clydeside had a booming shipbuilding industry; shots of Cunard's QE2 ocean liner nearing completion near Greenock, dated 1967.

He opened a brown envelope and out fell prints of Ashna: they were studio shots, posed artfully and beautifully lit, but with an undoubted sexiness to them, and one was a copy of the torn photograph revealed by Simran on national television. Rab knew that if they made his skin crawl, they would fill Ashna's parents with fury and disgust. They couldn't possibly avoid leaping to the assumption that Baldeep was, at the very least, grooming Ashna. Or worse. *What were you thinking, Dad?,* thought Rab.

Was there an innocent reason for the photographs? Without Ashna to testify to their innocence, they only cast suspicion on Baldeep's motives for taking them. Could he really have been involved in some way with the child of close friends, a kid who was young enough to be his grand-daughter? Rab had hoped for evidence to absolve Baldeep of guilt, but if he looked dispassionately at the photographs, the detective in him only saw signs pointing the other way.

He put the photos aside and opened a distinctive carton containing a video camera that was empty. Under the camera were two cassettes, hardly bigger than audio tapes, in their original boxes. The boxes were marked in neat, old-fashioned handwriting: *1989 1*, and *1989 2*. Rab inserted number 1 in the camera and fiddled with the controls, but nothing happened. He dipped into the same box for a mains adapter, which he attached and plugged into a wall socket. The little screen that

218

acted as a fold-out viewfinder came alive. With a growing sense of dread, he thumbed the *play* button.

At first the picture was indistinct and out of focus. A digital date appeared in the bottom right; it said 1/2/1989. February, four years before. The screen filled with blown-out white fuzz but gradually the auto-focus system hunted and pecked its way to sharpness. Rab saw his dad move backwards, presumably after pressing the *record* button. The auto-focus system's struggle continued as Baldeep backed into a chair. Rab knew the setting as his dad's attic office/workspace. Now lit by soft light from out of frame, his father gathered himself, looked straight into the lens, and cleared his throat. He spoke confidently and clearly:

'I have spent a fair bit of the last forty-odd years behind my cameras - and if I had had my way, it would have been a lot more. Now, for the first time, I begin a project that will see me in front of the camera. Call it an audio-visual diary. Just me talking, whenever I feel like it and about whatever takes my fancy. I am fifty-nine years old, which makes me five years older than my father was when he died. Other than a few photographs, I have only fading memories of a good man. Maybe I can record some things my son and my grandsons will enjoy when I am gone ...'

Baldeep stopped as the microphone caught a screeching voice coming from elsewhere in the house. It was Ruby.

'Baldeep! Who are you talking to? I know you are not on the telephone. Do you have someone there with you?'

Rab was startled by another intrusion, this time from the door of Ajay's flat, where a jangling electronic doorbell played Indian traditional music at a volume to frighten bus drivers on Dumbarton Road. As soon as the tune stopped, the door shook to the *polisman's knock*. In a break between thumps, a loud female voice made itself heard. Rab knew it right away. Constable Jane Ross.

'This is the police. We are acting in response to a reported break-in at this address. We know you are in there. Open the door slowly and take a step back, keeping your hands where we can see them. Do it now!'

Rab's eyes danced around the photos and the clutter spread across the floor. He ejected the video cassette from the camera and put it and the other one in his back trouser pockets, checking that they were concealed by the hem of his jacket. He wrapped the mains adapter cord around the camera, put it back in the box and hurried through to Ajay's bedroom, where he found a place for it on the top of a dresser. As he headed for the main door, the banging and shouting started again.

'Alright, alright,' he said. 'Hold your horses. I'm coming.' he said.

'Police! Open the door and take a step back!'

'Is that you Jane?'

He slid back the Yale lock and secured it with the snib before carefully opening the door. He even took a step back because he knew all about how adrenalin could lead to unwarranted violence. Jane Ross and another uniformed constable were shoulder to shoulder, one foot each on Ajay's heavy brush welcome mat, sticks drawn, held high.

'Whoah,' said Rab. 'Take it easy.'

'DS Singh!' said Ross. 'What are you doing here?'

'I could ask the same thing,' said Rab.

Ross and her colleague lowered their sticks. 'Mr McMillan from across the landing heard you break in and he dialled 999. Did you break into these premises, DS Singh?'

Rab showed them Aunty Ajay's key ring.

'There's been a misunderstanding. One of the locks is jiggered, so I had to use a bit of shoulder.'

Ross did not appear convinced. She read the name on the name plate. 'Is Agila Jayashankar aware that you are putting the shoulder to her door?

'I doubt it,' said Rab.

'What?'

'Relax, Ross. Auntie Ajay died a couple of months ago. She was an old friend of my folks. Never married, no relatives anywhere outside India. She left the flat to my mother Ruby and me.'

The other constable looked concerned. 'Jane, we will have to write this up,' he said. To Rab, he said: 'You won't mind if we take a wee look around?' Rab stepped aside and, after he retrieved bits of broken lock from the neatly tiled floor, welcomed them into the flat.

It took Ross ten seconds to discover the pile of photography materials in the spare room, and even less time to work out its importance.

'Is this what I think it is?'

'Surprised the hell out of me, too,' said Rab. 'You'd best call it in to DI Malloy. It might get you into his good books.'

'Wouldn't that be my lucky day.'

Rab held out the key ring.

'I'll leave you these. Got to go, things to do.'

'Hang on, DI Malloy will want a word.'

'Doesn't he always,' said Rab as he left the room. Ross tailed him to the bedroom on the other side of the hallway. Rab pretended to look around until he "found" what he was looking for. A video camera in a cardboard carton.

'The reason I came here today. Auntie Ajay promised it to the boys, and they've been craiking on at me to pick it up. The debut Singh Brothers film production is to be shot next Saturday at Firhill. The Jags versus the Buddies.'

Jane Ross was flustered. She had been out-manoeuvred, and worried about explaining herself when they got back to HQ.

'What do I tell DI Malloy?' she said.

'Tell him not to lose my keys.'

Chapter Twenty-nine

The section of the drive from McDonald's caravan that cut through town lasted no more than a few minutes, but as they were in one of the Argyll peninsula's few marked police cars, it drew enough attention to serve Sandy Woods' needs.

By the time they pulled into the police station car park, the jungle drums would be thrumming with news of the "arrest" of Iain McDonald, and soon half the town would be busy telling the other half what they thought was going on. Textbook it was not, but if Woods had believed there was any chance McDonald wasn't involved in the arson attack on Farty Caldwell's home and the vandalism of his car, he might have treated his suspect with a little more respect.

When he and McDonald and Constable Young entered the reception area, Woods was surprised to see Archie McCusker perched at the edge of a seat, keeping what looked like a nervous eye on the door. They hustled McDonald through to the back offices without pause. Woods was pleased to see Young angle his body between the two to prevent McDonald and McCusker from being able to exchange glances. The kid's a natural, he thought, not for the first time.

An unpleasant surprise awaited the Chief. A stranger in a thousand-pound suit sitting outside his office, poring over documents taken from what looked like an eelskin attaché case.

'You are?' said Woods, though he knew what was coming. The man was a regular on TV news bulletins.

He produced a business card like a magician pulling an ace of clubs out of nowhere.

'Jeremy Ambrose, QC.'

Woods looked at the card, printed on a grade of paper only seen in wedding organisers with millionaire clients and the offices of Queen's Counsels, or barristers. Archie had replaced his local minnow solicitor with a great white shark from Glasgow.

'My assistant can check my diary and arrange an appointment for whatever it is you wish to discuss, Mr Ambrose. At the moment I am simply too busy to see you.'

'I think you will find the matter causing you to be busy and my reason for being here are one and the same.' Woods watched the smug grin spread. The man had what Woods's dad called a kind face. The kind you liked to punch.

'You are here to represent Iain McDonald?'

'As well as my other client, Mr McCusker,' said Ambrose. 'Two birds with one stone, in a manner of speaking, Chief Inspector. Can I just say you appear to have a lovely little town here?'

'You just did,' said Woods. 'This way.'

In the interview room, Sandy Woods and Eric Young sat across the table from Iain McDonald and his lawyer, the mighty barrister from Glasgow whom they had both seen on television, often after securing not guilty verdicts for career criminals on charges the whole of Scotland knew they had committed.

The QC had spent half an hour alone with McDonald before consenting to sit for questioning.

'For the benefit of the tape,' said Woods, 'Iain McDonald has been informed of his detention under section two of the Criminal Procedure (Scotland) Act, 1980. Mr McDonald, you are detained on suspicion of having been involved in the crime punishable by imprisonment of willful fire-raising. You are not obliged to say anything, but anything you do say will be noted and may be used in evidence. Do you understand?'

'Aye,' said McDonald.

'Do you have any questions before we begin?'

'When do I get out of here?'

Ambrose raised a hand from the table, palm down, in front of McDonald. *Shut up*, was the signal. 'The police are legally entitled to detain you for no more than four hours,' he said.

'Thank you,' said Woods. 'Iain, when we talked to you this morning '

The immaculately manicured hand left the table again, and despite himself, Sandy Woods paused to allow Ambrose to speak.

'I believe you refer to when you barged, uninvited, into my client's residence.'

'Actually, Mr Ambrose, I think you'll find your client expressed no objection whatsoever to talking with us in his caravan. In fact, he made us tea. Delicious it was, too. Now, if I could ask questions without interruption?' The barrister's palm once again retreated to the table top.

'Iain, when we arrived at your caravan, you said you were just up – but later you admitted you had already been out in your car. Why did you lie to us?'

McDonald looked to his lawyer, who nodded. Here we go with an answer they cobbled together during their wee confab, thought Eric Young.

'It wasn't a lie,' said McDonald. 'I was a bit flustered, not thinking straight. Car problems. I explained.'

'So you did go somewhere in your car this morning. Can you tell us where you went?'

Jeremy Ambrose's hand rose from the table and did a side-to-side motion.

'No comment,' said McDonald.

'You also lied about not leaving your caravan on the night Arthur Caldwell's house was fire-bombed. You later admitted you did take a drive, supposedly to offset your insomnia. At what time did you go for this wee drive, and where did you go?'

Again, the negative hand signal from Ambrose.

'No comment.'

Woods leafed through some papers he held close to his chest. From the seat next to him, Eric Young could see they were minutes documenting a council meeting long ago consigned to history.

'I wish to inform you, Mr McDonald, that forensics examiners are already working at linking the bottles discovered at your home to those which caused the fire at Mr Caldwell's house.'

Ambrose's hand rose again, and this time the barrister drawled knowingly on behalf of his client.

'If indeed they ever find any evidence, I am sure you will have questions for my client's consideration, but until such time, Chief Inspector …' The sentence went unfinished. Insult to injury.

Woods didn't take his eyes off McDonald.

'Iain, do you think Mr Caldwell might recognise your voice?'

'He's been a passenger in my taxi often enough,' said McDonald. Another rehearsed response.

'Do you mean he might recognise it from taxi rides?'

226

'He might,' said McDonald.

'How about from two threatening phone calls he received on Wednesday afternoon?'

'No idea what you're talking about,' said McDonald, before he spotted Ambrose's hand leaving the table. 'No comment.'

'Those calls you know nothing about were both made from the same public telephone near Victoria Pier.'

Again, McDonald reacted before Ambrose could give him a signal.

'So?' Nervous.

'The area is well covered by closed circuit TV cameras, and along with telephone company records of the exact times and durations of the two calls, we are working on identifying anyone who used the public phone at those times.'

Globules of sweat formed on McDonald's forehead as he stared into the middle distance for long enough that Ambrose had to repeat his hand movement three times before it captured his client's attention.

'No comment,' said McDonald.

'Where were you on the night before the fire-bombing, Tuesday night?'

This time he got the signal to respond.

'At home.'

'That night Mr Caldwell's car was extensively vandalised, and the words "WE KNOW" spray-painted on it,' said Woods.

'Is there a question hiding in there somewhere?' said Ambrose.

'What did "WE KNOW" mean, Iain?'

'How the hell would I know? No comment.'

'Will our forensics examiners find paint to match the paint used on Mr Caldwell's car in your caravan or in your car, or on the clothes in your laundry basket?'

Woods never missed a beat, thought Eric Young, questions coming at McDonald constantly, in no predictable order, a Chinese water torture interrogation. Drip, drip, drip.

The hand signal was made and the "no comment" delivered. Ambrose butted in, eager to upset the flow of the Chief's questioning and to give the ever-more ragged McDonald a moment to regain composure and perhaps avoid a damaging over-reaction to whatever came next.

'Is this the best you can do, Chief Inspector? Forensic evidence you might find? What about any real evidence of my client's involvement in any sort of crime?'

He might as well have talked to the wall. Sandy Woods was still staring relentlessly at Iain McDonald.

'What was your involvement in the disappearance of Zoe McCusker?'

Ambrose leapt to his feet.

'We were summoned here to discuss the matter in which you suspected and in the absence of evidence, that is all it was, suspicion – that my client was involved in an offence. Now it appears you hope to use him to clear your entire caseload of unsolved crimes.'

Sandy Woods waived the right to hold McDonald any longer and showed them out through Reception. When he saw them, Archie McCusker began to get to his feet, but a shake of Ambrose's head made him stay seated. McDonald and Ambrose left the building and Woods retraced his steps towards the inner office. When he got to McCusker, he paused.

'Won't be long, Archie,' he said. 'I'll give Hen a shout when we're ready.'

Outside the station, McDonald stopped to listen to Ambrose:

'I have to get back in there,' said the lawyer.

'What the fuck do I do now?' said McDonald.

228

'Stay out of trouble and keep your mobile phone charged and switched on.'

McDonald got in a taxi and left without another word.

Inside the CID office, Sandy Woods huddled over a police radio. When Eric Young's voice at last came through, it was rough and distorted.

'That's him away, over.'

'Understood. Try to stick close without being seen. Keep me posted, over.'

Eric Young lowered the tinted visor on his motorcycle helmet, put the bike in gear, and rode off after the taxi.

Chapter Thirty

Rab didn't know what to feel, sitting alone in what for many years had been the family home. They moved into it shortly after Ronnie was born, a lovely old terraced house not far from Baldeep and Ruby's place. They could never have afforded it, but when Baldeep handed them the papers and said it was theirs, it would have been crass – and pointless – to argue. Such generosity from one set of grandparents gave Sheena's well-heeled father a kick somewhere painful, and he and Sheena's mother chipped in to fund a complete redecoration and new furniture. Some of the furniture was still here, looking tired from two boys spending their childhoods bouncing around on it, but the living room was home. Warm, comfortable, cosy home.

At first he planned to watch the tapes on the video camera's little pop-out screen, but before he pressed *play* Rab had a better idea. A drawer in the kitchen was filled to overflowing with old cables and plugs and adapters, and sure enough it had a spare set of three-prong audio-visual cables from a VCR. A couple of minutes fiddling at sockets in the darkness behind the TV got the camera attached, and after he plugged in the power adapter, he was away. He switched on the TV and felt smug when he recalled how to identify the channel for viewing the tape.

The television screen took him back to Baldeep's smoky attic office. The date on the bottom corner now said 24/2/1989. More than three weeks had passed since his father's first attempt at recording a video diary was cut short by Ruby's screeching. He wore his usual tailored shirt with the armbands, but his tie was loose and the top button undone. This was a state in which Baldeep would not normally have allowed himself to be seen in public. He stubbed out a cigarette in an ashtray needing emptying, exhaled a cloud of blue-grey smoke, and spoke to the camera.

'I only ever wanted to do one thing with my life. Be a professional photographer, emulate heroes of mine like Raghu Rai, Margaret Bourke-White and Eugene Smith. But thanks to pressure from my father, it wasn't to be, and now I do what I can to salve my bruised pride by taking snaps for myself and family and friends. One family friend, young Ashna, is determined to be an actress and dancer, much to the shock and discomfort of her terribly conservative parents, who remind me of my father when I was Ashna's age.

In Ashna I see flashes of my old self, a rebel spirit refusing to be quashed. Except that when I was a teenager, I allowed my creative desires to be beaten back by my father. I wanted to help her, but was fearful of what my good friends Dilip and Lala would think if they learned I was lending assistance to their daughter in betraying their wishes. But Ashna is so much stronger than I was as a teenager, and she begged me. The photographs were vital to her drama school application, and she saw no other way of achieving the professional results she needed. So in the end I found myself promising to help her with a series of portfolio shots and video sequences. I succumbed to Ashna's argument that the only way to get her parents to

231

support her wishes was to present them with the fait accompli of a place won at such a prestigious school, to make them proud of the achievement. After I gained her solemn promise to tell all to her mother and father as soon as she gained a letter of acceptance, I relented.

She is the most wonderful model, adventurous and blessed with grace and a natural photogenic quality unknown to most subjects: the camera absolutely adores her. Nobody knows about our photo sessions. Blessed too with the optimism of carefree youth, she tells "Uncle Baldeep" not to worry his pretty head what other people think. But I do worry, a lot – until I glimpse the joy my modest work brings to this young lady and my concerns disappear like puffs of smoke. But of course, we must keep our meetings secret because nobody will understand how an old man and a beautiful young girl linked by the joy of photography and creativity can mean anything to one another.'

On screen, Baldeep looked at his watch and sighed. This was clearly too much for him. He lit another Benson & Hedges before shuffling forward to turn off the camera.

The television screen went black even though the camera was still on *play*. Rab fast-forwarded it to find the next recording and found nothing, which meant the tape was more than ninety-percent blank. Rab felt robbed. He wished he could squeeze more minutes with his father from the tape.

There was one more cassette. He couldn't think why his father might move to a new tape when the first was barely used, but he swapped them over and restarted the machine.

Baldeep again. The date was 3/3/1989, making this recording about one week later. His dad looked even more weary, eyes tired, forehead lined and damp with sweat. Thinking back, Rab could hardly recall more than a handful of times when he had made the effort to take the boys around to

232

see their grandfather. He remembered promises to go together to the football or to watch a film at the cinema, promises often broken because Rab was too busy or Baldeep was too busy. Or because Rab couldn't be bothered spending time with his own dad.

On the screen, Baldeep backed away from switching on the video camera and sat on a stool that allowed him to lean back against the front of his desk. Again, he spoke to camera:

'It was never my choice, but all my life, artistic dreams have been suffocated by the demands of family and the business world. The results have been financial success beyond anything that even my father could have dreamed of, and my small family bring me pride and no little amount of joy. Still, I find myself wrapped in feelings of emptiness and regret over dreams unfulfilled. But at last I have found my muse. Nothing in my nearly sixty years has given me more pleasure than the time I have spent with Ashna, working as her co-creator of images and videos that bring me pure elation. And yet there is another regret: that, for Ashna's sake, this simple collaboration has had to exist under a cloak of secrecy. But that might be just as well, since nobody will ever understand how I live for our times together and pine for her smile when we are apart.'

Again, a blank space on the tape. Baldeep set out each time to record his thoughts, often finding himself returning to the lifetime disappointment forced on him by his own well-meaning father. And each time the creativity lasted for the briefest of spells. His speech was more halting than Rab remembered. Had he been in a downward spiral of depression that neither his wife nor his son spotted?

Rab sat, overcome with guilt and aching for his poor dad until the home telephone broke the silence.

233

'Hello?'

'I guessed you might be there,' said Sheena in a quiet voice. At work and not wanting to be overheard, thought Rab.

'I found something,' he said.

Sheena's voice dropped to an urgent whisper.

'And you took it with you? Malloy's having a fit; he wants Jane Ross suspended for not detaining you the moment she saw you going through the missing evidence. He suspects you took away something important, which leaves you wide open to a charge of withholding evidence. There's not much left of your career, Rab, but this could end it.'

Sheena's obvious concern for his welfare put a lump in Rab's throat, and he cursed himself for telling her he had found something, when the less she knew the better. Malloy couldn't accuse her of concealing something she was unaware of.

'You're better not knowing,' he said. 'There's something I have to do. I'll give you a call in a few hours.'

Rab disconnected the call before she could object and hurried from the house before she rang back.

Chief Inspector Sandy Woods and Sergeant Hen Henderson sat across the interview room table from Archie McCusker and his lawyer, Jeremy Ambrose.

'You again, Mr Ambrose,' said Woods. 'Is there no chance of a conflict of interest with you representing more than one suspect in cases that may be connected?'

Ambrose was wearing his smug face.

'My client requested that I come over to Dunoon to represent him because he felt that, instead of doing your best to locate his missing daughter, you find it easier to place him under suspicion. When Mr McCusker heard you were harassing Mr McDonald, he did what good friends do, and offered Mr McDonald my professional assistance.

234

Woods seethed inwardly. McDonald must have called Archie the moment Woods and Young left his caravan, and disconnected before they came back in to arrest him on suspicion of fire raising.

'This won't take long. I have one question, Archie,' he said. 'As part of our search for your daughter, my Glasgow colleagues have scoured national records for your wife, whom you claim moved to London more than two years ago. They were unable to detect any record whatsoever of Mrs McCusker being in the London area – or anywhere else – during the last two years.'

Archie took a breath to answer, but was stopped by Ambrose placing a hand on his forearm.

'We came here voluntarily to submit to questioning in order to aid your investigation into the disappearance of my client's daughter. And now you want to talk about his wife leaving him more than two years ago? Mrs McCusker could be anywhere in the world by now.'

Woods leafed through a sheaf of papers. 'Did I forget to mention that her passport expired several months before she was last seen, and that it has not been renewed?'

'You said you had one question,' said Archie. 'I'm waiting.'

'Aah, you remembered,' said Woods. 'Here we go: Archibald McCusker, did you, sometime in or around January 1991, murder your wife, Deborah Anne McCusker?'

As Sandy Woods was certain he would do, Ambrose took to his feet and hauled his client from the room, shouting streams of threats over his shoulder as they went.

But no amount of intimidation could take away what was burned in Woods's memory. The look of terror that froze Archie McCusker's face in the instant before his barrister went ballistic. Not anger at being falsely accused. Terror.

Woods and Hen Henderson watched from CID as, in the car park outside the building, McCusker remonstrated with Ambrose, who made placatory gestures for long enough to get Archie to head for his car.

'You know what you have to do,' said Woods.

'Keep a close an eye on Archie, and use the radio to keep in touch with yourself and Constable Young,' said Hen.

'We might get lucky,' said Woods. 'If McCusker and McDonald know anything about the disappearance of Zoe, maybe they will panic and lead us straight to her.'

'Or lead us to her body.'

'Try not to let them spot you.'

Fifteen years before, Stirling University felt a long way from anywhere, probably because Rab was living in Glasgow with his parents on a student grant and unable to visit his friend Frank in Stirling without changing buses at least three times. Back then, compared to Glasgow University, which measured its history in centuries and nestled in the middle of the city's West End, Stirling sat in the countryside. At ten years old it felt modern and austere with its few structures laid out in straight lines of cement.

Now, more buildings than he remembered had acquired a weathered patina and extensive campus grounds were thick with vegetation. The drive had taken less than 45 minutes, soundtrack provided by the Average White Band's first – and best – album. As much as he loved the music, Rab adored the idea of a band of young white Scots appearing on stage in America to play for mostly black audiences who knew their music from the radio, and who took to their seats in the auditorium expecting to be entertained by black soul musicians. Rab couldn't carry a tune in a bucket, but he knew a bit about confounding peoples' expectations.

236

The pedestal of what he assumed to be a modern art sculpture gave him something to lean against while fresh-faced kids streamed from a lecture hall in the main building. Guest speakers from the worlds of literature or television or film or human rights or environmental activism were attracted by reaching young, enthusiastic audiences, and held forth on Saturday afternoons, when lecture halls were unoccupied. Today's speaker was a loudmouth presenter of motoring television shows, known and seemingly admired for morally questionable opinions and famous for never encountering a racial or gender stereotype he couldn't embrace.

Stirling attracted students from all over the world, and the mixture of races and skin tones who streamed from the hall was like nothing Rab had seen anywhere outside of London. This was the kind of environment where he hoped his boys might flourish. He snapped out of his dream to see Simran Gupta standing in front of him. He was taller and more heavily muscled than Rab remembered, uncovered head cropped short and Bollywood-handsome face dusted with designer stubble.

'I've been expecting you,' he said, as he set off towards nearby parkland. Rab struggled to keep up.

'Why were you expecting me?'

Simran's stare seemed resolute, but filled with contemplation. He blinked continuously. Wired, thought Rab. Stressed out.

At last the young man spoke.

'You know, don't you?' He flopped onto a bench marked with a brass plaque explaining its donation by grateful graduates from China. It looked out over buttercup-speckled grasslands that swarmed with rabbits. 'How did you know to come to me?'

'Something had been bothering me for a long time, so I got one of the officers on the case to share some notes. Your alibi

237

had a hole in it you could drive a bus through, but somehow it was never followed up.'

Simran looked fearful. Rab went on:

'You attended the function at the Hilton that night, even arrived on time. You claimed that earlier in the afternoon you were at a video arcade in the city centre with two school friends, who backed you up. When the friends went home, you said you browsed the shelves at Tower Records before walking home to Dowanhill. Security footage at Tower Records picked you up, poring over Thin Lizzy records. Good taste in music, I thought.'

'So?' As if he didn't want to hear what might be coming next.

'Your parents said it was perfectly normal for you to walk home from the city. It's only a couple of miles, and even if you stopped to look in a few shop windows, you had plenty of time before the thing at the Hilton. But there was no way to prove that you walked – and nobody had ever worked out who Ashna had said she was going to meet that day.'

The young man closed his eyes and took a series of deep breaths.

'Then I got some help from Baldeep,' said Rab.

'Your dad?' Confused.

'He made a video diary I never saw until today. He talked about Ashna's plans to go away to drama school in England. He made it clear it was something your parents knew nothing about, and would never have supported.'

Simran shook his head, but Rab saw weariness rather than any kind of dispute over what he was hearing.

'I think you took a taxi back from the city centre. They're lined up outside Central Station, almost next door to Tower Records. A few minutes by cab to somewhere in the West End opens up plenty of time that was never accounted for. You met up with your sister, didn't you?'

238

Simran sat back and put his arms across his chest. Steeling himself. And out it came:

'You didn't have to live with her,' he said, eyes open now, glassy with emotion. 'Ashna was impossible. She did everything she could to make my parents' lives hell, everything a good Sikh girl shouldn't do.'

Rab looked at a young man whose absence of turban and whose hair style and designer stubble spoke of abandonment of the same faith he once held dear. Simran went on:

'I know she drank alcohol and smoked marijuana and went with boys even after she was expressly forbidden by my parents. She brought stress and pain and shame to our family. For a while at school she hung around with an orthodox Muslim friend and dropped loud hints about converting to Islam – for no other reason than because she knew it would drive my parents mad. And it did. She got the best education and private tutors Mum and Dad could afford, and still she rejected every attempt to encourage her towards a decent career. "I am not interested in going to university to do law or medicine just to make **you** happy," she shouted in their faces. Not Ashna. She lusted after fame as a dancer, or a fashion model, or an actress – or whatever she dreamed about that particular week. I saw a letter from the drama school acknowledging acceptance of an application our parents knew nothing about. She had gone behind their backs. The disrespect and the lack of trust she showed to her own parents would have broken them. You know what else?'

'Tell me.'

'The worse she behaved, the more invisible I became.' He dropped his elbows to his knees and stared at the ground. Unable or unwilling to maintain eye contact.

'Tell me what happened, Simran,' said Rab. He saw the young man's frame was shaking and he heard him sobbing. Through the sobs, Simran spoke.

239

'She's dead. It was an accident. I didn't mean it. I killed her.'

Chapter Thirty-one

Eric Young was proud of his little Honda. His mother had always hated the idea of him owning a motorcycle, and when he pleaded an urgent need for a way of getting to work at odd hours, she offered to sign for a loan on a decent car. But he wanted a bike.

One night when he stayed in town to have a couple of beers with a friend, they came out of the Argyll Hotel to find their old schoolmate Roy Campbell lying half-asleep on the pavement under a Honda CB200. Campbell did his drunken best to explain the bike had fallen over while he was trying to start the engine, as if the impromptu nap was the bike's fault. After they picked both man and machine from the street, Eric watched him stab repeatedly at the starter button, cursing like a trooper when nothing happened. Roy was struggling to get his leg over the seat to commence an assault on the kick-starter when Eric rescued a keyring from the ground next to the bike and asked if maybe this was the problem.

'Ya beauty,' said Roy. 'Ye're a lifesaver.'

'I'm the guy who's saving you from losing your driving licence,' said Eric. 'The key's not in the ignition, so let's pretend I'm not a cop and you are not in charge of the vehicle.'

He peeled the Honda key from the ring, handed over the rest of the keys, and sent Campbell on his way, wearily and without protest.

The next day Young was catching up with paperwork when Hen popped his big head around the office door to say he had a visitor. A sheepish-looking Roy Campbell was waiting for him in Reception to thank him for saving his life. Even apart from the threat he posed to himself by trying to ride home when he could barely stand, he needed his driving licence to run his plumbing business, and he needed the business to pay his mortgage, and his wife was pregnant with their second kid. The list went on. One drink-driving charge could have toppled a long line of dominoes.

Before Roy left, Eric scored a great deal on a lightly used Honda that had hit the deck only once, and even then while stationary and with a drunk to cushion its fall.

Because he was fairly certain McDonald was going home to Peninsula View, Eric was able to hold back and make do with an occasional glimpse of the private hire cab as it headed south. When it made the expected turning to go uphill, Eric waited until the cab returned and headed for Dunoon before he navigated the narrow road on the bike. Out of sight of the broken gates, he stashed the Honda behind a gorse bush and proceeded on foot around the perimeter wire until he came to a break with a clear view of the caravan. He congratulated himself for stopping at the Lost & Found cupboard to grab an old pair of binoculars. He unclipped a radio from his belt.

'Constable Young to control, over.'

The reply came instantly.

'This is CI Woods. What's going on?'

'The subject is at home, sir. I have a clear view, though from a long way off, over.'

'Keep me posted.'

242

Young found a tree to lean against while he wished he had brought a sandwich and something to drink. After about half an hour he listened in on a brief radio exchange between Hen Henderson and Sandy Woods:

'Henderson speaking. I have eyes on Arch- I mean my subject. Arrived home a few minutes ago, alone.'

'Understood,' said Woods. 'Anything changes, let me know immediately.'

Visibility with the binoculars improved when Young worked out how to focus them properly, and even more when he used his handkerchief to clean cobwebs from the optics. He watched as McDonald reached for a high shelf for an unopened bottle of Scotch, from which he splashed a large measure into a heavy tumbler. The VHS tape of Scarface lay on a countertop next to the window. McDonald picked it up, loaded the video machine, and flopped onto sofa with his drink. His favourite movie and a full bottle of whisky. Young could be stuck for a while. Even a flask of his mother's muddy tea would have been better than nothing.

Chief Superintendent George Quigley sat behind his desk while in front of it, Ken Malloy paced a groove in the carpet.

'He wants to bring in a suspect for questioning?' said Malloy.

It was less a question than an exclamation of disbelief.

'Think about it,' said Quigley. 'What's the alternative? Result or no result, Singh will face disciplinary action. In the meantime, we have a case to build, move forward.'

Malloy grimaced. Move the case forward. After years of it going nowhere with Malloy in charge. The gaffer was right. No new development, no matter how minor, could go uninvestigated. And Singh might have found the confession to break the biggest case of Malloy's career. This was going to hurt.

Rab pointed the Datsun onto the flyover that swept past Cowcaddens in the north end of the city centre. When they stopped at the traffic lights on the Charing Cross intersection, he reached into the footwell behind the driver's seat for a shopping bag. Inside were two bottles of Lucozade.

'Even if you're not thirsty,' said Rab, 'get one of these down you. The next couple of hours are going to be hard work, and you'll need to keep your sugars up. You'll probably be questioned by Ken Malloy. You know Malloy. He's a sneaky bastard, and he never misses a beat in the interview room.'

Simran opened one of the bottles and drank hungrily.

'One question,' said Rab. 'Between you and me, strictly off the record.'

Simran put the cap on the bottle.

'If you were so sure Ashna was dead, why did you go on *Crimewatch* and make such a song and dance asking for help from the public?'

Simran drained the remainder of the drink. Giving himself time to think.

'You would have done the same,' he said. 'I was protecting the only thing my mum and dad had left. The tiniest hope that Ashna is alive.'

Rab knew there was truth in what the lad said. Hope was the only thing the Guptas, Simran included, had to hang on to.

'Do you have a mobile phone?' said Rab.

Simran reached into his book bag and extracted a late model Nokia.

'Call your parents and tell them to meet you as soon as they can at Pitt Street police HQ, and to bring a good lawyer. When you're finished talking to them, I recommend you switch off the phone. You're not going to get a minute to yourself for a while.'

Rab did his best to be present in the interview room known by some as the "confessional box", but after suffering the indignity of Malloy laughing in his face he watched proceedings on a blurry CCTV monitor. Malloy and Sergeant Kosofsky conducted the interview. Simran sat beside the lawyer his parents had summoned. There was nothing the man in the suit could do to persuade Simran to refuse the interview.

Malloy saw them through the pre-interview formalities and tried to smooth proceedings by encouraging Simran to provide some background on the relationship he had with his sister. Simran obliged, paying no attention to the headshakes and sighs from his lawyer. Eventually Malloy moved on to the reason for the interview:

'Simran, you've explained how much you resented your sister, and why. I'd like you to take us to the night of March 17th, 1989 and explain again what happened. First of all, why did Ashna agree to meet you by the Clyde?'

'I never said we met by the Clyde. We met outside the Transport Museum at the Kelvin Hall because it was far enough from home not to bump into anyone we knew. We walked as we talked, and ended up next to the river.'

'Why did you meet?'

'To talk,' said Simran.

'Can you be more specific? What did you have to talk about?'

'About how she was tearing our family apart.'

Even on the small screen, Rab saw Malloy's shoulders stiffen. He was close, and he knew it.

'If I understand correctly,' he said, 'by the time you got onto the subject of how your sister was, in your words, "tearing your family apart", you were by the river bank. Where were you exactly?'

'There's a footpath right next to the water before you get to the Clyde.'

'*Before* the Clyde? Could you have been next to the River Kelvin?'

'What does it matter? It was four years ago.'

'If we took you there, do you think you could identify the spot?'

'I will never forget what it looked like.'

'In any case,' said Malloy, 'at that location, wherever it was, your argument came to a head. Am I right?'

After Simran took a deep breath, the words poured out.

'She wouldn't listen. I was trying to make her understand how much pain and anguish and shame she was causing our parents, and all she did was laugh in my face. She used to do this thing whenever I tried to talk about anything serious. She would dance around me, leering, poking at me with her fingers, showing the utter contempt she had for everything I said. It was her way to ignore me and belittle me and make me angry. I told her to stop. This was serious and she was treating me like a fool. She waved her fingers in my face and continued her stupid dance. I reached out to make her stop. I must have grabbed her neck. I was raging, shouting and screaming at her while I shook her.'

'How long did you hold her by the neck?'

'Long enough,' said Simran. 'I don't know.'

'A few seconds, longer?'

'I don't know. I remember letting go and she fell to the ground on a piece of the river bank where it sloped steeply to the water. She wasn't moving. It was dark and we were alone. I panicked and ran.'

'Where did you run to?'

'Back towards the Kelvin Hall. Not far. I was hardly gone before I knew I had to see if I could help her, maybe do CPR. I rushed back to where I left her, but she was gone.' He buried his face in his hands.

'Explain "gone",' said Malloy.

246

'Gone. No longer there. Not where I left her minutes before. The bank was steep and slippery. She had to have regained consciousness and slid into the river. I screamed her name, over and over, and ran back and forth along the bank trying to see her in the water, but the river was flowing fast. She was gone.'

Chapter Thirty-two

Rab got a fright when Sheena opened the door to the CCTV room without knocking.

'Did you give my number to a constable Young in Dunoon?'

They hurried to Sheena's office, where a phone lay off the hook, the light above one line fluttering.

'Eric?' he said.

'Sir, I'm watching Iain McDonald's caravan at Peninsula View. CI Woods put the frighteners on McDonald and Archie McCusker. Now Hen is watching Archie and I'm at McDonald's place.'

'Why the call?' said Rab.

'About an hour ago McDonald was on the phone, shouting and bawling. I'm too far away to hear, but I had him in the binoculars. He was unhappy about something. Here's the thing. Hen could see McCusker through McCusker's living room window. He was on the phone at exactly the same time, also having a heated discussion. They had to be talking to each other.'

'An hour ago? What's happened since?' said Rab.

'That's what bothers me, sir. It's gone quiet. McDonald was watching a video before, but it ended and now the TV screen's filled with snow. If he's out of sight on the sofa, he's asleep. He was drinking whisky. Started off with a glass, then went to slugging it straight from the bottle. He's fallen off the wagon and hit the ground hard.'

'Get over there, fast,' said Rab. 'Keep this line open.'

Sheena watched Rab keenly. Rab pointed to a second phone on her desk.

'Can you get me Chief Inspector Sandy Woods on another line?'

'Your boss in Dunoon?' she said. Rab gave her a raised thumb while, on the open line, he listened to Eric run as fast as his young legs could take him.

Eric sprinted straight to the window of the caravan living area and peered in. The sofa where McDonald had sprawled as he drank in front of the TV was empty. He ran around to the other side and found a bedroom window wide open, deep footprints in the mud below. He raised the mobile phone:

'He's done a bunk, out a back window,' he said. 'Hello? Are you there, sir?'

'Understood, Eric,' said Rab. 'Hang on a second. I have the Chief on another line.' When he reached for the other handset, Sheena pressed the speaker phone button.

'Sir? McDonald has done a runner. Your plan worked. You scared them into doing something stupid. Only problem is, you're not staffed for this.'

'However much good it will do with you in Glasgow, consider your suspension lifted, sergeant,' said Sandy Woods. 'Now what?'

'Do you have any friends in high places?'

There was nothing wrong with Sandy Woods' connections among the upper ranks. Less than 20 minutes later Sheena Ferguson sat strapped into the back seat of a police helicopter. Next to her were two of her best young uniformed colleagues.

She savoured the birds-eye view of the Clyde as its waters broadened towards the coastline. She had been in a helicopter once before, years ago, when the flight took the same route. That day the destination was the Faslane nuclear submarine base where they were to act as security for a visiting Westminster cabinet member scared of peace campaigners who for years had occupied protest camps outside the base gates. She recalled how, as the pilot pointed out the Waverley paddle steamer splashing leisurely twin tracks towards the Erskine Bridge, a radio call requested their assistance at an incident on The Cobbler, near the village of Arrochar.

The Coastguard helicopter was on a call-out to a trawler taking on water in the north Atlantic and the nearest mountain rescue team was more than an hour away on foot. It took them minutes to reach where a hiker lay still at the foot of a sheer drop. The absence of anywhere suitable for a secure landing didn't faze the pilot, who balanced a skid on a rocky knoll to let two of them jump to ground and scurry clear as the helicopter headed for the relative safety of the sky.

Wearing a first aid kit strapped to her back, Sheena and her colleague tackled a slope so steep it had to be negotiated on all fours. As they got closer to the crumpled figure, Sheena pictured her father, a keen hillwalker who often ventured out alone. At the time they hadn't spoken for months after she hit him with the double whammy of joining the police and becoming engaged to marry a Sikh.

When her colleague gently pulled back the hood of the accident victim to seek signs of life, Sheena took a dizzy turn so severe she nearly fell backwards down the slope. For an

250

awful moment she was certain the dead man, with his tousled white hair and neat goatee, was her dad.

Ten years later, from the back seat of a helicopter heading west along the Clyde, she still felt for the family of the retired schoolteacher from Prague, dead on the first day of his long-anticipated holiday in the Scottish hills. A family tragedy that put some perspective on a parent who refused to pick up the phone.

Chatter in her headphones. Rab, from the front seat next to the pilot, was talking by radio to Chief Inspector Woods in Dunoon.

'Most of the town has been out looking for her since first light,' said Sandy Woods. 'Everybody from the Coastguard to the Venture Scouts, even neighbourhood watch senior citizens. Volunteers are coming in from all over Argyll.'

'Inspector Sheena Ferguson and two of her constables are with me,' said Rab. 'What is the latest from Sergeant Henderson?'

'Hen says Archie is at home, making regular appearances at the front window, sometimes talking into a telephone.'

'Knowing he's under watch, and establishing an alibi?' said Rab.

'Possible,' said Woods. 'There aren't many hiding places on Alexandra Parade big enough for Hen Henderson. I want to bring McCusker in for more questioning, but without fresh evidence, his lawyer will have him back out the door in no time. In the meantime, if McDonald is hatching something, Archie is keeping well clear.'

'Eric Young has no idea where McDonald could have gone?'

'No sign of any vehicles missing, but McDonald's spent his whole life here, knows every blade of grass. Right now Young is tearing the caravan apart.'

Rab tapped an imaginary wristwatch for the benefit of the pilot, who mouthed "fifteen minutes".

'If it's OK with you, sir, Inspector Ferguson and I will join Constable Young in approximately fifteen minutes. The other two officers will continue on to the station and await your instructions.'

Rab watched Sheena run confidently from the helicopter to where Eric Young waited next to Iain McDonald's Chrysler.

Rab did the quickest of introductions, followed by: 'Anything?'

'Only this,' said Young. 'It was laid out on the dining table, as if McDonald wanted it found.' He showed them an Ordnance Survey map of the area. Peninsula View had been a feature on the landscape for so many years its boundary line was clearly laid out on the map. Young pointed to where the caravan's position was pinpointed on the map by a rough rectangle hand-drawn in blue marker pen. Another rectangle, this time in red, lay inside Peninsula View, but at the furthest point from the caravan.

Rab peered across the man-made plateau to the area of the red rectangle on the map.

'Any idea if there was ever any kind of building or shed over there?'

'That's exactly where I was standing for the better part of two hours when I thought I had McDonald under observation,' said Young. 'I didn't spot anything. By the way, McDonald escaped out the back.' He gestured towards the other side of the caravan.

'Show us.'

Young led them to where fresh footprints navigated the downhill slope through a slot cut in the perimeter fence. Within yards the trail disappeared into a dense thicket of regularly-spaced Scots pine.

'That is east,' said Young. 'From here to the coast is about two miles, most of it Forestry Commission land. After the trees, near the coast the main road runs north-south, and a few hundred yards on the other side of that is the shore.

Sheena poked among assorted junk cluttering the plot where the caravan sat. She lifted a sun-bleached tarpaulin to reveal a pile of creels.

'What are these?' she said.

'My uncle used to have a lobster boat,' said Young. 'These are lobster creels.'

Sheena looked sceptical. 'Two miles from the shore? What did McDonald do before he drove a taxi?'

Eric Young shook his head. 'I don't have a clue.'

Rab gestured towards Young's radio. 'Get a hold of Hen and find out.'

Sheena, eyebrows raised, looked to Rab for more information.

'Front desk sergeant,' said Rab, making the *yap yap* signal with his hand. 'Dunoon's answer to Sticky McCorrisken. Nothing gets past him.'

Eric Young, microphone held to his lips and the radio set to one ear, wandered around in search of a decent signal. Rab and Sheena heard him asking Hen to repeat himself several times. At last he returned to where they waited.

'Dunoon's own oracle says McDonald mostly worked as crew on boats working out of Dunoon; later he did some driving on contract to the American Navy before they pulled out. But get this: Hen says McDonald has a brother who works on North Sea oil rigs. Until a couple of years ago he had his own lobster creel boat, the *Crown*. It's still here, and Iain sometimes uses it in high tourist season when the good hotels pay top dollar for fresh lobster.'

Sheena beat Rab to it. 'Where is "here"?'

253

'Sorry,' said Young. 'Tied to an offshore mooring. It's much cheaper than a berth anywhere on the coast.' He saw them both give him a look saying *too much useless information.* He pointed to where fresh footprints ran down the muddy slope. 'Straight down there.'

'Radio Sandy and Hen,' said Rab. 'Tell them we need officers to get to the mooring as fast as possible.' He turned to Sheena. 'Don't suppose we still have a chopper at our disposal?'

She shook her head. 'It went straight back to Glasgow after dropping my men off at Dunoon. Already late for an appointment with some high heid yins from Edinburgh.'

He scanned the area. 'Where's your car?' he said to Eric.

'All I've got is my motorbike.' He gestured towards the Peninsula View entrance. 'Way over there, hidden behind gorse bushes.'

Sheena opened the door of the big American car. The ignition slot was empty, but knowing owners of these things loved to emulate their American movie heroes, she lowered the sun visor and a bunch of keys fell straight into her hand. She threw them to Eric, who leapt in and proceeded to drive it like he had stolen it.

The big car floated on too-soft suspension never meant for a road so tight. Tyres squealed and the rear end drifted as Eric did his best to keep all four wheels on the tarmac. Rab was in the back next to Sheena. If the rear seat was fitted with seatbelts they were nowhere to be seen, leaving them clinging to leatherette handles fixed above the side windows, like passengers in a runaway commuter train.

'You said the boat mooring is offshore?'

For a terrifying moment, Eric took his eyes off the narrow track to look at Rab in the rear-view mirror.

'Far enough offshore to prevent an extreme low tide dropping it onto the rocky sea bed.'

'How does he get out to it?'

'Probably a wee dinghy, either with an outboard, or failing that, oars.'

'If McDonald is already at the *Crown*, how do we get out there?' said Rab.

Eric threw the car into a horizon-defying left turn. They were now speeding parallel to the shore.

'I know where there's a boat.'

Chapter Thirty-three

When the radio call ordered them to head south along the coast, Hen Henderson summoned the two officers from Glasgow. Constables Strachan and Sweenie, both built like professional rugby prop forwards, were used to the discomfort inflicted by panda cars, and they somehow squeezed into the Ford Fiesta. They set off, siren blaring and lights flashing.

Dunoonites, unused to seeing a third of a ton of uniformed authority hurtling through town, stopped and gawked wherever they stood, even when they were in the middle of the street. At one point Hen had to negotiate an impromptu slalom course created by a young mother pushing twins in a pram and a little old man in a green parka who struggled to control a fat Labrador that threatened to pull him off his feet. As they passed, Hen wound down the window and shouted:

'Y'awright, Davie? Ziggy's grown into a handful!'

On the outskirts of town a car and caravan in front became a rolling road block, occupants oblivious to a two-tone siren loud enough to rattle windows. When Hen finally pulled off a dangerous overtake, they peered over to see young parents and kids in booster seats singing at the tops of their voices to *The Wheels on the Bus go Round and Round,* blasting from the car stereo. Hen acknowledged them with a jaunty toot of the panda car's horn.

Henderson was of the view this was a wild goose chase, probably invented by Singh to distract folk from how friendly he had become with Zoe McCusker. His disapproval of all things Glaswegian extended even to colleagues in uniform. When one of the two constables spoke – Strachan or Sweenie, he couldn't remember which was which – he struggled to remain civil.

'What are we on the lookout for, Sarge?' said Sweenie.

Henderson managed to make the sweep of a fat forefinger from forested hillside to the coast seem condescending.

'Suspect is believed to be on foot, running from up there to a point on the coast where we suspect he may have a boat moored offshore.'

'Description?' said one of the Glaswegians.

'Early forties – and Scottish.'

'Scottish?' said Strachan.

'Aye,' said Henderson. 'White like you and me.'

'As opposed to your colleague who also happens to be our boss's husband?'

The absence of a response pissed Strachan off.

'The same non-white guy who is running rings around you in the search for a vulnerable teenager?'

Henderson glared hard at Strachan for long enough to let the car come within inches of clipping a kerb.

'You watch your tone, son.'

'If you watch where you're driving, we'll keep our eyes peeled for a suitably *white* suspect.'

Strachan glanced at Sweenie, who sat in the back with his knees near his chin. Sweenie winked.

Strachan banged his head on the side window when the Fiesta made a sharp turn into a lane where, for a couple of hundred yards, bungalow-sized rock formations interrupted what was an otherwise unbroken line of sea view homes. As if trying to reassert himself, Henderson pulled to a halt fiercely. They scrambled from the car and he led them to where a crescent of grainy sand no more than 15 feet wide sat among yet more rock formations. Henderson pointed to a boat moored about 300 yards offshore.

'The *Crown*,' he said. 'It belongs to the suspect's brother. We have to get out there. Got a problem with that?'

Sweenie stared in the other direction. Nestled at the back of the tiny beach was a sturdy shed with no windows. The wood was long overdue some treatment, but the door solidly fixed with industrial grade fittings and not one, but two padlocks on recessed hasps. Casual vandals or opportunist thieves wouldn't have a hope of getting in.

'What's in there?' said Sweenie.

'No idea,' said Henderson.

'I think we should find out,' said Sweenie.

'Right now?'

'Right now.' Sweenie scanned the patch of land between the beach and the rocks. A lump of driftwood caught his eye, part of a tree trunk with broken limbs sticking out. He signalled to Strachan.

'Have you Glasgow folk ever heard of a search warrant?' said Henderson.

Sweenie spoke over his shoulder as he got a grip of the driftwood. As well as being incredibly heavy, it was jammed in a crevice between rocks the size of delivery vans.

'You'd rather come back and find a body in the shed you didn't check because you were worried about paperwork?'

As he spoke, Strachan got a sun-bleached piece of four-by-two under the trunk and set about working it loose. Henderson came to assist, and soon they took positions around a makeshift battering ram. The trunk was ponderous, with fragmented branches making an ideal grip near-impossible, but with Sweenie and Strachan on each side and Henderson's big arms wrapped around the rear, they would make do. Now it was all about weight and momentum.

'Hold it,' said Sweenie. He leaned forward to rap his knuckles hard on the edge of the door where the padlocks were fixed.

'Door opens outwards, and there is something solid behind the hasps.'

They took a half step back and focused on the side where hinges were hidden between the door and the frame. Six big police boots solidly planted, they swung the trunk back before driving it against the door. Nothing happened. They got into a rhythm and pummelled the same point over and over again. On the tenth swing, as their arms were about to give out, the ram went straight through, taking the lower hinge with it. They raised the trunk and attacked the upper part of the door until it too blew inwards and dangled by the padlocks. They dropped the trunk and examined a dark interior softly lit by sunlight bouncing off the little beach behind them.

It was crammed with commercial fishing gear latticed with cobwebs stretching from lobster creels hanging from hooks fixed high in the apex of the shed roof to tangles of salt-encrusted nets and to floats of a dozen different designs and hues hooked onto nails driven into one wall. One small area of floor was clear of junk. Hen Henderson edged closer and lit it with a pencil torch from his breast pocket. The light came to a halt on a galvanised bucket covered with a rough piece of plywood, and next to it sat a half-used toilet roll. Using one fingertip he raised the plywood for the briefest of moments and immediately wished he hadn't. The smell was sickening. A short distance from the bucket, a length of rope looped through a hefty U-bracket attached to a wall stud. With a handkerchief covering his hand, he assessed the tightness of one of the bolts. It might as well have been welded to the shed wall.

'Sergeant,' said Strachan. He pointed to the loose ends of the rope, where coils were formed from having been tied tightly. Inside the coils, bloody skin fragments glistened.

Henderson went back out to the doorway and raised the radio to his mouth.

'Henderson here. Come in please.'

The Chief replied instantly. 'Go ahead, Hen.'

'We are on the wee beach close to where the *Crown* is moored. There is a shed on the shore; it's probably where Zoe was held captive until recently.' As he talked, his attention was drawn to the *Crown* jerking on its mooring. Someone was onboard, moving around.

'Sir,' he said. 'We can see one adult on the *Crown*, moving around on deck.'

'Only one person?'

'So far as we can see from here.'

Woods sounded short of breath. 'Sergeant Singh or Constable Young, are you listening to this?'

A female voice responded. 'Inspector Ferguson here, sir. We heard everything Sergeant Henderson said.'

'Where the hell are you?'

'Pulling into a little marina where Constable Young says he can get us a boat.'

'Keep me posted, Inspector,' said Woods. 'Hen, you have to get out to the *Crown*. Any way, anyhow.'

Sweenie went to a dinghy pulled far enough onshore to avoid a high water line marked by seaweed in the sand and shellfish on the surrounding rock. He flipped it over to find a family of crabs scrambling over a pair of oars in the yellowed grass.

Sweenie and Strachan easily lifted the flimsy craft. 'Bring those oars,' Strachan said to Henderson, as they stumbled through sand toward the water's edge. Henderson did as he was told, his face a picture of incredulity. The wee dinghy didn't look big enough to carry one of them, let alone three.

Henderson squeezed into the seat at the bow of the dinghy, Strachan at the stern and Sweenie manned flimsy oars that rattled in shaky rowlocks. The little craft sat dangerously low in the water, forcing them to proceed with great care. From a crack in the fibreglass at their feet, rushing water formed an ever-deepening line along the keel. 'Get ready to bail,' said Sweenie.

'With what?' said Henderson. Strachan scooped seawater in his cap and Henderson did the same. While he bailed, he looked at Strachan. 'I was out of line there,' he said.

'Eh?'

'The crap about a white suspect. Totally out of line.'

'You've got a reputation in Glasgow,' said Strachan.

'I do?' said Henderson.

'The word is you're a bloody good cop,' said Strachan Sweenie nodded in agreement.

'But?' said Henderson. 'There's always a "but".'

'But you can be a bit of an arse,' said Strachan, 'Funnily enough, some at Pitt Street say exactly the same thing about Sergeant Singh.'

Chapter Thirty-four

The Chrysler barely fit through the narrow lane between tall walls preserving the privacy of showy sea-view homes. At the end of the lane sat a miniature marina. Young abandoned McDonald's muscle car dipping and swaying on its suspension, like a waterbed parked across three spaces in a six-berth car park, next to a flimsy jetty.

Sheena reached in to remove the car keys from the ignition while Eric trotted with Rab to a speedboat wrapped in a sun-cracked, yellow plastic tarpaulin. He tugged at a rope and the cover peeled off like the skin from a banana. *Dad's Delite* was a wooden speedboat long past its prime. Judging by the clutter of gear on its deck, someone now used it for fishing.

Eric Young may have been reading Rab's mind: 'Belongs to a pal of mine,' he said. 'Loves the fishing, and I sometimes tag along.'

Rab watched him drop to his knees and fumble behind the dash to emerge with two keys wired to a flotation device shaped like a cartoon fish. He used one key to free a heavy padlock keeping a well-worn Mercury outboard attached to the boat and elevated clear of the water. At its business end the propeller was no stranger to rocks, but Eric soon had it in the water.

'Let's go,' he said. Rab stepped gingerly into the craft and offered his hand to Sheena, who waved it away and hopped aboard like she had been doing this all her life. Rab had forgotten she spent many childhood weekends off the coast at Largs, sailing her father's Mirror dinghy. When Rab, Sheena and the two boys once took the ferry from Largs to Millport, the boys were in awe of Mum's stories of doing the same crossing single-handed in the ten-foot wooden sailing boat she helped her dad build in his garden shed. Rab didn't admit it at the time, but he was quietly awestruck, too.

The outboard coughed to life, Sheena cast off the lines holding them to the jetty, and they took off much faster than Rab anticipated, the boat rapidly getting onto the plane and tipping him back into his seat. Sheena perched on a fibreglass bench behind Eric.

'How far is it?' said Rab.

Eric pointed south to the nearest headland. 'The other side of that point. Can you get me a life vest from under there?' He jabbed a finger at the storage area beneath the prow. Rab fished out a contraption of mouldy orange fabric and blocks of polystyrene. Eric alternated hands on the wheel as he shrugged his way into the clumsy vest.

'Thanks,' he said. 'I can't swim a stroke. Terrified of the water.'

'I'm not sure I wanted to know,' said Rab into the rushing wind, one protective hand on his turban. With the other hand he dug through gear lying in a stem-to-stern tangle. From a metal bucket he extracted a knife, sharpened so many times much of the blade was gone; it tapered from fish-oil-stained handle to a needle-like point. He put it on the deck next to a six-foot wooden pole with a metal hook at one end. From the darkest recesses of teenage memories built mostly upon adventure fiction, he plucked a word he hadn't seen or thought of in a long time. The pole might be a gaff.

He looked at Sheena sitting comfortably, short dark hair ruffled by the wind. Neighbours, he thought. For the first time in the ten years they had been with the police, they were ignoring rules thanks to another word cops were fond of. Exigencies. Officers who were closely related never worked as "neighbours" on a case, but, thanks to Sandy Woods's pull with people on the upper floors at Pitt Street, and because of the exigencies of the Zoe McCusker case, Rab now sat a few feet from his wife as they dashed towards the as-yet unknown fate of a vulnerable teenager.

Eric Young helped jolt him back to reality.

'There!' he said.

They skirted a rocky headland on one side of a deep, narrow cleft in the coastline. At its landward end was a sliver of sand and a solitary shed. Even from a quarter of a mile away, Rab could see the shed door hanging askew. Eric steered for the one vessel at the seaward end of the cleft, a modest fishing vessel attached to an offshore mooring. Despite the flat calm sea, it jerked wildly as a crouching figure ran around topside.

Sheena reached over and tapped Rab's knee. He followed her finger to where, like characters in a child's picture book, three large uniformed men crowded a dinghy that gradually approached the *Crown* from landward, under the power of oars manned by Constable Sweenie. Its gunwales barely proud of the water, the dinghy looked like it could sink at any moment.

Eric powered *Dad's Delite* in a rush at the other vessel before taking it in a tight arc that made them veer sideways. A short burst of reverse thrust from the outboard brought them to a near halt. Sheena looked impressed and Eric Young seemed relieved. The manoeuvre put the speedboat and the dinghy at

90 degrees to the *Crown*, mere yards away. After the din of the outboard, the silence was a shock.

The figure they had seen scrambling around the deck emerged from below. It was Iain McDonald. From behind a boat anchor and several yards of chain fixed to his neck and chest with a length of hairy rope wrapped around a blood-soaked Sensational Alex Harvey Band t-shirt, McDonald stared at Eric Young.

'Did you find the map?' He was out of breath, pale as a cartoon ghost, eyes unfocused.

'We did,' said Eric, who blipped the Mercury outboard's throttle as if to stop them drifting backwards. Behind him, Sheena saw he was keeping them and the dinghy with the three uniforms far enough apart to prevent McDonald from being able to keep them both in view at one time. Sweenie used oars that in his grasp looked like lollipop sticks to softly draw the dinghy closer to the far side of the *Crown*.

'We got the map,' said Rab. 'You're cooperating, and that's important. It will help you later. But you need to tell us, Iain. Where is Zoe?'

McDonald lost his footing. He wore no shoes and his feet were slick with blood. For an awful moment Rab thought they were going to lose him over the side. Wrapped in chain, he would sink like a stone, but he somehow regained a stable stance. His face blank, he stared at Rab.

'You saw the red X.'

'On the map? Yes, we saw it,' said Eric.

'There you go. The red cross marks the spot.'

Rab felt his knees buckle. Surely not.

'Are you talking about Zoe?'

McDonald seemed to want to take a moment before responding. On the other side of the *Crown*, Hen Henderson crouched near the bow of the dinghy, threatening to take all three uniforms into the water. None of them wore a life vest.

'Her mother,' said McDonald. 'The lovely Debbie. My life's not been worth living since Archie woke me in the middle of the night, begging for my help. He said it was an accident, she fell and hit her head, but he knew you lot wouldn't believe him and it was me he came to when he needed help.'

Not Zoe, thought Rab. But they still needed to find Zoe. In McDonald, Rab saw one of society's terminal losers, a lonely, not-very-bright, unattractive alcoholic swallowed by fresh self-hate for having fallen from the wagon. Rab also had to consider Jim Baxter's accusation. Was McDonald a paedophile? Was his life shaped by the disgrace of criminal urges, at the same time shaming him and making him feel a victim of his urges? Was he going to kill himself? Not if Rab could help it. Not before they found Zoe.

'If you testify that Archie made you help bury his wife,' he said, 'you'll get a break in court. It's not over, Iain. But where's Zoe? Is she OK?'

'You don't understand,' said McDonald. 'It is over. I've nothing left. Nothing.' He stepped over the shallow gunwale and the water swallowed him without so much as a splash.

Rab fired himself through the gap between Eric and Sheena and hit the water belly first. The visceral shock of the cold sea fired him into life and he followed McDonald's descent. If the water was deeper than ten or twenty feet, he would never get near the other man, but as he traced a spiral line of disturbance in the water he saw McDonald had already come to rest in thick, shallow kelp on the rocky bottom, a few feet below. Without an anchor to help his descent, Rab had to kick hard to get among the kelp where he locked two hands onto the rope crossing McDonald's chest. McDonald's eyes were open, but showed no sign of knowing Rab was even there, let alone struggling with the knots in the thick rope. Rab felt a stab of pain when he tore a fingernail loose.

266

McDonald's eyes snapped wide in pure terror. He clamped his hands around Rab's biceps in an instinctive longing for survival, a death grip that could be the end of them both. Rab was running out of oxygen and out of time.

At the surface, Hen Henderson made a cutting motion with one hand as he screamed at Eric Young.

'A knife?'

Eric reached down to where he had seen Rab place the gutting knife. He sent it in a tumble-free arc towards Henderson's outstretched hand. Hen plucked the handle from the air and plunged knife-first into the water.

Something in Rab's peripheral vision made him turn his head in hope, only to see a rippled upward line of orange fabric from his unravelling turban, the end reaching for the surface, where he could make out the light of the sky and the dark undersides of three boats. An explosion near the surface became the dark shadow of Hen Henderson coming at them head first, in full uniform, grim faced and with an ugly knife in one hand. Rab fought the deadly instinct to let go of the last breath in his lungs. He knew it would mean never seeing Sheena again, never again taking the boys to the football or the cinema. He closed his eyes and hung on. With McDonald's hands locked onto his upper arms, he couldn't go anywhere if he tried.

When the end of Rab's turban came to the surface Sheena nearly crumbled, but Young had brought the speedboat alongside the *Crown*, and she leapt across the gap. She watched as the stream of bubbles ascending the fabric became ever more faint.

In the end, daylight shining through his tightly closed eyelids brought Rab back. He opened his eyes, still expecting to see the barnacle-encrusted undersides of boats far out of reach, but instead was rewarded by the glare of open sunshine and a sky blue enough to make him cry. He blew out the last spent air from his lungs and roared as he filled them again, not with water, but with fresh sea air and the certainty that life was still his to embrace.

His hands were wracked with pain from gripping McDonald's triceps. He must have transferred his hands to them when Henderson went to work on the rope with the knife. He was relieved to see Hen treading water a few feet away, gasping. McDonald made a choking noise and vomited sea water and partly digested food. Rab wanted to kill him. He released one hand and with it he clattered the side of McDonald's face.

'Where is Zoe!' he screamed. 'Where is she, McDonald? What have you done to her? Speak to me you bastard!'

'Rab! Rab!'

A big hand surrounded his and another pair of powerful arms wrapped around his chest. Sweenie and Strachan treaded water like synchronised swimmers with Rab and McDonald in their embrace.

'Rab!'

The voice. It was Sheena, perched in the stern of the *Crown*. She too had someone in her arms. Zoe, shell-shocked but alive, wrapped in a grubby tartan rug, tears coursing down her wee face. As Sweenie and Strachan steered Rab and McDonald towards the stern of the *Crown*, Zoe silently mouthed a message to Rab.

'Thank you.'

Chapter Thirty-five

By convincing him there was no way to stop her being there, Zoe left Rab with no choice but to take her along to Peninsula View. She grudgingly agreed to remain next to McDonald's caravan and what seemed like miles of crime scene tape, long fluttering sections trailing in the wind like decorations on the world's ugliest kite.

From cobwebbed shadows under the caravan, he extracted a couple of folding chairs, wiped them down with a Black Sabbath T-shirt hooked onto the corner of a window frame, and asked her to sit. She refused, and for the next three hours paced a groove in the dirt. She hardly took her eyes off the far corner of the clearing, where police vehicles from Dunoon and Glasgow sat like circled wagons around the excavation of the spot marked on a map with a red rectangle by Iain McDonald.

A lot had happened in the 48 hours since Sheena found Zoe traumatised but unharmed on the *Crown*, since Rab and Hen Henderson saved Iain McDonald from a coastal kelp bed, soaked in blood from multiple slashes on his wrists. While crime scene specialists and forensic scientists sifted through Peninsula View soil with the painstaking care of archaeologists parting the dust at Pompei, Rab hoped to get Zoe to open up.

'Are you OK with the McCraes?' he said.

'Sarah's being a pal and Hilary can't do enough for me. Thanks for that.'

There had been one other option, but Rab was haunted by Zoe's thoughts on foster care. *If you put Archie away I'd end up in a foster home. I'd kill myself first.* Rab had to bang heads with Social Services bureaucracy to temporarily place Zoe with the McCraes.

'You need to be with friends.'

She treated him to a wry look. 'Did you mention to the nice friends not to pester me with too many questions, to let me talk about things when I was ready?'

'You're going to have too many people bothering you,' he said. 'You need time to take all this in.'

'Will I have to go back to school?'

'It's something you'll have to face eventually. You're too bright not to be making the best of school.'

'What will happen to them?'

Them. She wasn't ready to use their names.

'They are both in big trouble. Iain is going to testify against your dad, but no matter what, they are going to jail for a long time.'

'How did you work it out?'

'The only available piece of hard evidence helped, thanks to you.'

Zoe's eyes shone with tears.

'I heard Archie snooping around. He must have known about the envelope I found, so I hid it in the photo frame. I hardly got the frame back onto the bedside cabinet when he barged in and wanted to know what I had done with the envelope. It took him about half a minute to find it, and when he ripped it out of the frame I thought my last hope was gone.'

'Luckily he didn't spot the fragment caught in the corner of the glass,' said Rab. 'I suspected him all along, but

270

couldn't prove anything until that piece of necklace turned up. Thanks to you.'

'It didn't matter where my mum went. She would never have left the necklace behind. She must have told me a hundred times it was her favourite possession in the world. She never took it off, not once.'

'You confronted your dad about it?'

'Told him I knew he must have killed my mum, and now there was evidence.'

'Why didn't you tell me?'

'I was going to, but I was waiting for the right time. Then Archie took my mobile phone away and the next thing I knew, I was tied to the wall of a shed with a bucket to pee in.'

Rab could hardly imagine the psychological damage Zoe had suffered from having her suspicions about her father confirmed in such a brutal way, even after the years of abuse. How many hours did she lie in the shed, knowing her own father was waiting for the right moment to kill her? He made a mental note to ask Social Services to hurry up with counselling.

'I have a question,' said Zoe.

'Ask.'

'What did poor Mr Caldwell do to deserve what they did to him?'

'They were trying to be clever. They knew Dunoon police station was understaffed, and I was the new boy who didn't have a clue about anything. Archie wanted to divert police resources away from looking for you, but all he succeeded in doing was getting attempted murder added to his long list of charges.'

'Because you were having none of it,' she said.

'Not just me. I was suspended, remember. Constable Young took a helluva chance following my lead while I was stuck in Glasgow.'

Zoe looked thoughtful. 'What's his name? Eric?'

'Eric Young.'

'I owe him a thank you.'

'If you're in the mood for paying debts, don't forget you owe me two empire biscuits.'

He got a smile, at last.

'Now it's my turn,' he said. 'One more question, but don't worry, you don't have to answer it if you don't want to.'

'Alright.'

'What you claimed about your dad coming in to your bed,' said Rab. As soon as he spoke he knew he had made a mess of it.

'What do you mean "claimed?" ' said Zoe in a shout that turned heads of forensic archaeologists hundreds of yards away.

'Sorry. Bad choice of word. I believe you, but if you are going to testify in court about this, lawyers will do their best to make **you** out to be the liar.'

'**If** I am going to testify? Fucking right I am going to testify. What was your question?'

'You just answered it for me,' said Rab, his head turning towards new activity and raised voices coming from across the dirt plateau. He fumbled for the volume control on the radio clipped to his belt. Too late.

'Forensics to DS Singh,' called a voice, loud and clear. 'Be advised we have found a body.'

Zoe tried to set off in a sprint, but before she ran three steps, Rab held her tight while she twisted and wailed herself hoarse.

Chapter Thirty-six

Ruby Kaur was not a person whose heart often skipped a beat at the sound of visitors. But this time when the bell rang, she hurried to the hall, smile beaming. She threw the door wide and her face fell at the sight of her three visitors decked out in orange and yellow.

'My boys!' She dipped down to hug her grandsons, knowing as she did the days of having to crouch for a hug were not going to last much longer. At the rate these lads were sprouting, she would soon need a box to stand on. Stuart returned her hug with warmth and when Ronnie did his best to get it over with, the ever-alert Ruby subjected him to a few extra seconds locked in her perfume cloud. It wouldn't teach him a thing, but it gave her a few more seconds in his grasp, however reluctant it might be.

Behind the lads towered her other boy. Rab leaned forward for a kiss and delighted Ruby by not calling her by her name. It was a courtesy he tried but often failed to observe when the boys were around their grandmother.

'Hello, Mother,' he said. 'Three hungry Partick Thistle fans here, looking forward to some delicious home-cooked fare to fuel their fires while they relive in excruciating detail exactly how the mighty Jags tore the poor Buddies to pieces, albeit during a scoreless draw otherwise bereft of entertainment value.'

'Come in, come in. I've been cooking like the hired help all afternoon.' She waved her grandsons through the hallway and hissed at Rab:

'How many times have I told you about all that horrid football stuff? Do you take pleasure in parading your sons in public looking like riff-raff?'

Rab answered in a low voice. 'If it's a hissy fit you're after, I will tell you the cost of those shirts. Now what about food you spent all afternoon preparing?'

When the boys were happy stuffing their faces with the best Indian food in the West End, Ruby sat with Rab, drinking tea.

'Now tell me the real reason for the visit,' she said.

'It's not enough that I bring the beloved grandsons to visit their grandmother?'

'Don't get me wrong, Rabinder,' she said. 'I look forward to hours cleaning food debris from my furniture and carpets. But why **are** you here?'

'I need your help.'

'See!'

'Score one to Ruby,' said Rab, notching the imaginary point in the air with a fingertip. 'Do you remember a few years ago when the Guptas were climbing the walls because Ashna was getting too friendly with a classmate, a girl from an orthodox Muslim family?'

It was Ruby's turn to purse her lips in mock exasperation.

'That would be Fatima Hamed. I remember Lala didn't stop fretting about it until her family moved to England. Somewhere in the north. Started with a 'B'. Bolton, Bradford, maybe Barnsley?' Her eyes burned with curiosity. 'Why do you ask?'

The taxi ride from Burnley station to the community centre took a few minutes, but for first-time visitor Rab, the trip was an eye-opener. He was used to Glasgow, where Asian faces and costumes were relatively rare, seen mostly in the neighbourhoods of the main mosque or the Sikh gurdwaras. Even though he knew Lancashire had been a magnet to south Asian immigrants over the decades, he was still surprised to find himself in a community where Asian faces, rather than being the exception, were in the majority. Even his taxi driver was a Sikh who seemed perplexed by Rab wanting to visit the community centre. When Rab asked why, the driver replied in an impenetrable Lancashire accent, something about the predominance of fookin' Muslims in that part of town.

When the cab stopped in front of a slab-sided two-storey building, Rab dug into his pocket to pay the exact fare stated on the meter. He spared the driver a lecture about how he saw sectarianism in Glasgow every day and didn't need to experience it coming from a fellow Sikh. He might need a taxi back to the station later.

The community centre may have been run on a tight budget that didn't stretch to an occasional coat of paint. The swing doors with mesh reinforcements holding together cracked security glass creaked loudly before taking on a life of their own and slamming behind him. In front of the entrance was a cork board covered with a scattershot array of notices, some computer printed, others hand-scrawled. They touted macramé weaving, private yoga lessons in the comfort of your own home, culinary classes in a range of Asian and Afro-Caribbean cuisines, meditation and pottery instruction, and a lead guitarist wanted for an Indi-Pop covers band, *No Heavy Metal Plonkers!*

Taped to the wall below the board was the information he sought. A sign with a broad arrow pointing left to the *All India Modern Dance Troupe Rehearsal (Fatima)*.

A sequence of similar pointers led him round a corner to a double doorway spread wide to allow air into a windowless dance studio. Inside, an instructor led nine students through an energetic and bewilderingly unpredictable sequence of moves they seemed to know rather well.

Rab lingered in the corridor where he could watch without making himself too obvious. The instructor was a young Asian woman with bleached spiky hair. She was barefoot, wore light cotton trousers in a maroon shade Rab associated with Tibetan monks, and a sleeveless singlet top showing off an array of jangling jewellery, some of it clinging to her wiry biceps. Even at a quick glance, it was obvious her students, an even mix of genders, were all ethnic Indian, their clothes hinting at a range of faiths. Like the troupe name said: *All India.*

The instructor was good. She called out every move in a code Rab could not follow and delivered personalised shouts of encouragement to individual students. The building blocks of her dialect were a curious mix of Punjab, Lancashire – and Glasgow.

The music from a boombox came to an abrupt end and she brought proceedings to a close with a plea not to miss tomorrow's 'last rehearsal before the big show next week'. As students filed from the room chattering excitedly, Rab stepped into the doorway. There was a pause before the instructor spoke.

'Uncle Rab,' she said.

'I have something I think you will want to see.'

From a small backpack, he extracted Baldeep's video camera, opened the viewfinder screen and hit the "play" button. She came close to get a good look at the small image on the screen.

276

In one corner, the digital date read: 22/3/1989.

Baldeep seemed worn out and his forehead and scalp gleamed with perspiration as he stared into the lens and spoke in a tired monotone.

'*Five* days since anyone saw Ashna, and I cannot stay silent any longer. As I have already discussed in an earlier video recording, she came to me a few weeks ago, seeking advice. She was worried her parents didn't understand her. She thought they didn't care about the gulf between what she wanted to with her life and what they wanted of her.

'When she told me this, I made a terrible mistake. One I will forever wish I could reverse. I told her my single biggest regret was adhering to my father's demand that I pursue a business career. As a result, despite making a success of business, my entire adult life has been filled with regret over not chasing my one real dream, that of being a photographer. Even worse, when my own son Rabinder declared he wanted to be a policeman, instead of providing support and encouragement to a young man making his own way in life, I stood back and let his mother treat him to an endless barrage of obstruction and complaint.

He paused to draw a handkerchief across his damp brow and to clench and unclench his teeth and move his jaw from side to side, before steeling himself to continue.

'I told Ashna to chase her dreams with all her heart, and not to worry, because her parents would come to appreciate that her happiness and theirs would eventually become one, never mind if it took months or years to happen. I set aside four thousand pounds for her first year of tuition fees at a wonderful private school of drama and dance in England, and helped her prepare her application for the school.

'But now she has disappeared, so far without touching the money I put in an account for her. At first I told myself she would be back in a day or two. Now, five days later, I fear for the poor, mixed up girl, and feel such pain for her parents, who love her dearly and have told me through floods of tears of their only wish in the world, that she might come back safely and allow them to make amends. Tomorrow I will see Inspector Malloy, tell him everything I know, and show my shamed face at the home of Dilip and Lala to beg for their forgiveness.

'What was it Robert Burns said? "The best-laid schemes o' mice and men gang aft agley." My scheme wasn't even clever. I'm sorry Ashna. I'm sorry Dilip and Lala.'

He closed his eyes and pulled at one arm and shook his head as if trying to offset dizziness before he moved unsteadily to turn off the camera and the picture went black.

Ashna choked back sobs.

'He looks terrible. Why was he sweating so heavily? What was wrong with his mouth?'

'I showed this to a doctor friend. He said Baldeep was almost certainly displaying signs of an impending stroke or heart attack. He told me if he saw a patient with those symptoms, he would be on the phone to the ambulance service right away, and warning the hospital of the likelihood the patient was having a major coronary episode. Dad died in his office not long after he filmed this. He never had a chance to speak to DI Malloy.'

'Malloy has been on TV talking about Simran.'

'Your brother is in a black hole of guilt and grief,' said Rab. 'It hasn't been made public, but he confessed to killing you. The Procurator Fiscal doesn't know if a murder charge will get thrown out of court, confession or no confession. In the meantime, Simran has been charged with serious assault and other offences related to interfering with a police investigation. Now he has been released on bail. A murder charge remains a possibility – and Malloy is pushing hard to make it happen. Malloy wants a result, wants the case closed.'

Ashna seemed to need time to take all of this in. Rab looked around the room and said:

'How did you pull this off? Do you have any idea how hard we looked for you?'

'I hid under a full burqa for six months in a retreat for battered women. Then my friend Fatima's parents took her back to Pakistan for good. We already looked like sisters, so she gave me her passport and a copy of her birth certificate. A whole new identity. No more Ashna Gupta.'

So simple, yet it had fooled them all.

'The money,' said Ashna.

'What money?'

'The four thousand pounds your dad talked about. It's gone. After I got out of the retreat—'

'Baldeep wanted you to have it. He would have loved to see you dance today, watch you teach your students. He would have been proud of you.'

'I still feel bad about the money,' she said. 'I have something else to tell you ...'

Chapter Thirty-seven

As Ken Malloy's partner, Brygida Kosofsky would normally be privy to all discussions related to their caseload, so when word came from Quiet Man Quigley's office that the gaffer wanted to see Malloy alone, she was far from pleased. Maybe the boss wanted to protect Malloy's professional pride, because in this job, professional pride mattered. Personal feelings were different. Not even the Quiet Man gave a shit about Malloy's feelings.

For three straight days since the story broke, she and Malloy had been confined to office duty, under strict orders to say not one word to the press. They remained stuck to their desks and absorbed every available morsel of news about the sensational re-emergence of Ashna Gupta. The tempest-like media coverage had yet to subside, never mind the paucity of new information available in a story still being treated as breaking news. Despite every tabloid hack in the country waving money in search of leads, even the red-tops were stuck regurgitating old anecdotes. Ashna had voluntarily declared herself fit and well, and a police press release said she had been living in England since shortly after she disappeared. Attempts to exploit rumours of a Burnley connection were met with an unbreakable wall of silence in the Lancashire Indian community. Nobody knew anything more.

With thousands of hours of police time failing to produce meaningful results, the re-hashes were never going to make Malloy and his colleagues look good. With depressing predictability and infuriating regularity, the Plod word dominated headlines and opening paragraphs.

The dearth of new details was partly explained when an advertising campaign exploded all over primetime TV, breathlessly declaring the WHOLE SENSATIONAL STORY would be exclusively revealed in one Sunday tabloid. Yours for only 50p. Be sure to reserve your copy.

Brygida wondered how long it would take for the story to leak about Ashna's visit earlier that morning to a Preston police station. A tip from Lancashire colleagues had done nothing for Malloy's mood, as it seemed Ashna's account of the night she went AWOL was at odds with her brother's. She claimed that after they exchanged harsh words, she physically assaulted Simran, prompting what she insisted was no more than a "minor scuffle". At no time had her brother choked her, nor had she ever fallen to the ground. According to Ashna, when Simran left her next to the River Kelvin, instead of lying prone on a river bank, she was upright, unhurt and perfectly able to leave the scene under her own power. Brygida suspected Ashna was being a little creative with the facts in order to protect Simran.

Malloy's hope of prosecuting charges against Simran had been based entirely on his recent confession, but what had previously been a murder case without a body had turned into a minor scuffle with no injuries. Brygida knew the press were going to tear Malloy into even tinier shreds, and as his partner for the last 18 months, she knew she could forget about promotion for a long time.

She watched Malloy slink from the Quiet Man's office and trudge despondently to their table. He threw down morning editions of tabloid newspapers fanned out like an oversized card trick, every lurid front page dominated by the Ashna story.

Malloy's pain was compounded by how, for the few days before the Ashna story broke, Rab Singh dominated the front pages in his new role as the media's pet policeman, the hero behind the dramatic rescue of Zoe McCusker. FROM SUSPECT TO SAVIOUR was the one Kosofsky and her colleagues enjoyed most. Copies of the page appeared everywhere Malloy turned, pinned to notice boards, taped to toilet doors and held at eye level by fridge magnets in the staff break room.

'At least we're getting out of the office,' said Malloy, after he sat down. 'Gaffer's orders. We have to be seen at the bloody parade, be the face of a force committed to the well-being of the Indian community and eager to share in the Gupta family's joy.'

'Why is it,' said Rab, 'you never see a female television presenter with matching collar and cuffs?'

Sheena had heard the line at least a hundred times. She dug her elbow into his ribs as the boys looked at them quizzically. Awkward questions were imminent.

They occupied a raised podium erected outside the gurdwara every year to give lucky temple members an unobstructed view of the procession. Immediately in front of them, a news presenter with streaky blonde hair and suspiciously brown eyebrows did her best to pronounce strange words as she stumbled her way through an on-camera intro to the Vaisakhi Festival parade. Sheena recognised her as Claire Christie, the presenter who had interviewed her outside

282

Ruby's home. She was surprised to realise only a few days had passed.

'Every year, around this time,' said Christie, 'Glasgow's Sikh community enjoys a Lunar New Year parade linking the city's gurdwaras, or Sikh temples. The colourful spectacle is very much looked forward to by Glaswegians of all faiths.'

'However, this year, an unprecedented level of anticipation has turned the atmosphere here in Glasgow's West End feverish.' She paused to let the cameraman take in the temple guests on their podium, and to focus for a few seconds on a heavy press contingent, corralled behind temporary metal barriers on the opposite pavement.

Looking nervous among those on the podium were Dilip, Lala and Simran Gupta. Not far away, Ruby, Rab, Sheena and the two boys were equally restless.

Noise from the approaching parade meant the presenter had to work hard at putting on a show of excitement.

She swept one palm at the temple. 'Viewers might recognise the Gurdwara Ravidas Sikh temple as the centre of one of Glasgow's biggest mysteries in recent decades – the disappearance four years ago of fourteen-year-old Ashna Gupta, whose family worship at the temple. Just under seventy-two hours ago, the nation was shocked to learn Ashna is alive and well. Today she returns to Glasgow to lead a Lancashire dance troupe in the Vaisakhi festival parade, which as you may be able to hear, comes closer by the minute. Today's crowd are anticipating what promises to be an extremely emotional, heart-warming occasion to remember.'

The cameraman lowered the camera from his eye and Claire followed him to a point on the pavement where colleagues had somehow reserved her a kerbside spot with a short step ladder overlooking the street.

Stuart Singh, meanwhile, was hanging off Rab's arm.

'When is she coming? How will we know her? Is she a dancer? Is she our Auntie Ashna, or some kind of a cousin or something?'

'You remember Ashna. Simran's sister,' said Rab. 'She'll be leading a dance troupe from England. You'll see her in a minute.'

They all waited as a guard of honour in matching orange costumes and turbans and solemn faces paraded past to respectful applause from both sides of the street. They led an ornately decorated covered float that carried, protected from whatever weather Glasgow threw at them, the Sikh book of scripture called the Guru Granth Sahib. Around the edges of the float, a handful of senior Glasgow Sikhs who waved majestically at people they knew in the crowd lining the route.

The Guru Granth Sahib float was followed by a pick-up truck barely large enough to carry one man making a huge kettle drum shake to a hypnotic rhythm. Behind it marched a band of musicians playing reed instruments fighting a losing battle with the clamour of the drum. At the back of the band a short gap was commandeered by an elderly western hippy wearing enough jewellery to fill a pawnshop window. She pirouetted ecstatically, long, rainbow-painted fingernails flitting through her flowing grey hair.

'Is that Ashna?' said Stuart.

'Not yet,' said Sheena.

Rab knew the big moment was coming when half the press corps took mobile phone calls. The TV presenter was on the top step of her little ladder, talking animatedly to the camera as the din from the reed band was overtaken by speakers roped to the roof of a battered Datsun.

'That's your car,' said Stuart in a near-scream, drawing looks from everyone on the podium. Rab grinned at his son. Earlier, Ashna had called in a panic. The old van they brought to carry their sound system was broken down. Could he help?

Rab recognised the music from the rehearsal in the Burnley community centre. Sikhs who packed the pavements on both sides of the road and leaned out of apartment windows burst into deafening applause and unbroken cheers.

Ashna was back.

The All India Modern Dance Troupe was well-named. Clad in wildly contrasting costumes representing a selection of the cultures and faiths of the Indian subcontinent, their routine appeared unstructured to the point of chaos. Rab had watched them rehearse, and knew it had taken endless dedication and toil to make the routine appear haphazard, yet never cease flowing for a moment.

As a rule the parade never stopped, but Ashna slowed her troupe's progress and waved urgently to the podium. At first Rab interpreted it as a signal to him, but it soon became obvious she wanted Simran to join the dancers. Her brother leapt to street level, dashed through an opening in the crowd and embraced every dancer in the troupe. After he hugged Ashna, she took him by the hand and trotted to the front of the podium. She stopped, fixed her gaze on her parents, put her palms together and bowed.

'Namaste,' said Ronnie. 'Also known as "pranaam".'

'Respect for your elders,' said Stuart.

'Exactly,' said Rab.

As Ashna dashed off to rejoin her disappearing dancers, the press corps, not known for their patience and buttressed by the mob competitiveness of their English brethren, knocked over the metal barriers, barged through a brass quintet playing the theme song from a Bollywood blockbuster, and aggressively invaded the personal space of everyone on the podium.

From the top step of a shuttered furniture store Brygida Kosofsky watched the scene unfold, touched and impressed by Ashna's gutsy maturity. In the space of a minute she had respectfully shown her parents she was a grown-up 18-year-old who was making her own way in the world. Her uncovered spiky bleached hair delivered a message about her take on strict adherence to their faith, and her public embrace of Simran and show of respect to Lala and Gupta illustrated a potential for broken bridges to be mended.

Now she saw Ashna's path back to her dance troupe being blocked by an overweight photographer, camera strobe flashing obtrusively in her face. Shoulder to shoulder with the photographer, a reporter thrust a tape recorder close enough to make Ashna flinch and shouted questions that met with zero response. Brygida's instinct was to wade in and help, but the crowd was too thick, and in any case, police interference with the press was to be avoided at all costs. She glanced sideways to gauge what Malloy was thinking. He was gone.

Malloy got lucky. Natural lines in the crowd of onlookers allowed him to cover a lot of ground in a short time. When he got to the two reporters, he saw they worked as a team, crowding Ashna one moment, stepping sideways the next to prevent her from slipping past to get back to her troupe. He heard the reporter shout questions calculated to draw angry replies ripe for misinterpretation.

'Why did you abandon your family, Ashna? Don't you care how much pain you caused? Do you hate your parents?'

Ashna remained stony faced. Perhaps sensing that they were to come away empty-handed, the photographer tried another tack.

'How about you show us your tits?'

With the briefest sweep of his foot, Malloy took the legs out from under them. The sound of camera equipment smashing to the pavement drew a cheer as Malloy reached down to the photographer.

'Let me help you, mate!' he said. The photographer stretched out to grab Malloy's hand. As if by accident, the hands failed to connect and Malloy's came to rest on the camera that moments before was thrust at Ashna's face. Somehow the back of the camera opened and the film canister ejected, a spiral of exposed film twisting in the daylight.

'Wow, sorry!' said Malloy.

Ashna skirted the mini tangle of bodies and for a moment her eyes met Malloy's. She blinked her thanks and ran towards the troupe.

Malloy found himself being crowded gently by Sikh teenagers who wanted to shake his hand.

On the gurdwara podium, for the first time in years, Dilip and Lala wept with joy while on the street, Simran continued to dance deliriously.

'He's a shite dancer,' said Stuart.

Sheena did her best not to giggle.

Around the outer edges of the platform, men and women from the temple formed an unbroken circle around Dilip and Lala, blocking intrusions from microphones or cameras. Accents from all over Britain yelled entreaties to Ashna's parents, begging for the merest snippet to be turned into a headline for tomorrow's front pages. The cramped podium wasn't made for their number or their aggression.

Although Sheena was off duty, she knew she had the keen eye of one of the sergeants in charge of keeping the peace. With the slightest of head movements and a miniature Nike swoosh with one fingertip, she called in the troops.

Rab watched with pride as the press were none too gently informed they had overstayed their welcome. As the journalists faded from the podium, two big uniforms stopped before him. Rab reached behind and pulled a reluctant Ruby to his side.

'Mother,' he said. 'I want you to meet two of the young officers who helped save my life.'

Ruby's face went from sourness to adulation. Taking their hands in her own, she assured Constables Sweenie and Strachan they could look forward to the best home-cooked Indian food of their young lives, any time they were in the West End. They only had to ask Rabinder where to find her.

'Thank you both very, very much,' she said.

The constables were somewhere between pleased and embarrassed.

'Sergeant Singh was the real hero of the day,' said Sweenie.

'Oh, you don't have to tell me, I know,' said Ruby. 'I can't begin to describe how proud I am of my son.'

Rab sneaked a glance to where Ronnie watched the scene through the eyepiece of his grandfather's video camera. This was going to make Ruby squirm for years.

Other Titles by Ron McMillan

BETWEEN WEATHERS, Travels in 21st Century Shetland (non-fiction)

Yin Yang Tattoo (contemporary crime fiction)

Bangkok Cowboy (contemporary crime fiction)

Bangkok Belle (contemporary crime fiction)

Ron McMillan began writing in Seoul, South Korea when he became a freelance journalist and photojournalist in the fevered run-up to the 1988 Seoul Olympic Games.

During a decade based in Hong Kong, he travelled throughout Asia on assignment for magazines in North America, Europe and Asia, visited Mainland China almost fifty times and made five 'tourist' visits to isolated North Korea. As well as appearing prominently in *Time*, *Newsweek*, *L'Express Magazine* and the *New York Times Sunday Magazine*, his photographs gained notoriety in North Korea. To this day, visitors are watched to ensure photographs of the giant statues of the Great and Dear Leaders never cut them off below the knees.

Ron later wrote and illustrated articles in travel, airline and business magazines and Sunday newspapers before travelling around the Shetland Islands in the autumn of 2005. *BETWEEN WEATHERS, Travels in 21st Century Shetland*, the first travel narrative about Shetland since Victorian times, was published in 2008 by Sandstone Press. It remains in print.

In 2010, Sandstone Press published *Yin Yang Tattoo*, a crime novel that earned the unusual distinction of having its invitation to the Hong Kong Literary Festival rescinded. '*Altogether too highly coloured for our kind of festival*,' said the festival chairman. *Yin Yang Tattoo* and two Thailand-set crime novels, *Bangkok Cowboy* and *Bangkok Belle*, are available as eBooks and paperbacks on Amazon.

Don't Think Twice is the first in a series of Rab Singh books to be set in different parts of Scotland in the 1990s.

Acknowledgements

I owe a debt of gratitude to a considerable number of friends who have been generous with their help and advice and patient feedback during the writing of the first book in the *Call Me Rab* crime series. If I fail to thank you all individually, forgive me.

Officer A, a retired Central Scotland police officer, put me right on multiple matters procedural and legal, as well as providing precious details on how officers interact in the workplace. Without his patience this book would never have come about.

Ajay Close in Scotland and Bobbie Darbyshire in London gave me the encouragement I needed to get started on the book. Micheal Woods in Chiang Mai, Thailand, Mark McTague in Baltimore, USA, the ever-itinerant Sarah in Thailand, Korea and England, David Donald on Koh Samui, and Rose Sloan Ford in Lerwick, Shetland provided valued input when faith was flagging. Fellow Scot and author Suhayl Saadi shared specialist insight that helped me avoid stepping on too many cultural landmines.

And finally, Louise Aylward in Totnes did a wonderful job of proof reading and copy editing the manuscript.

Printed in Great Britain
by Amazon

10145616R00166